LEGO ME

STEPHEN KANICKI

Black Rose Writing | Texas

The author grants the final approval for this literary material.

First printing

This is a work of fiction. Names, characters, businesses, places, events, and incidents are either the products of the author's imagination or used in a fictitious manner. Any resemblance to actual persons, living or dead, or actual events is purely coincidental.

ISBN: 978-1-68433-987-7
PUBLISHED BY BLACK ROSE WRITING
www.blackrosewriting.com

Printed in the United States of America
Suggested Retail Price (SRP) $19.95

Lego Me is printed in EB Garamond

*As a planet-friendly publisher, Black Rose Writing does its best to eliminate unnecessary waste to reduce paper usage and energy costs, while never compromising the reading experience. As a result, the final word count vs. page count may not meet common expectations.

To Dana, my love, my life, my muse.

Other Titles from

STEPHEN KANICKI

The Seven Experiments

There Are No Saints

LEGO ME

-Chapter 1-

The faithful flocked to the Lily Dale spiritualist community in yearly summer pilgrimages while born-again Christians marched outside the gates holding protest signs, and chanting: *Satan be gone.* As a child, I had a front-row seat to this clownish display of clashing beliefs.

I had no sympathy for the Christians. They were ignorant and self-righteous; two qualities I hated. As a young boy, I couldn't resist yelling, "Hail Satan," at them while flashing the devil horns with my index and pinky fingers. They yelled back that they would pray for my soul. "Gee thanks."

I liked the psychics and mediums, however—they were fun to hang out with, told fascinating stories and, ironically, were more compassionate than the Christ followers. They never shared their weed, however—I was too young—but I scavenged the partially used joints they left behind. Still, I viewed them as entertainers and freaks. No reasonable, intelligent person would believe this nonsense, I reasoned. From an early age, I was both reasonable and intelligent, some would say precocious, and I believed in science and my ability to shape this world as I pleased.

Still, I held fond memories of the place. My Aunt Sandy lived here in the seventies; she was a psychic or a medium; I'm not sure what the difference was. Her specialty was the Tarot. She charged an insane amount for the time, like sixty dollars for a thirty-minute reading on everything from relationships to career, and God knows whatever else came up. I didn't pay too much attention to her career, though I secretly wished she wasn't deceiving people or if she was, I hoped she helped them. Her clients always had smiles on their faces after a session, so I think they got something out of it. Happiness and comfort are well worth the price of admission. I've paid a lot more and received a lot less in my lifetime.

My mom was sort of Catholic and took a dim view of Aunt Sandy's career and her psychic friends. Spirituality frightened Mom. She thought psychics were part of a dark underworld controlled by the Devil and his evil minions. Fortunately, I didn't subscribe to her Christian beliefs. God and Satan were fictional characters created to keep the masses in check. Besides, Aunt Sandy was always nice to me. She was mom's younger sister, a hippy-type, and a freethinker, who smoked pot back when it was truly illegal. She played chess too, not well—I could beat her by the time I was six—But she played and that endeared her to me.

Despite Mom's dim view of the spiritual community, she let me visit my aunt during the summers. I think mom wanted me out of her hair for a few months. I was a precocious boy and asked a lot of questions she couldn't answer. I was a young Sheldon before there was a young Sheldon, a genius with—I like to believe—social skills.

"Why don't you visit Aunt Sandy this summer?" Mom said after I interrogated her about our solar system.

"Yeah, okay. Cool!"

Aunt Sandy never gave me a reading, but her psychic friends would visit and give me free readings comprising general, multiple-choice questions that could apply to just about any boy: Do you have a cat, a dog, a frog? See? I knew it! They were odd people; very nice, just odd; kind of like Aunt Sandy. What do you expect from individuals who claim to talk to the dead?

One of my aunt's friends differed from the rest. Her name was Carrie; she had short dark hair and wore black, plastic-framed glasses. She reminded me of Velma from Scooby Doo. Carrie told me specifics that couldn't be deduced from my name, sex or age, and there was no Google back then, so she couldn't look me up on the internet. Carrie told me things about myself that I didn't even know. She said I had a guardian angel. He was my deceased brother, Tom. I thought I caught her in a fib, and I smugly told her I had no brothers living or otherwise. Later, Aunt Sandy confirmed I indeed had a brother who passed at birth before I was born. Mom never told me about him, and his name was Tom. Aunt Sandy swore she never shared this with Carrie, and I believed her.

Carrie also knew I wrote a book. Not a lot of kids write books, but I had this crazy idea that I was a writer at eleven, and I wrote a story about a NASA space mission that went horribly wrong, my version of Apollo 13. I wrote it in pen on lined notebook paper and stapled the sides for a makeshift binding. I had told no one this, and it's not something you can easily guess, like, "You must like baseball, kid?"

Still, I was dubious and thought I knew everything. Religion and talking to dead people, they were the same beliefs to pacify the minds of the ignorant masses to make them feel better about dying. I never thought about death in those days. I was young and bulletproof. Besides, *someone would find a cure for death by the time I got around to it*, I thought. It was possible. They found cures for many horrible diseases. Why not cure the most horrible disease of all: rotting six feet under for eternity?

Aunt Sandy was generous and gave me money to buy whatever I wanted at the gift shop. I usually bought gum and candy there, but they also stocked tarot cards, angel cards, crystals and incense. I didn't believe in the magical, fairy world accouterments, but they were intriguing. One time, I bought a crystal because it looked cool; it was polished to a high gloss and felt good between my fingers. It was supposed to help my energy and clear my chakras, whatever that meant.

Sometimes, I'd have money left over, and I'd treat myself to a cheeseburger from the little pavilion restaurant in the center of town. I remember they had garlic soup, too. That was a thing back then, garlic soup. It tasted good.

Lily Dale was pretty in the fall. I walked down First Street and admired the fall colors, and I recounted the wonderful times I spent here. I used to wander these streets like it was my personal playground when I didn't have a care and everything was new and exciting. It's when a day lasted forever.

It looked different. Maybe it's because I see it through adult eyes, or maybe it's because it was more rundown. I walked past a row of little, yellow and pink houses in need of a paint job. My Aunt's house was on Third Street not too far from the bookstore; just a few blocks to go.

My legs were tired and sore. However, hope spurred me toward a friendly face. I trusted Aunt Sandy. Besides, she's all I had. I had no friends and no other relatives. The police were not an option. They were looking for me. I murdered someone.

Perhaps murder is not the right word. I wasn't sure anymore. I thought what I destroyed was my creation, a machine I made with my hands. Yet machines don't bleed; do they?

I pictured my girlfriend, and for a moment, her sweet face made me smile, but then I remembered; Tracy was untrustworthy, and she despised me. I recalled her blank stare; the fear stretched across her face as if she were seeing a warped version of me. Aunt Sandy was my only option.

The life of a loner was harsh, but it didn't bother me most of the time. I had lots of time for chess, electronics, my toys, and computers. But when I needed help, these distractions were worthless. I couldn't talk to my electronics. A chessboard didn't provide food or shelter.

I was a rat stuck in a trap-filled, dead-end maze. And I must live knowing that I was the author of my predicament. I could have left well enough alone, but my hubris got the best of me. I was confident and smart, but ignorant; my wanton, self-serving pursuits were better suited for an addle-brained chimp than a man of science. Yet, it was my scientific mind and my hunger for knowledge that brought me to my plight.

I moved mindlessly down a dusty brick road with its street sign missing. Dilapidated houses sat stoically on either side of the road; their windows, dark and foreboding, instilled dread in me. My God, what's happened to this place? It was out of season before the faithful arrived, but it appeared all the psychics had packed and moved away before winter. It's nothing like I remembered. It was bright and cheerful. People would greet you in a friendly manner and offer a Namaste blessing; that's what I needed, a friend, a blessing. Instead, I got empty streets, a regular ghost town (no pun intended). What could Aunt Sandy do for me? A pull like a magnet drew me nearer to my destination. Safety and peace of mind were close by.

I walked down another block, past old houses with peeling pastel paint. It was late afternoon, and the ambient light faded fast under a threatening October sky. Everything appeared grey, and I pulled my collar up and my cap down in deference to the fall chill. And then, up ahead, a soft glow cascading through a window caught my eye. I approached the cottage and read the number on the door: 108.

I arrived: 108 Oak Street. Aunt Sandy's house. I saw a sign hanging next to the door:

Reverend Robert Cole—Readings: Walk-ins Welcomed

I took a step back and surveyed the place. It was the right house, the right address, the right location, the same peach-colored paint, peeling and chipping away like modern art.

My breath turned rapid and shallow; my mouth felt like cotton. I didn't know what waited for me on the other side of the door, but I summoned my courage and rang the doorbell. A few moments passed, and I heard the wind buffering through the eaves, causing them to strain and protest under the pressure. I turned to leave when I heard the door open with a loud creak reminiscent of a haunted mansion. I turned back around, hoping to see Aunt Sandy's smiling face. Instead, a prototypical, grandfatherly figure greeted me. He looked to be in his late sixties with shocking white hair that contrasted against his dark skin. He squinted at me and cocked his head to the side. I've grown accustomed to strange looks, so I shrugged it off. I must have looked like a bum with my dirty skin, unkept hair and scraggly Rip Van Winkle beard. The man looked frightened by my appearance. I smiled at him, but this only raised his apprehension.

"What—who are you?" he said. "What do you want?"

"My name is Dr. Lance Ziegel. I don't know what I'm—well, when I was a little boy, I spent my summers here, in this house, with my Aunt Sandy. Do you know my Aunt Sandy?"

The man's eyes were wide. He shook his head from side-to-side but said nothing.

"Well, that's okay," I said. "She used to live here, but it seems she moved."

"You say your aunt lived in this house?"

"Yes. I'm sure it was this house. It was a long time ago, during the seventies. I was a little boy back then. I used to spend my summers here in Lily Dale."

The old man looked past me as if I wasn't there. He appeared to be looking for something or someone else behind me.

"Who sent you?" he said.

"What? No one sent me. I was looking for my aunt and a place to stay."

"Your aunt?"

"Yes. That's right. Aunt Sandy."

"You say she lived here, in this house?"

"Well, she did back in the seventies and eighties. I lost track of her after that, went to college, and you know I never kept in touch. I mean, we never kept in touch. At any rate, she may have moved, or she may be dead for all I know."

The old man looked at me with piercing grey eyes that seemed to penetrate my skin. I guessed he had few visitors that time of year.

"That's remarkable," he said.

"Well, not so remarkable. People lose touch, you know. Anyway, I'm sorry to trouble you."

"No, no. It's no trouble."

"I saw your sign; you're a psychic, right?" The man nodded his head. "My aunt was a psychic. She specialized in the Tarot. She used to give Tarot readings here."

"Tarot. Yes, I understand," the man replied in a mechanical tone. "She used to give Tarot readings."

"Yes, well," I said, while backing up. "I'm sorry to have bothered you."

A breeze kicked up and rustled the dead leaves near my feet. I pulled my collar up and wrapped my coat against my chest as I turned to leave.

"Wait," he said. "It's getting late, and it's cold. It might storm later. Why don't you come inside for a spell?"

I didn't like the company of strangers, but the old man seemed friendly, and I had no place to go. Aunt Sandy was my last hope, a long shot that didn't pan out. Besides, the October chill cut through my light jacket like a knife. I was nearly out of gas and completely out of money; sitting alone in a cold car while I waited for the authorities was my only other option. I nodded my head and accepted his invitation.

The old man led me inside, past the foyer and into the parlor room. This was the same parlor where Aunt Sandy met with clients. It looked different, but I recognized the bones beneath the new decor. The old man gestured for me to sit in the worn leather chair while he sat in a paisley cloth chair across from me. He crossed his legs, then uncrossed them, and for good measure, crossed them once more.

The room was lit by half-drawn blinds, and by the soft glow of a lamp resting on an end table just to my right. The rich, dark wood paneling echoed the illumination and kept us in partial darkness. I looked around, trying to pick out details, but my eyes had trouble adjusting.

The old man leaned forward, and I felt his eyes scanning me from head to toe. I was a little self-conscious, but my disheveled appearance was the least of my worries.

"I am Reverend Bob Cole?" he said, startling me out of my trance. "What may I help you with, young man?"

He called me young man. I'm fifty years old and hardly think of myself as young, but being fifteen years his junior, I guess I fit the description. I liked the Reverend. His voice was soft, and his face warm and inviting. He spoke with a Brooklyn accent, which was quite endearing, but unusual considering we were nine hours away from New York City.

"Uh, I don't know," I said nervously. "Like I said, this was my aunt's house. I remember being here. This was the parlor where she gave readings. Down the hall, and to the right is the kitchen and through the kitchen is a door that leads to the side porch. Upstairs are the bedrooms. There's two. A master and a guest. The bathroom is upstairs too."

The Reverend nodded his head up and down. "That's remarkable," he said.

It was the second time he used the word, and I asked him why he thought it was so remarkable.

"I don't know," he said. "I guess you can have such vivid memories of the place when you—you said when you were a boy?"

"That's right. I was about ten, eleven. Did you know my aunt?"

"I never met her. My wife and I purchased the house twenty years ago, but it was empty. We never met the owner."

Lines and wrinkles populated his face, but his expression glowed with compassion and empathy—something I sorely needed. For the first time in twenty-four hours, I could breathe.

"Would you like a reading?" he said.

His offer surprised me. I had no interest in voodoo or witchcraft or any other such practice, but I didn't want to sound rude.

"Yeah, okay," I said.

"My fee is one hundred dollars for a one-hour sitting."

I forgot; like any other Lily Dale psychic, he does this for a living and wants payment.

"I—I don't have a hundred dollars," I stammered.

The reverend raised his voice. "Oh! Well, well," he said. "Today is Tuesday, right?" I nodded my head in agreement. "I forgot to factor in the Tuesday Special. Today, it is—is it seventy dollars?" He paused a moment to gauge my response. I shook my head. "I see. Is the special today fifty dollars?"

"I have no money," I told him.

Reverend Cole stroked his chin. Then he spoke to me in a gentle voice. "What brought you here today?" he said.

"I was hoping to see my aunt."

"Is that all?"

Those eyes of his. They looked past my facade and uncovered the truth inside me. I lowered my guard and told him there was something else.

"I'd like to hear your story," he said.

"I told you. I have no money."

"It's okay, young man. I want to hear what you have to say."

"I don't know where to start."

"What did you say your name was?"

"My name is Doctor Lance Ziegel."

"Bob," he replied with a smile. "You may call me Bob."

"Okay, Bob. I don't know what I'm doing here. I need help and I thought my aunt could help, but I'm not sure if she's alive or dead. I suppose I haven't been a good nephew. I never bothered calling or writing or visiting in nearly forty years. She's—well, she's probably dead. She would have been that age. My mother passed, you know."

"Perhaps it's fate," Bob said, smiling. "Perhaps I'm the one that's supposed to help you."

Bob leaned in. I tried to look into his eyes, but the dark shadows streaking across his face obscured them. "Relax, young man. I see you're shaken and troubled. I can help."

"How?"

"Well, I'm a psychic."

"So?"

"So, maybe your problem is beyond the physical world?"

"That's possible."

"Perhaps, Lance, your dimension falls short, and you must enter mine to find the solution."

"Perhaps," I said.

"So, that's where I come in. I may have a spiritual solution. You know, every problem has a spiritual solution."

I nodded my head. Even though I was a man of science, my story had no scientific explanation, none that I could think of. What did I have to lose? I had reached the end of my rope.

"Okay, let's give it a go," I said.

"Now, just so you know," he said. "I'll be bringing things to you, things to look forward to, things to watch out for and things you'll need to decide on. Understood?"

I would have laughed at him a few weeks ago. Now, I clung to his words, embraced them like centuries-old wisdom not found in any textbook.

"Yeah, I understand," I said.

"That's fine," I said.

The Reverend's face took on a serious expression. "Lance, I'll ask you to join me in prayer, and we'll see what comes forth. Okay?" We both closed our eyes and bowed our heads as he prayed in a singsong voice: "Dear heavenly mother, father, God. As we ask for the parting of the veil from one side to the other, we ask our spirit-loved-ones, our teachers, and our guides to come forth with words of wisdom, peace, love, understanding, and healing for which we pray, Amen."

"Amen," I echoed.

The Reverend's eyes grew keener, and his broad smile faded to a compassionate grin. "Son, what's troubling you?" he said. "Take your time and tell me your story."

"Yeah, I'd like that. But I don't know where to begin. I'm afraid you'll think I'm mad."

The Reverend's smile returned. "Well," he said. "As Winnie the Pooh said, it's always best to start from the beginning."

-Chapter 2-

I divided my robotics' students into two groups. Each group must build a team of soccer playing robots capable of beating the other group's team: the winning robots earn their builders an A.

Robots must be no taller than twelve inches and should be humanoid, complete with arms, legs, and a head—they must look and act like little human soccer players scurrying after the ball on the soccer pitch. Oh, and they must construct their robot bodies from Legos. That was my added twist to keep things interesting. Soccer robots will rule the world—that sort of thing.

The little bots made me laugh as they waddled around, homing in on the little ball and trying to kick it into their opponent's net on the specially designed mini playing field I constructed for them. They could never compete against the Brazilians. Instead, they looked more like a six-year-old pee-wee team, whiffing and kicking the air or picking daisies off to the side. Sometimes, you couldn't tell what the little bots were supposed to be doing. They'd huddle together, lock arms and square dance while the ball lay undisturbed on the other side of the field. Sometimes, a bot would walk into a side wall repeatedly as if looking to escape; some gave up altogether and laid on their backs while their arms and legs pawed the air. The futility on display outraged my more serious students, but I told them to relax. It was a learning process, and a highly entertaining one at that.

My students needed Lego bricks to build their bots, so I went to the Lego website to place the order. That's when I saw the clicks-to-bricks program. Download their free, proprietary software; design something, anything: puppies, toasters, cars, tanks, boats, buildings, star ships, you name it. Submit your design to the Lego Corporation, and they'll send all the bricks and instructions to bring your Lego creation to life.

It was an ingenious marketing tool dreamt by the good people at Lego. Soon, my overactive imagination envisioned the possibilities. That's when I got the idea: I'd build a lifelike replica of me, my doppelgänger, made entirely of Lego bricks. At first, it was a lark.

"Hey," I said to my class. "I'll place the Lego Man behind the podium. Let him teach and see if you can tell the difference between it and me." No one laughed, and I dismissed the idea for the nonsense it was.

But a few days later, I revisited the website. I was curious and delusional enough to think I should make my Lego twin. The examples provided on Lego.com only fueled my aspirations. There was the standard fare: vehicles, houses, space stations, animals. But there were creative designs too, like Lego shoes, Lego dinosaurs, Lego clocks, Lego cameras, and Lego people—busts and torsos, but no full-sized specimens. The possibilities seemed endless. If you could imagine it, you could make it from Lego bricks. It made my neurons fire like an addict jonesing for his next fix. I needed to explore more.

I devoted the next several days to studying the Clicks-to-Bricks program, or more like immersed myself into the world of Lego brick construction. I watched online video tutorials and downloaded the free software as I prepared to build my Lego Man. Progress was slow at first, and I spent those embryonic stages learning their software. I wanted to create a lifelike image that popped from the screen in three dimensions. My skill set made me uniquely qualified for the task. I was more than a professor, a scientist, a robotics engineer, an expert coder, tinkerer, and a damned fine chess player. I was also an artist, and well acquainted with illustration, graphic design, and sculpting. I took figure drawing classes in undergrad school and took pride in the left-right, yin-yang brain I had.

The learning curve was steep at first, but I progressed through the design phase quickly as my knowledge and confidence grew with each passing hour.

My project needed a name. I called it Lego Me.

Over the next month, I descended into this weird and wonderful world of Lego building block construction. It sounds ridiculous, I know, but that's what twenty-plus years of teaching and research does to a person. New challenges were at a premium. Life had lost its luster. I could teach my students in my sleep. Sometimes, I think I was sleepwalking through my classes. I needed something new, something exciting, something that diverged from the sameness. Lego Me was it.

A stroke here, a tweak there brought me closer-and-closer to my likeness. In two weeks, I had a humanoid frame mapped on my computer screen. It was approximately my height and build—I made him slightly taller than my six-foot, two-inch frame and more muscular than my thin and shapeless body. Over the next several weeks, I refined my creation with delicate, nuanced pen strokes. I made him anatomically correct, complete with a Lego penis, Lego balls, and a nice, bulging Lego ass—my girlfriend, Tracy, always complained about my flat ass, so I made a better one for her. I made Lego Me completely nude, so I could clothe him later for a more realistic effect.

It seemed silly, but who cared? It was fun.

I worked slowly and meticulously on the face. I spent long hours shaping his features, capturing nuances, which made me, unmistakably me. As I progressed, I evaluated my creation with an artist's discerning eye. I edited and made corrections as needed. When I executed a brilliant stroke, I'd click save several times. I layered micro fine detail to remove any doubt in the beholder's eyes. If it looked like me, I kept it. If not, I discarded and tried again. I wanted a twin, a doppelgänger of sorts. He'd smell like me too if I had my way.

I spent four hundred hours over an eight-week period fashioning Lego Me in pixel form. In the end, my hard work paid off. The face staring back from my screen was at once satisfying and unnerving. I was Narcissist staring into a pool of water, tracing the outlines of a well-defined cheek bone that matched my own, and I felt the primal urge that humanity had longed for: to create himself in his own image.. This wasn't a lark anymore. It was my passion. I can't explain it, but it was as though my life depended on Lego Me. It sounds strange to me now as I relate this story.

With virtual Lego Me complete, I placed my order and waited for the parts to arrive. For a week, I obsessively tracked my order online, checking my cell phone every half hour. When it finally arrived, I met the UPS driver halfway up the walk. I scribbled my signature and took possession of two large boxes. They were plain brown and hid the magic contained within. But I knew.

As soon as the packages were safely in my living room, I tore one open with the enthusiasm of a little boy on Christmas morning. My eyes lit up when I saw the white Lego pieces. I still had to scavenge the other parts: actuators, sensors, a power supply, and a chipset from other bots to make Lego Me function; hours of programming still lay ahead, but this was a good start.

Seventy-five thousand pieces, I mumbled to myself while shaking my head. *Seventy-five thousand pieces?* What am I doing? Am I mad? I was giddy as a madman.

And the cost—I'm not rich by any means, and Lego bricks aren't cheap. It was a good thing I was single and childless because children are so expensive and wives, too. Spouses carry the extra burden of practicality. A wife would never indulge my hobby. I'd live shackled like so many other men. I pitied my married brethren. Even so, my indulgence embarrassed me. What if it doesn't work and I wind up with a worthless pile of children's building blocks at my feet, another failed attempt at making something from nothing? What kind of fool would I be then? These dark thoughts were the normal insecurities of an artist staring at a lump of clay, or a writer confronted by a blank page. I had to dive in. Something would come of it, something good. I kept telling myself this.

I dragged the boxes down to my laboratory. Well, it was my basement that I converted into a lab of sorts. It's where I built my bots, computers, machines, and other toys. The lab was dark, and reminiscent of a 1930s monster movie, but I liked it that way. It was quiet and outfitted with every tool I could afford. I called it my second home within a home; it even had an operating table I procured from a doctor friend of mine. He didn't say how he came to possess it. I didn't care, and I didn't ask. I asked him how many people died on the table and he just shrugged, and so I thought little of it. Many wonderful machines were born on that table, and it was the perfect bed to birth my Lego Man.

That evening, I began the assembly phase. The instruction book was as thick as an automobile manual and with seventy-five thousand Legos staring back at me, I felt the daunting weight of the task at hand. Accounting for all the pieces took most of that first night. The next morning, I called in sick even though I felt fine. I wanted to work on Lego Me.

For weeks I toiled in my lab, assembling the bricks every evening after work. That is, if I went to work. My students had a lot of cyber days that semester, at home projects that stood in lieu of class. No one seemed to mind. When I worked on Lego Me, I lost track of time. I'd glance at my watch and see it was three in the morning, which meant I had worked on my creation for nine hours straight without eating or taking a bathroom break. Nine hours felt more like nine minutes and dark cloth covered the windows, so I could never gauge the passage of time. I'd double check my cellphone and my laptop and they all said the same thing: *you're obsessed.*

I worked through a veil of pot smoke and amidst empty beer bottles. My lab smelled like stale underarm, a repugnant stench that I first ignored and eventually came to embrace. It looked like a homeless man had broken into my basement and was squatting there.

Building Lego Me was the closest thing to pregnancy I could experience with all its joy and exhilaration and none of the discomfort— well, there was fatigue and blinding headaches brought on by the long and tedious labor. I knew it was an inanimate object, but to me, there was something deeper at work, as if there were a soul waiting in the shadows to inhabit the plastic body.

It was difficult and sometimes frustrating work. The manual, which was supposed to provide step-by-step assembly directions, was written in broken English. Having degrees in both computer science and robotics and being a proud member of the male sex, I announced I had no need for directions. I ripped up the directions and confidently chucked the pieces into the garbage. But Lego Me proved to be the Rubik's cube from hell, a game invented by the devil himself to torture me. A day later, I desperately rummaged through the trash and tried to fit the ripped pieces back together.

Still, I persisted with bulldog determination. Some might call me stubborn or pigheaded. What else could I do? I was in too deep, the time, the money I invested. I might end up with an unfortunate, malformed amalgamation of Lego Bricks, but I'd see this through no matter what.

So, I labored obsessively, night-after-sleepless night, hour-by-hour, breathing life into the Lego Me while Steely Dan, Eric Clapton, and Jimi Hendrix played in the background. I suffered during this time, ignoring food, rest, and personal hygiene for days on end—days that turned to weeks.

My reflection shocked me. My eyes were dark and sunken, and my already pale skin turned a sickly, ashen hue, not normally found in nature. Lines cut deep into my face and portrayed an old man that contradicted my fifty years.

"Where the hell have you been?" My girlfriend, Tracy, said. "I barely see you. We don't have sex anymore."

I couldn't tell her the truth. She wouldn't understand. I'm not sure I totally understood.

"Sorry, Hun. I've been preoccupied with—with work," I told her. "I'll make it up to you. I promise."

My days looked like an endless, circular line with no beginning or end. Mondays blurred into Tuesday, weekdays into weekends. I slept occasionally in fitful, sporadic spurts, maybe an hour here and there, in my laboratory and not always by choice. More than once, I nodded off in my chair in the middle of a delicate operation and with the nub of a burnt-out joint hanging from my lip. I dreamt of Lego Me. I saw him fully assembled, in my image, a handsome brute, if I say so myself. He was made of Legos, but he always appeared to me as flesh and blood, organic, pliable, breathing, heaving as if taking his first breath. I'd gaze into his eyes and think he could talk. In one dream, he spoke to me. He asked me why I was doing this, and why did I feel the need to build a creature in my image. My mouth opened, but I could not make a sound. Instead, thousands of tiny rat bots poured from my mouth. I begged them to stop, but my words coagulated into a jumbled mass in the back of my throat. Startled awake, I gasped for air, and clutched my throat, and when I opened my eyes, I saw the pile of Lego rubbish lying on the operating table. I still had a long way to go.

I suffered mood swings, though I was never prone to them before. One moment I'd feel light and enthusiastic, and the next moment, I'd feel the weight of a mountain on my chest. This undertaking was frivolous to most. It shouldn't have mattered, but to me it was everything. I didn't want to fail, but more importantly, I couldn't fail. And so I plodded forward to my inevitable end.

Two months passed, and I forced myself to take time off. I needed a break for my survival and mental health. I stayed away from my lab for an entire week. I bathed, shaved, and ate proper meals. The time away gave my frayed nerves a chance to heal. I called Tracy and took her out to dinner and a movie. For the first time in a long time, I relaxed and thought of something else other than the Lego mannequin lying on the operating table in my dark basement.

However, when I returned to the lab, something was off. I had left Lego Me in a decidedly unfinished state, with head, arms, and legs haphazardly strewn about. He looked like the victim of a gruesome, chainsaw murder minus the blood. His face was, well, it was there in form, but it had no personality; it looked like the hockey mask that Jason wore. His arms were stumps reminiscent of the Venus de Milo. This is how I left him, and this is what I expected to find when I returned. Yet, as I descended the stairs to my lab, I saw the white sheet draped over what looked like a fully formed body. The hair on the back of my head stood on end as I approached the table. I pulled back the sheet and immediately dropped it. My eyes were playing tricks, but I had not imagined it. Lego Me was whole.

His face was still a template, but his head, legs, and arms were attached to the torso. How did this happen? I hadn't touched him in a week. I had not even entered my lab, and yet someone had worked on him. But if not me, who?

I'll admit, I drank more than usual during this time. I smoked a lot of pot too, but THC helped me solve complex problems while stifling that critical little prick that sat on my shoulders. Maybe I over indulged; that and a lack of food and sleep, made me forgetful. At any rate, what lay on the table was undeniable. Time fast forwarded. The mannequin was complete, and I was a full month ahead of where I previously thought. Who was I to argue?

With the end in sight, I worked faster and more feverishly than I did before. Teaching was a nuisance that distracted me from my true passion. I'm not proud to say, but my students were on their own. On the rare occasion I showed up, my mind was back home, in my lab, and thinking about Lego Me. I was getting odd looks from students and colleagues alike. Perhaps they wondered about my absence or disheveled appearance. I blamed it on my health, feeling under the weather and all. Teaching was once a source of pride, but now I was someone I loathed when I was a student: a bad, self-absorbed teacher. I couldn't help it, so I buried these feelings.

The winter cold gave way to warm, spring air and with it, Lego Me emerged like a butterfly from its cocoon. I felt chills when I was around him. I don't know why. There was nothing particularly frightening about Lego Me. He was a humanoid figure with articulating arms and legs. He'll move autonomously when I get around to coding; otherwise, he was just a big plastic toy, a glorified and expensive GI Joe doll made from Legos.

Every day, a new face emerged beneath my skilled hand, until one day, I saw myself in him. At first, the sight of my doppelgänger lying on the operating table sickened me. It's hard to explain, and I know I sound melodramatic, but if you were alone with your Lego twin, you'd feel the same. I'm sure.

Finally, after months of meticulous work, I finished. Well, with the assembly phase, that is. I was a proud father. It was worth every struggle, every headache, and every sleepless night. What stood before me was pure brilliance. I made him from Lego bricks, but when I took a step back and squinted, he looked like I chiseled him from a solid block of marble. He was a work of art worthy of the Academia Gallery, standing tall on a podium next to Michelangelo's David. So, I'm joking, of course, but he was magnificent, and I couldn't stop admiring my Lego man. I've created a lot of art in my life—illustrations and paintings—but Lego Me was my crowning achievement to date.

The Reverend sat through my story silently, intently. His eyes were enormous, and his face lit up like a flashlight.

"Wow! That's an incredible story," he said. "So, you built this thing from scratch, and it turned out good? It really looked like you?"

"Well, I made it from Legos," I said. "But all things considered, yeah, it was a fair likeness."

"And tell me again please, why you did this?"

"It started as a lark," I said. "You know, something fun to do. Plus, it was a nice creative outlet."

"That's fantastic. I wish I were artistic." He paused for a moment before speaking again. "That is a remarkable story."

"Well, there's more to it," I said.

Reverend Cole asked me to proceed, but I was hungry and thirsty, and I told him so. The Reverend's eyes grew remarkably wide, and he shook his head, smiled and offered me coffee and leftovers—an Irish stew his wife had made for dinner. I asked if the Irish in Irish stew had anything to do with whiskey. He said it did.

"Maybe I'll start out with a glass," I said.

"You mean you want a glass of whiskey?"

I hated to impose on the old man, but he seemed amiable enough, and I needed something to calm my nerves.

"Yes," I said. "If it's not too much trouble."

The Reverend stared into my eyes. His expression turned rigid and inquisitive. Finally, he snapped out of his trance, stood up, and walked over to a desk where he produced a key hidden beneath a sliding drawer, then used it to open a side cabinet. From here, he took out a large bottle filled with a brown fluid.

"This is fantastic stuff," he said, trying to hold back a laugh, but failing miserably at it.

"Oh, I hope it's not too much trouble," I said. "I'm fine with the cheap stuff. I just need something to calm the nerves."

The Reverend waved me off, then he walked over to a little dinette parked in the corner and retrieved two medium glasses, which he filled halfway. After handing me a glass, he took his chair across from me and stared at me as if waiting for me to drink first.

I smiled nervously at the reverend, then I held up my glass and announced cheers. The Reverend laughed, then we reached out and clanked glasses. Oh, that burning sensation; it felt like eternal Hell fire as it trickled down my throat and into my gut, and yet, the sensation was pure joy. In a few moments, my insides felt warm, like a cozy fireplace on a winter's eve. I looked at the Reverend and noticed he was still clutching his glass.

"What's the matter?" I said.

"Nothing."

"Then why aren't you drinking?"

"Oh, uh, it's Mrs. Cole. I'm really not supposed to be drinking. She wouldn't like it if she knew."

"Oh? Where is Mrs. Cole?"

"Upstairs," the Reverend said gesturing towards the staircase with his glass. "She's napping."

"I won't tell."

The Reverend smiled and took a slow pull from his glass. "Ah, that is smooth," he said in a raspy voice. "Why aren't you drinking?"

I squinted at the Reverend. "What do you mean?" I said. "I am drinking."

"Yes, of course," the Reverend said, taking another sip.

"I'm sorry. I've been doing all the talking. I know nothing about you. How long have you been a medium?"

The Reverend sat back in his chair and took a deep breath. It appeared the alcohol was taking effect on both of us; he looked warm and fuzzy, the way I felt on the inside.

"Well, I've been a medium my entire life," he said. "I remember when I was a little boy in my crib, an elderly man with white hair visited me. I didn't know who he was, but he was kind and would look in on me when I was alone and crying for my mom."

"Was this man a spirit?"

"Yep. I was at my grandmother's house one day and saw a picture of him, and I asked my grandmother who he was. She told me that was my grandfather and that he passed months prior to my birth. I told her I had seen him before and that he visited my crib; she just gave me a condescending smile."

"I was never a believer," I said. "Then one day, I met a psychic; she told me things about me I didn't even know. She was a friend of my Aunt. Aunt Sandy was the one I asked about when I first came to your door. She used to live here, and I used to come visit her during the summers."

"Oh, I see. No, I just recently became a part of the Lily Dale assembly. I passed my certification a few years ago. Was your aunt a psychic?"

"She was." Reverend Cole swirled his glass before taking another sip. "Reverend," I said. "You see dead people right, people who have passed, relatives, my mother, and father?"

The Reverend stared blankly at me and nodded his head.

"Good," I said. "Do you see people around me? Are they here with me right now?"

The Reverend stared at me for a long time. He shook his head and smiled, and said he wanted to hear more.

-Chapter 3-

I showered and dressed, then I dressed Lego Me in my work clothes: a button-down, white shirt, gold-colored jeans, and a blue tie with yellow polka dots. He was the spitting image of me right down to his Haines boxer briefs just in case we got into an accident. I didn't want anyone to think he was a crude Neanderthal. It was the first time I saw him clothed. He looked dashing, a regular old college professor. I even lent him my professor's jacket, the one with the patches on the elbows. What a difference the clothes made. Twelve feet blurred the lines between man and machine. If I squinted, I couldn't tell if it was me or if it was Lego Me. He was ready for his teaching debut.

I laughed when I pictured my student's faces. I liked practical jokes; I loved making people smile while they learned. That's my teaching philosophy: get their attention and then teach them something. This would get their attention. I've been a poor teacher these past several months. I felt bad, but I believed it was worth it. To prop Lego Me up in front of the classroom, and make him move his arms and walk a bit—how inspirational for them, I thought? To say, *look at what I've achieved class, and now you can do the same or better.* This magnificent creature will inspire you. When I was a student, I would have killed for a professor like that. This was my gift to the robotics class, and it was just the first iteration.

Lego Me's articulating parts were perfect for traveling. He had movable joints; his waist, wrists, knees, and ankles could bend into a seated position or locked for standing. Even his head swiveled from left-to-right. I placed him in the front seat of my Subaru and buckled his seatbelt.

"We need to be safe," I told him.

I positioned his smiling face—I designed him with a permanent, eat shit grin—towards the passenger side window to capture the attention of passing motorists. *I'm such an asshole*, I thought as I began our hour-long commute to work.

The winter drive was sometimes brutal and dangerous, but this was early March, and I caught a break today with spring like temperatures. The warm air, and Steely Dan lifted my spirits: *Are you reelin' in the years? Stowin' away the time...*

I felt fine, and Lego Me seemed to enjoy the ride.

"You Okay?" I said. Lego Me didn't respond. "I'll take your silence to mean all is well. Maybe we can play chess tonight. Would you like that?"

My Subaru peeled away the miles. The scenery flashed by in bursts of color and light, while my fingers tapped out the beat to Reeling in the Years. "Almost there," I said. "Another 15 minutes."

I turned my head to get his reaction. Lego Me staring straight ahead at the road in front of him. *That's odd*, I thought. I positioned his head to face the passenger side window. A loose neck joint and a bumpy road must have turned it. Well, there'd be adjustments. He was just born.

We arrived in the parking lot at 7:20 am. "Time to teach," I said to Lego Me.

Getting Lego Me from the parking lot and into the classroom was going to be a challenge. I programmed him to walk, but he moved like a toddler, with short, unsteady steps that threatened to deposit him in a heap at any moment. My code was fast, dirty, and rudimentary. I still had a lot of work to do before he looked somewhat normal traversing a short, flat distance. Besides that, the building where I taught was old, had many stairs, and long hallways, and one rickety elevator in the building's distant corner. To make things worse, my class met on the third floor. My only recourse was to place Lego Me across my back and carry him to the third floor.

"You and me, bud," I said as I firefighter lifted him onto my shoulders. "Fuck!" I yelled. "You better lay off those late-night snacks, Lego Buddy. You've put on weight."

He didn't feel that heavy when I placed him in the car, but I was feeling his ponderous weight hauling him up those stairs. I never thought a bunch of Lego bricks could weigh so much.

As planned, we arrived at the classroom well before the students. I needed time to set him up before anyone else got there. I went to work quickly, placing him into position behind the podium. Then I took out my cellphone and opened the App I had developed. Using the app, I turned his head from side-to-side, and everything seemed fine. I worried his loose neck would interfere with his cranial articulation, but it had not. Next, I moved his arms and hands and ran him through a series of gestures that closely matched my own. I talk with my hands a lot and so I thought it would be funny if Lego Me did the same. I straightened his tie and gave him one last inspection. His usual cheerful countenance seemed off. He appeared worried.

"Aw, don't fret, Lego Buddy," I said. "You'll do just fine. I'll be right behind the door, watching you."

The classroom had a side door used only by faculty. It led to a back stairwell, which, I presumed, was there to facilitate a hasty exit in case a class didn't go well. The door had a small glass window, which I could peer through for an unobstructed view of the classroom. This is where I waited.

A few minutes later, the first arrivals entered the classroom and took their seat. I watched closely in anticipation of the excited and surprised faces, but they never came. Instead, my students looked stoic and sleepy-bored. Hardly anyone acknowledged Lego Me and if they did, it was with a forced smile and a nod of their head. Besides that, there was nothing, no laughs, no inquisitive or perplexed looks, just blank faces. One-by-one they came in and sat down. Some took out their cellphones, but no one bothered to snap a picture. They were sitting, waiting for the lecture to begin like any other class on any other day.

It wasn't the reaction I hoped for or expected. Where were the laughs, the smiles, whispers, and shaking heads? These students acted like I was standing at the podium instead of a big Lego Man.

And then, all at once, as if on cue, the class came to life. Heads rose, eyes lifted, and bodies shifted in their chairs. Books came into view, and pages turned, first left and then right, and then left again as the students searched the pages of their textbooks for some unknown reason. Lego Me stood at the podium in the pose I had placed him in. Were my students that dumb, or so blind they could not tell a big Lego dummy was leading the class?

I turned my gaze downward and stared at my shoes. "What the fuck?" I whispered beneath my breath.

I turned my attention back to the classroom and saw the students were fully engaged. I mean, they had suddenly come to life and almost looked interested in what was happening in the room. Some eyes lifted toward Lego Me in studious concentration. They were clear and bright and filled with wonder. Other eyes peered into the textbook, while their fingers frantically scanned the words. And then, suddenly, it happened; the reaction I had been waiting for finally arrived. The room erupted with laughter; bodies rocked in their seats. It was infectious, and I joined in.

I turned away from the window again. "Jesus Christ!" I whispered.

I knew some of my students were slow, but how long does it take to catch on to a practical joke, and why was the class reaction so sudden and mutually affecting? It was as though I was teaching and made one of my silly jokes.

I looked back at the class. The din of laughter had faded. Faces were now twisted in concentration as if the students were solving a complex problem. Then I noticed Lego Me. He gestured with his right hand and arm. It was a slight shift to be sure, but it stood out in stark contrast. Lego Me adopted a new pose. I must have bumped the controls on the app before I put my cellphone into my jacket. That had to be the explanation. What other existed? Perhaps it was another loose joint.

It was unbelievable—how they seemed to hang on Lego Me's every word; but he did not speak. How could he? I had not programmed him to do so. He didn't have the hardware for speech. I hadn't installed a speaker or a soundcard. He was mute and would remain so until I made the necessary revisions. Yet, Lego Me, my alter ego in Lego form, mesmerized the class as if he cast a spell. Instead of questioning the joke, they looked at him with admiration. *What the hell?* They were never this attentive when I taught.

I turned my back to the class and slid down the door before taking a seat on the cold linoleum floor. Sweat beaded and dripped down my forehead and into my eyes, causing them to sting and tear. I loosened my collar and tie to get a breath of air. What if I threw the door open, barged in and stood next to Lego Me? Then I'd question their mental state and their ability to differentiate between a plastic toy and a flesh and blood human being. I decided that wouldn't be prudent and so I remained hidden.

There had to be a logical explanation. Had they gone mad? Was this a type of mass hallucination? Perhaps it was me. Maybe I was the one who was imagining things. That must be it. I'll look again and see a bunch of bored students picking up their books and leaving, happy to get out of class. But when I stood and looked through the window again, I saw nothing of the sort. The students' heads were down and they were writing. Occasionally, one would look up and place their pencil in their mouth before returning to their work. If I didn't know better, I'd think they were taking a test, but what test? I wasn't even in the classroom to assign one. A plastic dummy stood at the podium. Any normal student would have laughed and shook their head in disbelief and then I'd come out of hiding and say, "Hey class, what do you think? Let me show you what I did." Then I'd show off his mobility, and I'd project my code on the screen and we'd go over his functions and subroutines and I'd assign a project to modify the code and make it better. That's how it was supposed to go.

But none of that happened.

I waited for that aha moment that never came. Then, it happened again. I did not see him move, but there he was, one hand resting on the podium, the other pointing to a student. I checked my phone. The app wasn't running. No jostling great or small could have triggered his movement. I thought it was a hardware problem. His actuators activated on their own; the battery probably caused an electrical spike.

Yet, the students sat through it all; their stoic faces cast on Lego Me as if he were acting out a scene from Hamlet.

They were playing games with me. It was retribution, payback for my shitty teaching efforts over the past several weeks. Their stoic faces were a mutiny. I turned my back to the door, sat down and checked my cellphone. There was a text message from Tracy.

Hey Lance. Get your phone back?

What?

Your phone?

What about it?

You said it was missing stolen?

Tracy went on about my phone and tried to convince me we had a conversation about this on our last date. I told her it must have been her other boyfriend, but she was unamused. I was thinking Tracy was the delusional one.

Well, I'm glad you got it back

Yeah sure

It was time for class to end, so I stood up and had another look: still the same students, still the same dry, humorless faces. I looked at Lego Me and the hairs on the back of my neck stood on end. Lego Me had both hands raised above his head, and his palms turned towards the heavens as if reaching for God. All eyes were locked on him, including mine.

The Reverend's smile faded. His chin rested on his thumb and forefinger, and deep furrows spanned his forehead. Did he think I was mad? Any sane person would. I thought I was crazy; perhaps that's a good sign I wasn't. There was still hope for me, and that somewhere there was a reasonable explanation. God knows what it is. I had spent long hours contemplating an answer.

It seemed like a dream, but I was awake through it all. Yet, the absurdity seemed to defy reality. What should have been a room filled with bewildered college students was nothing of the sort. These young men and women weren't confused. No; not in the slightest. I have never seen them so alert, so attentive and well-mannered in deference to what amounted to an oversized Lego doll. How? Who were they listening to? Who inspired them? I had pressed my ear to the glass in the door and yet, the only thing I heard were the muffled sounds of shuffling feet, turning pages and the occasional dropped pencil.

After a long dramatic pause, the Reverend spoke. "Why did you stop?" he said. "I'm intrigued."

"I want to get your impressions," I said. "What are you thinking? Do you think I'm insane? Do you believe what I'm telling you?"

The Reverend's warm laughter filled the room and lifted my heart. "Lance," he said. "You're not crazy. I know this much."

"Yes, but do you have any initial thoughts you can share? You're a psychic. Tell me, what do you see? Am I possessed or something?"

Reverend Cole's eyes lit up, and I knew I had struck a chord.

"What is it?" I said.

"Lance, it's like that movie: I see dead people. But..."

The Reverend stopped and bit his lower lip.

"But what?" I said.

"I'm going to be honest with you, Lance. Ever since you came to my door, I haven't seen any spirits around you."

I took a moment to think about what this meant. Why shouldn't he see spirits around me? Carrie read me when I was a child. She saw my dead brother; the one I didn't even know existed. Perhaps it was the Reverend.

Not all mediums were equal. There were good ones and bad ones. Perhaps the Reverend was a bad one.

"I don't understand," I said.

The Reverend took another sip from his glass. "Why aren't you drinking?" he said.

"What?"

The Reverend pointed to my glass. "Don't you like my bourbon?"

I stared into my glass and swirled the ice cubes around. "Sorry," I said. "I was lost in my story. The bourbon is fine. Very fine."

"What happened after that?"

"What do you mean?"

The reverend leaned forward, propped his elbows on the table, and rested his chin on clasped hands. "I mean, what happened after class?" he said. "Did you finally reveal yourself to your students?"

"No. After my students left the classroom, I walked in, and I, well, I sat down for a minute, trying to collect my thoughts. Then, I hoisted Lego Me on my back, and carried him to my car and off we went. I canceled my other classes that day. I was in no mood to teach. It was odd because I thought bringing him back down the stairs would be relatively easy. But the Lego mannequin seemed to have put on another fifty pounds in a little over an hour."

The Reverend's face grew taught. "Yes. Yes," he said. "But what about the next day or the next day after that? Surely, someone must have said something to you. I mean, you placed a Lego man in front of your students for Christ's sake."

I shook my head back and forth. "Not a thing... not a damn thing," I said. "My next class met two days later, on a Thursday. No one mentioned Lego Me, and I said nothing. The students filed in, sat at their desks and turned in their homework, a perfectly routine convention except for..."

"Except for what?"

"I hadn't assigned homework."

-Chapter 4-

I rationalized and explained the events away.

My students were ridiculous. No big revelation. Eighteen- and nineteen-year-old kids are this way, just one of many maladies that curse today's youth. There were a lot of other explanations: It was a morning class; they were tired, disinterested, bored; they lacked an inquisitive nature or had the visual acuity of a blindfolded mole trapped in a sensory deprivation chamber. I don't know. Pick one; pick them all. One was as good as the next. I know this much: I am not insane. I placed a Lego Man in front of my class to entertain, to provoke, to conjure ideas, to initiate thought and conversation, but mostly to inspire and yet, not one—not a single one mind you—appeared to notice a static figure was standing behind the podium where a living, breathing soul should have been.

Perhaps after twenty years of teaching, I should have known better. Each passing year, cohorts seem to be dimmer than the batch before them. You practically must jumpstart their hearts with a car battery to get so much as a rise from them. But this, well, this shook my sensibilities to my core. What can I do? I am a mere mortal and there are limitations to what I can accomplish. If my class could not recognize a practical joke when they saw one, then so be it. Maybe the joke wasn't that funny. I'm persistent, however. I'll try again, this time with a new victim: Tracy. She won't let me down.

It was date night, and I prepared Lego me with a fresh change of clothes and a spritz of cologne. A new bowtie completed the effect. Yes, he was a dashing brute with rugged, Hollywood good looks, complete with a cleft chin. I have a cleft chin. It's one of my outstanding features, so naturally Lego Me had to have one. If I squinted hard enough, the line between Legos and human flesh blurred. *It was time to have some fun.*

Tracy and I were struggling. Okay, struggling is a kind term. We were bickering and fighting a lot. Our conversation had dried to a low ebb. It reminded me of my parents, and what really upset me was that I vowed never to become them. I was going to find a wife who I got along with and who shared my passion for life and thirst for knowledge, someone who could match my intellect and challenge me at chess. Well, that never happened. Instead, I met Tracy a few years back.

I called Tracy number ten because she was my tenth online first date. The others were miserable failures. Tracy was different. We met at Barnes and Noble for coffee, and four hours later, we were still talking. That's how long our date lasted, four hours, and all we did was talk and drink coffee. A few weeks later, we were in a relationship, and she teased me about how long I nursed a cup of coffee and what a cheap first date it was.

Statistics show that sex usually occurs after the third date. Tracy and I were right on schedule. It was date number four, and it was on my blue sofa. I never looked at that sofa the same way after that. Tracy and I became a thing, and we have been together for three years. While she lacked the intellect and scholarship I was searching for, she was the first woman I could talk to. I mean really talk to and enjoy the conversation, the give and take, the kibitzing. She kibitzed a lot, and I returned the favor in kind.

We spent wonderful times together in Bemus Point on the shores of lake Chautauqua. We'd get stoned and make a spectacle of ourselves, shopping in the quaint little specialty stores, laughing too loud and pretending to be husband and wife. One of the store clerks asked our names and Tracy told her with a straight face that she was Bonnie and I fell into line and said I was Clyde. You should have seen the expression on the poor clerk's face.

Tracy and I had a lot of fun. However, like most good things, it didn't last. Lego Me exasperated things, but it was happening before him. Ours was a distance relationship, about an hour's drive separated us. The long commute bothered her, especially in the wintertime, when the brutal weather made it difficult to see each other regularly. I was okay with it. Absence makes the heart grow fonder and all of that, but she had a hard time with it and couldn't understand why I was so unbothered.

"Don't you want to see me?" she'd ask.

"Well, of course I do. But what do you want? I live in Falconer, and you live in Smethport."

We talked about marriage and even looked at a house together. But then Lego Me came, and he made a tense situation worse. I take the blame. I was spending a lot of time on my project and that really set her off. She accused me of loving Lego Me more than her. I didn't listen. Instead, the back of my ears burned, and I went into my *that's ridiculous* speech. Well, it was ridiculous. Lego Me was a project I worked on during the long, cold winter. Okay, yes, I spent more time with him than I did with Tracy, but that was circumstance. It had nothing to do with love or the lack thereof.

I don't absolve myself of anything. There's no doubt I could have been a better partner to Tracy. I could have been more caring, more sensitive to her needs. I regret not spending more time with her, but she didn't see how important this project was. The scientist and creator in me took over, and this was my form of self-expression, my art. Why couldn't she understand? I would have loved her company while assembling Lego Me, and I often extended her a heartfelt invitation.

"Why would I want to spend time in your dingy basement watching you play with your little plaything?" she said.

"It's my lab, not a dingy basement," I said. "And Lego Me is not my plaything. He's a passion of mine and I wish to share my passions with you. I wish you could understand that."

But nothing I said appeased her. Our passion faded, but I still had feelings for her and I wanted to makeup for the past six months. I had been careless and selfish, but tonight would be different. Tracy will get to meet Lego Me for the first time. She'll see. She'll come to know what a wonderful specimen he was and all that work I put into Lego Me will open her eyes. It's one thing to describe Lego Me, but to see him, to hear his actuators high-pitched whine as he walked, or stumbled across the room, was the only way to appreciate him. Tracy will see my passion and the dedication it took to bring Lego Me to life. Then, we'll laugh; we'll open a bottle of wine and enjoy a romantic evening together. It was all set.

It was nearly six, and the tension morphed into exhaustion. Lego Me's skintight black tee stood in stark contrast to his alabaster white skin. I sat next to him on the sofa and placed my arm around his shoulder. He and I had a father-to-son pep talk.

"Don't be nervous," I said. "Just put on a smile and give her a real surprise. She's been kind of surly lately and we want to show her a good time. Okay?"

I heard the side door squeak open. "This is it," I told him.

There was a look in his eyes. I'll never forget it. His wide, stupid grin faded in front of me; he was frightened, like he was before his teaching gig.

"You'll be fine," I said, patting him on the shoulder. "I'll be down the hall and out of view if you need me."

I hurried out of the living room and took my place down the darkened hallway several feet behind the sofa. I squatted to keep myself small and unobtrusive.

"Is anyone home?" I heard Tracy call out.

Tracy stepped cautiously into the living room, then she saw Lego Me and stopped. Her face tuned white and smooth, and I clenched my teeth to suppress the nervous laughter.

This was the reaction I was expecting. After a few seconds, her puzzled look melted into a big grin. *That's it*, I thought. She gets it, not like my numbskull students.

I was tempted to come out of hiding right then and sweep her into my arms. She looked stunning dressed in her short, tight black skirt. Her smooth, long legs screamed sex to me. But the joke hadn't fully played out. I watched as Tracy, still smiling, stepped towards Lego Me. Then, she cocked her head to one side like I've seen her do a thousand times before in response to a silly joke or a bit of ridiculousness that escaped my mouth. She bent over and tugged and straightened Lego Me's collar. It was so typical of her. I'm sure she had OCD and couldn't stand having a single thing out of place. Oh, God, I thought. This was going to be a special night. We will put the last six months behind us.

I was ready to reveal myself and end the ruse, but Tracy surprised me. She dipped her left shoulder and allowed her sweater to slink down her arm. Then she removed it altogether and tossed it on the floor. Her bare, bronze skin looked taut and smooth. It took my breath away. I was afraid my beating heart would give me away.

Tracy took a seat next to Lego Me. He looked like a sixteen-year-boy about to lose his virginity to a cougar. As I watched the scene unfold, that sick, uneasy feeling in my stomach returned. It was like I was reliving the events in my classroom a few days earlier.

I nearly gasped when I saw Tracy wrapping her arms around Lego Me's neck. She laid her head gently against his chest and used it as a pillow. Her eyes were closed, and her face was angelic. My breathing turned labored as I watched the two figures mold into one. That's when I saw it: Tracy's head moving in sync with the rise and fall of Lego Me's chest. My eyes were not tricking me, and I was in my right mind. This is what I witnessed. My blood turned cold. Lego men cannot... they do not breathe. I struggled for an answer, but I had nothing.

Time seemed to speed up. Tracy's head craned around his. They embraced; he positioned his lips across her lips as if to plant a kiss. Then they kissed. It reminded me of Rodin's sculpture—beautiful if it wasn't so bizarre.

His hands clumsily fondled her breasts, squeezing them hard through her blouse. I watched in horror as he worked his mouth down her neck while he grunted and snorted like a pig at mealtime. Tracy responded with a soft moan. Her cheeks turned bright red as she became more-and-more aroused. I thought about how clunky and ragged his hands looked against her soft, curvaceous body. The sheer madness taking place on my sofa caused me to fall into a trance.

And all I could do was watch helplessly as Lego Me helped her out of her blouse. Tracy reached around her back and undid her bra. It fell gently to her waist. Lego Me tenderly brushed his nose across her areolas, causing her nipples to grow taught and stand at attention. Then his right hand slipped between her legs before disappearing between her thighs. They kissed passionately, and I watched their bodies twist and writhe like two entangled serpents. Lego Me lifted his hand from between her legs and tugged hard on Tracy's skirt. The skirt gave way and fell down, along with her panties. The two garments lay tangled at her ankles. Then she lifted her feet and wiggled and squirmed until she broke free. Tracy was naked except for the high heels.

Tracy fumbled with Lego Me's belt buckle. It took her a few clumsy seconds, but she finally loosened his pants enough to slide them down his thighs. Lego Me, well, I don't know how to say this, but just to say it; he was aroused. Tracy's hands looked child-like next to Lego Me. She stroked him gently, and after a few seconds, her fingers glistened like morning dew on the grass. Lego Me was on fire. He rose swiftly and confidently and positioned Tracy on her stomach. Then he grabbed her hips and lifted her butt. From my vantage point down the hall, I saw everything. They left nothing to my imagination. I turned away as the sight was making me nauseous. The sounds coming from my living room, however, told the rest of the story in vivid detail. I had to cover my ears.

The Reverend's glassy-eyed stare and gaping mouth conveyed his doubt. This was a bad idea. I should have—I should have kept my mouth shut. The door was just a few feet away, but I had nowhere to go. So, I waited for him to respond or call the authorities, whichever he was inclined to do.

"Jesus," the Reverend finally said.

"Yes, that's an understatement."

"I don't understand. How was this happening, Lance?"

"I don't know."

"What were you thinking while this was taking place?"

"I don't know. I was thinking it was the most incredible thing I'd ever witnessed. It was insanity times ten." The Reverend nodded his head. "She never moaned like that when I made love to her," I said.

"Yes, well, there's that," the Reverend said as he ran his fingers through his hair.

"Do you see... do you see why I needed to talk to someone?"

"Yes. It's good you came here."

His soothing baritone voice put me at ease. I decided then to trust the Reverend. What other choice did I have? Relatives were dead; friends were absent or never existed. The Reverend was a sympathetic ear with a kindly face.

"You believe me?" I said. The Reverend nodded his head. "Tell me what you see, Reverend. What do you think happened? Is this supernatural? Is someone playing a trick on me?"

The Reverend held up his hand. "I'm 67 years old, and I've seen and heard a lot of things I can't explain," he said. "There are so many things in the spiritual world and even in the natural world that remain a mystery to us mortals. I don't know. I've heard stories of Demon possession; dolls imbued with life, a soul—a very dark soul or dark energies, as I like to call them. We can't rule out witchcraft, voodoo, mass hallucinations, spells..."

"Yes, but you're a psychic. What is your Spirit-Guide telling you? What are your impressions?"

"Spirit is telling me there is more to this story, a lot more, and that I should listen to the rest before saying anything."

My patience was thin, but I nodded my head. The past month was agonizing, brutal even. I wanted to go back in time and undo the mistake. My doppelgänger brought me nothing but heartache. I had a good life. I didn't always see it before. But from this miserable vantage point, I see I had everything I needed, everything a man could want: a career, a flawed but workable relationship, my sanity, my dignity, my pride, respect. To any ordinary man, this would have been more than enough, but for me, a void festered like an ulcer despite my accomplishments.

I was born with a longing in my heart, one that could not be filled through societal norms. From an early age, I looked at people around me—perfectly fine people, mind you—and despised them for the normal lives they led. They were boring, and I never wanted to be like them, and I vowed I wouldn't. While other students studied in study hall, I'd go to the library and read about famous people. Einstein, Oppenheimer, Ford, Edison, Van Gogh, and Gauguin were my heroes. I liked science fiction too. I read Frankenstein when I was twelve, and I empathized with the doctor, not the monster. Doctor Frankenstein was dissatisfied with the status quo and so he explored, studied, and sought new ideas about life and death. Sure, he had a god complex, but that's only because there was no other God. We are the miracle. We are the Gods, and we must understand this if humanity is to obtain new heights.

Yes, I know there was another moral to the story: leave God matters to God. It was lost on me. What if a man lives and dies and leaves nothing but fragments of himself behind—his offspring—to do the same? History won't remember him, and so what's the point? Oh, I'm not criticizing those who lack the ambition to do anything more than to live and work and survive. My mom and dad were those people, and they were wonderful parents. A person could not ask for better. But that's not me. My purpose was greater. But the pursuit of greatness devastated me. Building that Lego Man, I see now, was a mistake.

"Tell me something," the Reverend said. "When you looked at Lego Me, what did he look like? I mean, did he appear to be human with human form and flesh?"

"He looked like a Lego Man," I said. "A big, stupid, Lego Man made from a child's building block."

-Chapter 5-

My bedroom was dark and disorienting. I wrapped my arms around my shoulders and rocked myself back and forth while I recalled the dream. Rats. They were roaming freely in my living room, crawling over the couch and over me, sniffing the air with their wet pink noses. One sunk its pin-sharp teeth into my flesh, and drew blood; it oozed from my arm like red honey. I thrashed the varmint against the arm rest until I broke free. When I awoke, I still felt its teeth on my arm. I'm a big believer in dream interpretation. I wondered what that one meant.

After a few minutes of feeling sorry for myself, I stumbled to my feet and walked down the hallway. The house was dark except for a faint light emanating from the kitchen. I checked my cell phone. It read *10:45 pm*. I was sleeping longer than I thought. I stepped tentatively at first, allowing my eyes to adjust to the light. When I reached the living room, I saw the sofa where hours before I witnessed the bizarre images that haunt me to this day. My brain tried to process everything, but I couldn't make sense of it. I was a scientist by trade and yet, science had no explanation for what happened. At least not my branch of science. Perhaps this was something for the medical field to decipher, or more accurately, the psychiatric community. But I wasn't crazy. I realize, however, every raving lunatic locked in an asylum believed as I do. In that case, I'm in dubious company.

A feeling came over me; that feeling you get when you're being watched. I turned my head to the right and saw him. He was naked and stoic, like a statue. His feet were spread apart. Both hands rested on his hips and he looked like a perverted version of Superman, striking an arrogant pose. All that was missing was the cape. He looked at me with that dumb, eat shit grin of his; the same one I had given him several weeks prior. He now used that smile against me; mocking and taunting me as if I was the plastic Lego dummy and he the master.

My body coiled and tingled. My fight-or-flight mechanism was in full charge. I wanted to retreat to the safety of my bedroom, but my feet were cemented to the floor, and so I stood there and did my best to keep calm while I studied him for clues—anything that would help me piece together the broken fragments of my reality. I watched for the telltale rise and fall of his chest or any other signs of life to indicate he was something more than a glorified robot. Nothing. In fact, besides his unusual stance, or the fact he was standing at all, there was nothing out of the ordinary. What stood before me was the familiar Lego Man, the one I had built from scratch. He did not breathe or move. He was inert as the furniture and, no one in their right mind would mistake him for anything else. And yet, I saw what I saw.

I took a deep breath and walked up to Lego Me. I placed my hand on his face and walked my fingers across his seams. Then I worked my way down his neck and shoulders. His interlocking Lego bricks, which I carefully laid just weeks prior, gave him the strength of an anvil. *My work*, I thought. This is what I've made.

"Who are you?" I whispered. "And what have you done with Lego Me?"

I studied his lifeless eyes and tried to break down the problem into its varied components. I thought about hackers. They were all around us, hijacking our computers, cell phones, and bank accounts. Was it possible that someone hacked my phone, had taken control of the app, and was orchestrating Lego Me's movements, his behavior? Of course, it was possible, but it didn't account for what I saw, not even close. It would be like someone hijacking a model airplane and ordering it to land in Cuba for a ransom. That couldn't happen. Lego Me was a piece of art designed with limited functionality and movements. He couldn't—you know, he couldn't do what I saw him do and besides, how would that account for Tracy's reaction? How was she mixed up in all of this? She must have seen him for what he was, and yet she was complicit in this madness.

I kept returning to my mental state. I must have imagined the entire incident, or I did not see what I thought I saw. Tracy was never here. She was a ghost, a figment of my imagination. Lego Me was another apparition, and I cast them both into a devilish movie in my imagination. Perhaps I needed my head examined; I've been told as much before. But before I called the school's counselor, I'd inspect Lego Me and take him apart if necessary. I spent so much time and energy on him, but there was no alternative. Something inside of him that was making him act peculiar and if it wasn't him, that left me with one other explanation: I was suffering from a serious case of psychosis. Either way, I had to find out.

"You wait right here," I said sternly.

I went down to the lab to prep for surgery. I found the solvent needed to melt the cement that held the Legos together. Then I found the hammer, screwdriver and hacksaw and laid them neatly on my workbench. The thought made my stomach turn, but I had no other recourse but to crack him open like a lobster. I had to check for anomalies. At the very least, he needed to be dismantled so as not to cause harm to any other human being. Lego Me was a menace and I had to return him to the pile of Lego bricks from which he came. What had I done unleashing this monster into the world? I thought about my poor Tracy. Would she ever forgive me? I could not undo the pain I'd caused. The best I could hope for was to make amends.

When I returned to the living room, Lego Me was no longer standing. Instead, he was lying on the couch with his arm draped over his eyes as if he were napping. I didn't imagine it. He was upright and standing when I left and now he was vegetating like he had a long day at work.

My cheeks grew warm; perspiration rolled down my forehead and into my eyes, causing them to sting. I wiped my brow and stood there for a moment as I gathered my resolve.

"C'mon, boy," I said as I took hold of his leg.

Adrenaline was on my side, and I used it to pull the big Lego thug from his cozy couch. If I couldn't carry him down to the lab, I'd slide him across the floor and throw him down the steps if necessary. With one leg in tow, I turned and pulled him toward the basement door. Lego Me's hard shell scraped the hardwood floor and made a cringing sound similar to fingernails on a blackboard. Then there was a jarring stop. I yanked harder, but he wouldn't budge. When I looked back, I saw Lego Me had grabbed the edge of the kitchen wall. His knuckles were white as he strained to keep his grip.

I took hold of both legs, one under each arm, and leaned back with all my weight. It worked. He let go of the wall, but then he lunged forward and grabbed my wrist. His plastic fingers tightened and sunk into my flesh as he pulled me towards him. I had no chance against him in a wrestling match. I was fifty pounds lighter, plus his actuators had the crushing power of a trash compacter, and if he had a mind to, he could have turned my bones to dust.

I was never in a street fight, but I've watched mixed martial arts (MMA) on TV. Well, it wasn't much, but it was all I had. I let go of his ankle and bent my arm into a chicken wing—a trick I learned from watching MMA. Then I launched my elbow against the side of his jaw and heard the satisfying thud of bone meeting plastic. It was like hitting a baseball on the sweet spot; I didn't feel a thing. His head snapped back; his eyes rolled back and all I could see was the white. He looked possessed. My victory was sweet, but short-lived. The first blow signaled the start of battle.

Lego me shook his head as if clearing the cobwebs. Then he looked at me and conveyed his intent. That's right; a face made from a child's building block projected feelings and emotions. His narrow, red eyes, his wrinkled forehead, and flared nostrils—he wanted to kill me, but I wouldn't give him the satisfaction. Instead, I threw my two hundred pounds on him, wrapped my thighs around his torso and from this mounted position, I rained lefts and rights down like lightning bolts from heaven. A few good shots made their way through, but his Popeye-like Lego arms blocked the majority. Besides that, I was getting the worse of it. Flesh and bone were no match for glued-in, interlocking Lego pieces. After a few seconds, the pain and exertion slowed my offensive. My arms felt like lead, and I had to sit there, catch my breath and weather the onslaught.

I maintained leverage by squeezing his torso tight with my thighs—another trick I got from TV. Otherwise, he would have knocked me cold with one punch. Instead, most of his blows landed weakly on my midsection and were more annoying than damaging. Unfortunately, Lego Me soon figured this out and grabbed my shirt to draw me in close—I figured he watched the same MMA shows I did. Then he used his free arm to land short elbows on the left side of my face. These shots landed against my wet temple and I heard the rhythmic slap, slap, slap of a drum. I tried to defend myself, but all I could do was close my eyes and paw the air in front of my face; it was a feeble attempt, and any compassionate referee would have stopped the fight. Unfortunately, there was no referee, just me and Lego Me locked in a life-and-death battle. No one to save me except me.

This beating went on for several seconds, and then suddenly, in answer to a prayer, it stopped. I opened my eyes. Lego Me's arms were stretched out wide like wet noodles. He lay impotent and was panting like a dog in dire need of a drink.

I considered resuming my assault, but thought better of it. It was time to get up, get out, and run.

The Reverend's face was white. "What the hell?" he said. "What did you do next?"

"I left. I got the hell out of there. I was so scared. I drove to my office at the University and spent the night there."

"You didn't call your girlfriend?"

"And tell her what? I saw you fucking the big plastic dummy I made in my basement and that I got into a fight with him. No fucking way." The Reverend's eyes glazed over, and he stared blankly at me. "Reverend?" I said.

"Yes. I'm listening. Go on."

-Chapter 6-

"Welcome to McDonald's. May I take your order?"

The young female clerk behind the counter was too chipper for 7:30 a.m. But when she looked up and our eyes met, her jaw slid open, and her skin turned pale. Was she a former student of mine?

By now I've grown accustomed to surprised faces. It may have been paranoia, but there was something more to it. I felt it when I walked into the restaurant. Old people and children stepped back as I approached. The bolder ones stood their ground and gawked; some snickered. I hadn't seen a mirror in some time, but I imagined how I looked: disheveled, unshaven, unkept, and now a mouse under my left eye from the fight with Lego me. In less than two weeks, I went from a respected college professor to a broken-down prize fighter. I understood their reaction, but it was unwelcomed all the same. I wanted to be alone, to order my breakfast and nurse my wounds.

Besides my half-shut eye, my back hurt from sleeping—or trying to sleep—in my office. Thank God it was Saturday. I couldn't imagine standing in front of a classroom after what happened last night. Trying to string two coherent thoughts together in front of an audience was unthinkable. I dreaded Monday.

Despite my anxiety, my appetite was strong, and McDonald's breakfast looked oddly wonderful.

"Yes," I said to the girl. "I'll have a sausage, egg and cheese McMuffin, an order of hash browns and a small coffee."

The girl giggled, but dutifully punched in my order.

I never thought of McDonald's as comfort food, but today, it was the closest I'd get. Besides, I needed some sugar, carbs and coffee to jumpstart my heart, to help me think clearly. That's what I needed. A rational mind to place the puzzle pieces. It was like trying to solve a giant, unwieldy Rubik's Cube from hell. No one could help. It was up to me to figure this out.

Luckily, I'm a scientist, and this is a science problem, I reasoned. All I had to do was apply basic troubleshooting principles to the problem, much like I would find and fix a computer bug. There appeared to be a glitch in the cosmic code, a malfunctioning universe, a tear in the dimensional fabric through which I've unwittingly stepped. Insert the corrective code or replace the defective chip and everything will return to normal.

A scientist starts with a hypothesis. Here's mine: I'm crazy, as in batshit crazy. That made sense. I didn't feel crazy. I felt no different than before this bloody mess started, but that meant nothing. If I were crazy, I wouldn't know it. Does anyone know if they're insane or not? I think that's the definition of insanity. People don't know how abnormal they are and the ones that know are, well, normal.

Drugs, hallucinogens in particular, could be another explanation, but I have taken nothing like that in years. Well, besides pot; I smoked weed occasionally, but I never heard of marijuana causing these types of hallucinations. If it did, that would be some killer weed. I drink occasionally, but nothing that should lead to psychosis. I wish it were that simple. If I were crazy or drugged, I could get help. I could get this thing fixed.

"That will be $7.95," the cashier said, snapping me back to reality. I nodded my head and swiped my debit card.

"Sorry. It was declined," the girl said.

"What? What was declined?" I said.

"Your card came back declined. Would you like to try again?"

"Uh, sure."

I had recently been paid by direct deposit. There should have been plenty of money on the debit card to cover the purchase. I swiped once more.

This time, the girl gave me a pensive look and bit her lower lip. "Sorry. It's coming back as stolen," she said.

"Stolen! That's my card! I'm a professor here at the university. It's not stolen!" I grew angry and frustrated and every eye was trained on me because I was talking too loudly. The young girl behind the counter was visibly agitated; I caught myself and tried to calm down. "Sorry," I said. "Can I try another card, please?"

"Of course," she said.

I swiped another card. She didn't tell me what the error code was this time, but her eyes told me it was nothing good. Anyway, I didn't care what the reason was. I didn't want to know.

"I have cash," I said. "You take cash, right?"

After paying for my meal, I used my cell phone to check my accounts. They were locked. I couldn't access any of them. A chill ran down my spine. Suddenly, I realized something very troubling. I was alone in this world, a piece splintered from the larger whole like a Lego brick lost beneath the sofa. The irony made me laugh.

I didn't know what any of this meant, but I had my suspicions. I dialed my landline back home. The phone rang twice and then I heard an unfamiliar voice on the other end.

"Hello," the voice said.

I felt like I was going to be sick. "Hey! Asshole!" I shouted into my phone.

"Who's this?"

"It's me!"

There was a brief silence. "Oh. Hello," the voice finally said. "You're talking."

"Well, of course I'm talking. Why wouldn't—Oh, never mind. Who the fuck are you?"

"Who am I?" Lego Me said in a quiet voice. "Come home and I'll tell you. You see, George Bailey, you had a wonderful life. You just didn't know it."

"That Fuck! That fuckin' Fucker!" I shouted. "He was mocking me with a line from my favorite movie!"

I felt an angry tear form in the corner of my right eye. It dangled precariously for a moment before cascading down my cheek.

"And the credit cards... he stopped your cards from working?" the Reverend asked.

"Yes. Well, I think so. I had plenty of money on both cards, but they were reported stolen. It's a type of social engineering where hackers impersonate you and steal your accounts and lock you out. That's what I'm thinking this is. Either that, or some type of demon possession. What do you think?"

"Uh... I have fresh coffee," the Reverend said. "Can you... I mean do you like coffee?" the Reverend said as he hurried towards the counter.

"Yes, I'd like that. If it's not too much trouble."

I watched the Reverend pour our coffee. "Do you take cream, sugar?"

"A little of both would be nice."

The Reverend returned with coffee, and store-bought cookies layered on a platter. He set them down on the table and motioned with his hand to help myself.

"Eat something," he said.

I took a cookie and dunked it in my coffee. I was hungry, and food was comforting. We sat in silence for a few moments before he spoke again. His voice was soft and reassuring.

"Lance, you told me you're a professor. You teach robotics at a university. Correct?"

"Yeah, that's right."

"Well, what in the world of technology, computers, or science could explain how a Lego bot can act like he did?"

I asked the same question before, but never came up with a reasonable answer.

"I don't know," I said.

"Could someone be playing a trick on you, Lance, one of your students, perhaps a colleague? The Lego's could be programmed to move like humans. Could that explain what's going on? Somebody got to your Lego Me and reprogrammed him?"

"Well, sure, but this goes beyond any robot I've seen. The artificial intelligence in this thing is unbelievable and is more advanced than our current technology, like fifty years or more. Besides, who besides me would have the skill set to do this, and when would they find the opportunity? I made Lego Me in my lab. I kept him in my basement, in a locked house. No one had access to him but me."

"Well, I'm just throwing ideas about, Lance. I'm trying to help stimulate some thoughts that may lead to a solution."

"Reverend Cole, thank you for helping me and for believing in me. It means a lot," I said.

The Reverend looked at me—stared is more like it. I felt his eyes trace every contour, as if he were studying me like a lab rat. I took a sip of coffee, and this seemed to amuse him.

"Reverend?" I said.

"Oh, yes, yes," he said, startled from his trance. "You're most welcome."

-Chapter 7-

I was afraid to return home, and my office was no longer an option. Lego Me had the lock changed. It was him alright. I went in one afternoon after I thought he'd left. My key didn't work. I pounded on the door and kicked at it a few times and then I noticed a sheet of paper on the floor, half-slid beneath the door. I picked it up and read the title page: *How to design and analyze the electronics related to the weak signal acquisition, particularly electrophysiology.* Dan from my robotics class wrote it. He scribbled a note to me.

Sorry this is late, professor.

That's quite alright, Dan. I hadn't assigned a research paper. In fact, I had assigned nothing lately. I'm not proud to say, but I've been derelict in my duties over the past several weeks, given my obsession with Lego Me and my recent, apparent mental breakdown. I crouched to my hands and knees and placed my ear to the ground to get a bug's eye view beneath the door. There were several more papers strewn on the floor, each bound in a clear plastic binder made for academic papers. They gave me chills.

I stood up and peered through the glass window insert for a better look. My office looked like a deranged scientist had taken it over. Boxes, Legos, electronics, and incomplete bots scattered on the floor, desk, and bookcase. An unkept office I could tolerate, but the mutilated Lego bodies with their half-finished torsos, disembodied legs, and arms turned my stomach. I scanned the darkened room and saw an arm sticking out of an unmarked brown box and a leg partially covered by canvas. I never saw the head.

Then, something caught my eye, a movement between the shadows. It looked like a rat crawling over the boxes, stopping, and sniffing the air, before resuming its search for a hidden morsel. Only the rat wasn't real. It looked robotic and made from Legos.

I checked the door once more and gave it one last kick before turning to leave. I got about halfway down the hall and ran into one of my students. It was Melissa, something or other. I forgot her last name, but I was happy to see her. Not that I was fond of her as a student or anything like that. I was just happy to see a familiar face.

"Melissa," I said. "Melissa. Hi. How are you?"

She didn't respond. Instead, she stood there with a stiff back and that blank, pale face that was becoming too familiar.

"Melisa. I—I want to say how sorry I am. I know I haven't been much of a teacher lately. We still have another month left in the semester. That's enough time to fix your code and get your soccer bot working."

I smiled as I spoke, but she was unmoved. Her wide eyes stared blankly at me.

"I know I must look awful," I said.

I reached for the mouse under my eye and told her I had fallen off my bike and that I was okay. Then, I noticed the paper she was holding in her hand and asked it her what it was.

"It's a research paper for Doctor Ziegel," she said.

"What—what do you mean, a research paper for Doctor Ziegel? I am Doctor Ziegel, and I didn't assign a research paper. Have you lost your mind too?"

I noticed we had an audience: students and colleagues had stopped in the hallway and were gawking at me. I took out my handkerchief and wiped the cold sweat forming on my brow.

"I—I didn't mean that. Here, I'll take it," I said, reaching out my hand.

Melissa turned and shielded the paper with her body. The hallway closed in on me. People inched closer. Some laughed, and some looked perturbed. That's when I saw Lego Me standing at the end of the hallway. We made eye contact, and I felt a chill run down my spine. He put his head down and marched toward me with determination and bad intent. I didn't think. I just turned my back and exited through the side door. I ran down three flights of stairs, bounding three and four steps at a time and when I got to the bottom, I ran out the door and toward the parking lot. My fifty-year-old body was long past its prime, but I felt like an Olympic-class sprinter as I made my way across the lawn and to the safety of my car.

I was low on cash. I wore the same smelly clothes every day, washed in public bathrooms and raided restaurant dumpsters for food. One can eat swell on the garbage meant for scavengers. Each passing day, I lost more-and-more of my humanity. In a week, I looked more like a flea-bitten rat than a respected college professor.

Lego Me had taken over. I couldn't go back to work, and I had no friends at the university, no colleagues I could trust. All my life, I was a loner. I'd come to work, teach my classes, conduct my research, and leave. But in these desperate times, I had no one to confide in. No one could help.

I drove around town at night trying to collect my thoughts. Traveling the side streets of the sleepy college town was therapeutic, but I had to stop. Gas was low, and I had no money. I parked at a local picnic spot not too far from campus and near the lake. I slept there and tried to pass the time by playing chess in my mind's eye. Despite the stress, my intellect was still intact. In fact, my memory and cognition were never stronger. It felt like my brain was on steroids. When chess became boring, I put my head back in the rest and tried to stop my brain. It was no use. My mind spun out of control, like an overclocked CPU processing a billion threads per second. I'd sweat and my stomach churned like a wonky motor. More than once, I opened my car door just-in-time wretch and puke onto the gravel. Hardly anything came out.

My car was my prison. I wanted to step out and walk by the shore and allow the breeze to wash over me and cool my tired brain. But whenever I was in public, I drew the same peculiar looks from strangers. Okay, I was a mess, dirty and disheveled, my grimy face, and my unkept beard. I looked like what I was, a homeless man living out of his car. Still, I expected sympathetic stares laden with pity or general disinterest. After all, there were lots of bums walking around town. No one paid them much mind. I never did. Yet, when people looked at me, they froze; their eyes narrowed. I read a hint of fear and wonderment on their face. Some would stop and pull out their cell phone, and that was my cue to run, to cower like a scared rabbit.

I had my car, the clothes on my back, and my cell phone worked for the time being. It was a pleasant diversion to play games on and study old photographs, my past life, as I called it. I texted Tracy, but I got autoresponder back: *this user has blocked you.* The message gave me the sad chills, but I didn't blame her.

Lego Me texted me: *come home.*

I blocked him.

One day, I received a disturbing text message from the Lego Corporation. It was an order confirmation, like the one I got for the Lego Me pieces. The invoice was for a 9mm Lego gun that was designed and ordered from the Clicks-to-Bricks program. I hadn't placed any such order. In fact, I hadn't been on their website in weeks, and I had designed nothing since Lego Me. I wasn't about to start another project after all I've been through. Besides, my bank accounts were locked, so I couldn't pay for the order. Yet, someone designed and paid for a 9 mm gun. The parts were scheduled to arrive in two days.

I had enough. My life hung in the balance. I needed to talk to someone trustworthy, and that's when I decided to visit Tracy. I should have gone to her sooner and told her everything. She could help. Maybe I had lost my mind; she would know what to do. I could forget about her as a girlfriend. That part was over. What I needed most was a friend, just a friend.

I confronted her at her workplace in the parking lot. She was exiting her car, returning from lunch, I presumed. She saw me approach and offered me a crooked smile.

"Hi," I said.

Tracy cocked her head to the side. "Hello," she said. She studied my face like she was seeing it for the first time. Her weak smile dissolved into a perplexed expression. She looked like she was trying to solve a riddle. Apparently, I was that riddle. "Can I help you?" she said.

"Can you help me? It's me, Lance. Don't you recognize me?"

And then I saw him. The bastard. He exited the passenger side of the car and walked behind Tracy. He stood close to her, wrapping his thick Lego arm around her small waist as he pulled her in close. I had a good, long look at him. I studied his face and tried to grasp what others saw. He had the telltale ragged edges of a Lego sculpture, the one I made in my basement. He was plastic, scarred with seams formed by the conjoining Lego bricks. His skin was not human. It was ragged and yet strangely pliable. It moved and twisted with the subtle nuance of actual flesh, but it made my flesh crawl.

This odd couple stared at me. They looked at me as if I were the freak.

"Lance, he's scaring me," Tracy said.

Tracy stepped behind Lego Me and used the brick monstrosity as a protective shield. That's when I knew she was talking about me. I was frightening her, as if I were the Lego Monster.

Lego Me stood there, silent and defiant. His muscles bulged and twitched beneath a tight-fitting shirt—it was one of mine. I sized him up and quickly determined I was no match. That night in my living room, I got some good shots in and avoided catastrophic injury. I was lucky to escape with my life, but I didn't want to press my luck.

"It's me," I said to Tracy. "I'm Lance. This—this monster is made of bricks. He's been imitating me. He's pretending to be me. Can't you see that?"

Tracy said nothing; instead, she stood close to Lego Me and clutched his elbow.

"So, Tracy didn't even recognize you?" Reverend Cole said.

"No," I said. "Worse than that, she looked frightened... by me."

The Reverend ran his hand through his white hair. "What did you do next?"

"I left. There was no point in staying. I wasn't going to accomplish anything."

"Did you hear from Lego Me again?"

"Oh yeah," I said. "He called the next day."

-Chapter 8-

I was asleep in my car when my phone rang.

"Hey, it's me," the voice said.

"Who are you?" I said.

"I want to help, Lance."

"Yeah? Like hell you do. What else are you going to do? Shoot me? Kill me?"

"Lance, why don't you shut up and listen for once in your life? That's your problem. You think you're smarter than everyone else, and okay, maybe you are, but it doesn't mean you have to be an arrogant prick about it." Lego Me took a deep breath. "It's my fault," he continued. "I'm an arrogant prick, so why shouldn't you be?"

I gripped the phone tighter. The one thing I took so much pleasure in creating, I now wanted to destroy. "What do you know about me and my life?" I said.

"Come home."

"Home?" I laughed into the phone. "Why? So you can finish the job?"

"I was merely defending myself. You were the aggressor."

I had to pause and collect my thoughts. Either I was imagining things, or I was having a full-blown conversation with an overgrown toy. A Lego man, the one I conceived and delivered in my basement lab, was speaking to me in a calm, reasoned manner. This wasn't Siri voicing pre-fed lines in response to auditory cues. Lego Me was coherent, intelligent, and thoughtful, and he flaunted a remarkable display of human consciousness and self-awareness. Yet, he was a machine looping through an instruction set, arrays, logic, routines, sub-routines, classes. Someone obviously connected him to the Internet. That's where he got his information on me and possibly his vocabulary, too.

His programming was remarkable, sublime even, and would pass the Turing test: the test used to determine if a machine could fool a human into thinking it was human. I'd proudly take credit for it if I could. But I had not programmed his AI. My code was quick and rudimentary: move joystick forward to walk forward, back to step back. That was about it. He shouldn't speak, let alone think, and behave as a normal person. And if I hadn't programmed him, then who? Who, besides me, possessed the skill set? I worked at a university, yes, but I was the resident AI and robotics expert. People came to me. They asked me questions. I did the research. I taught the classes. I wrote the papers on advance artificial intelligence and robotics. I'm not a braggart. That's just the way it was, and yet all these facts pointed to my deteriorating mental state. It suggested I was not actually having this conversation, but imagining it.

"But you're a Lego Man," I said.

My words sounded feeble and reactionary, and I saw Lego Me in my mind's eye, raising an eyebrow and smirking.

"Lance, come home."

"No."

"I have money for you."

I perked up at the sound of money. It was probably a trick, but I was nearly broke and completely desperate.

"How much?" I said.

"Two-hundred. I know it's not much, but it's all I can spare."

Without friends, nor family, my options were few and so I accepted.

"Who are you?" I said. "What's going on?"

"Look. We'll meet. I'll give you the money, and we can discuss it then. Okay?"

"I want to meet in a public place. How about Wegman's supermarket in Lakewood?"

"No. Come home."

"Why not Wegman's?"

"People will stare. We won't have any privacy."

"You mean they'll stare at me?"

"Look, just come to the house."

I paused, then I told him it was Wegman's or nothing.

"Fine," he said. "Wegman's. 2:00 PM, Tuesday in the food court."

It was past the lunch hour, but there were enough people in the food court to make me feel safe. I purchased a coffee and took a seat at a table next to a window.

A few minutes later, Lego Me entered the food court. He was dressed in a pair of my blue jeans, my maroon, long-sleeved shirt, and my herringbone blazer—the professor jacket, as I affectionately named it.

He was a grotesque figure with his Lego-brick-skin and rigid, awkward gait reminiscent of a walking corpse. Nothing about him was natural. He looked like what he was: a Lego man. Yet, as he moved through the food court, he didn't seem to warrant any extraordinary attention, and that was extraordinary. He appeared to be another face in the crowd, just another shopper on a Tuesday afternoon, casually strolling through the food court, looking to meet a friend for lunch. He was normal to everyone else. To me, well, I saw the devil for what it was.

Indifference could be explained by people's jaded view of technology. We walked around with minicomputers perpetually glued to our ears. Most people texted between bites of food and sips of coffee. That's why a big Lego Man hardly drew a passing glance. Even the store had robots, cute things rolling around, and cleaning the floors like dutiful little slaves.

Shoppers were used to them, and they may have thought Lego Me was just an upscale version of a cleaning bot.

The Lego dummy spotted me and strode up to my table. He was confident and arrogant. I could tell by the way he carried himself. However, his eat-shit Mona Lisa grin was absent. A serious, more business-like expression replaced it. My heart thumped beneath my shirt, but I reminded myself I was safe. Lego Me wasn't foolish enough to try something in a public venue, but if he did, I was prepared.

"Have a seat," I told him. "Are you hungry? Would you like something to eat? Can you eat?"

Lego Me waved me off, then he sat across from me and folded his brick arms across his chest; there was a hint of compassion in his eyes. They were blue, like mine.

"Is that Polo?" I said, forcing a smile. "It smells nice. It works well with your natural plastic body odor."

Lego Me was unamused. He shook his head and asked me what I was talking about, and I told him never mind.

"I got the money for you," he said.

"Good."

"I said two-hundred, but I was able to spare an extra fifty."

"Well, that's just great. What about my house?" I said.

"What about it?"

"Well, it's my fucking house!" I said, pounding the table.

I felt everyone's eyes on me. I didn't imagine it; they were all staring, so I waited for things to return to normal before I spoke again.

"It's my fucking house," I whispered.

Lego Me spoke in a hushed voice like a father might talk to his young son. "Lance, that was your old life. You have a new life. You'll have to adjust. I'll have to adjust."

"Adjust? How? By living out of my car, broke, jobless, accepting handouts from the likes of you? What are you anyway?"

"What do you mean?"

"I mean, someone got to you, programmed you. Who was it?"

"Lance, I—"

"Don't get me wrong. I think it's quite remarkable. I should submit you for Turing testing."

"Turing testing?" Lego Me said, shaking his head.

"Yes. It's a test of a machine's ability to fool a human into thinking it's human."

"I know what the Turing test is."

"Then, why did you ask?"

"It's just that—"

"Well, whomever programmed you, did a fine job. If it weren't for your appearance, I'd never guess you were silicon and code, bits and bytes cleverly organized to trick the mind into thinking you are an organic brain. Congratulations. You pass. Did you hear that whoever is listening? As a scientist, I'm jealous and intrigued. Who's responsible? I'm not angry or anything. I just want to meet the person or persons responsible for this engineering feat."

I was only half-lying. I wanted to meet the individual, or more likely the team responsible for Lego Me, and congratulate them on their fine work. Not only had they programmed Lego Me's AI, but they did so beneath my nose and in my house. Yet another part of me wanted to strangle the miserable bastards. They ruined what was supposed to be a playful project. It was a causality that altered my life in the worst possible way. I had hardly anything left except the dirty, smelly rags on my back, a cell phone and a car that was nearly out of gas. I wanted to meet the hackers, shake their hands, and then bust them in the mouth. No. I am not a violent person. It's not in my DNA. But like any other human being, pushed to my end, I will fight with everything I have.

"Did you know I was born with a birth defect?" I said. "Hypoplastic left heart syndrome, HLHS. The left side of my heart didn't form fully, so they had to crack my chest open when I was a baby to repair it. Imagine that: a little baby laid out on a gurney, spread open like a lobster like a grade school biology experiment from hell. Would you like to see the scar? It's quite impressive actually after all these years; it looks like a big zipper."

"Yes," he replied in a matter-of-fact tone. "I also remember the time you were knocked unconscious after falling off your bicycle. The doctor had to stitch you back together to fix the hole in your head."

I reached for my temple and ran my fingers across the narrow bump just above my eyebrow.

"How did you know that?" I said. "How could you? That's not public knowledge. It's not Googleable."

This was bigger than I imagined. Lego Me was tapping into private medical databases and looking into my health history. He had to be. Either that, or someone fed him the information.

"May I?" Lego Me said while extending his hand.

He was asking to touch the scar above my right eye. It was an odd request, but I let him more from curiosity than anything else.

Lego Me raked the back of his fingers against my scar. It didn't hurt. The accident was several years ago and the scar, along with the memory, had faded. I felt his fingers drag across my cheek and toward my right ear. I moved quickly out of pure instinct and grabbed his wrist. It was remarkably supple.

"What are you doing?" I said.

"Nothing. Let me go, please."

I pushed his hand away and released my grip.

"Where's my money?" I said.

"I have your money, but listen to me, Lance. You're not well. You're not thinking right. Something's happened. Something got mixed up. We don't know what it is, but we want to help."

"We? Who's we? Who are you?"

"If you just come home with me, I'll show you. We can fix you."

Yeah, I thought. You'll fix me good. Sometime, somewhere, I pissed somebody off and now they were exacting their revenge. Perhaps it was a former student; I've had a few demented ones over the years. What could I have done to make someone want to ruin my life? This was way beyond any practical joke. It wasn't funny. It was just cruel, a pure evil genius that robbed me of everything I loved, everything I ever knew, leaving me penniless and without recourse. A simple robbery would have been much kinder. Why not tap into my bank accounts, my savings, drain them dry, and leave me to wallow in the wake? Why take the extra steps: steal my job, my identity, my lover and leave me homeless? Was it because they could? Did these arrogant pricks simply want to prove their hacking mastery in a show of superiority?

I stared into Lego Me's deep-set eyes. Why was he giving me money? There was no reason for it. Whomever was controlling him had my money, and they weren't concerned whether I lived or died, so why offer a bone?

"So, you have money for me?" I said. Lego Me nodded his head. "Why?"

"What do you mean, why? Because you need it."

"So, what if I need it? You've already stolen everything. My house, my checking accounts, were locked. What about my house and Tracy? I'm surprised you haven't cut my cellphone service, or is that next?"

"No one has taken your house and the checking account was frozen for your own safety, so you wouldn't hurt yourself or someone else. And your cellphone will remain in service. I want to maintain contact with you, especially in your delusional condition. If you only come back home with me. You'll see. You can stay in your house, your bed. I'll explain everything and we can fix you."

"Excuse me, but it's not me who needs fixing. There's nothing wrong with me."

"Lance, listen to—"

"Where's my money!" I shouted. "You said you have money for me. Well, let's see it."

Lego Me's eyes dropped in resignation, then he reached inside his jacket. His Lego hand fumbled beneath his garment, and he seemed to take an inordinate amount of time.

Sweat poured down my cheek, and well, I couldn't take a chance. In one coordinated motion, I lifted my jacket away from my chest and reached for my gun. It was that quick, that easy. I held the 9 mm in front of my face and took aim at his chest. My hands shook, but I managed to disengage the safety. For a moment, I did nothing, said nothing. I just watched silently as his eyebrows lifted slightly and his eyes grew wide. I don't remember squeezing the trigger.

The report reverberated throughout the café like a thunderclap. I never shot a gun before. I didn't know what it would sound like. The bullet ripped into him with a loud thwack—lead slamming against hard plastic. Lego Bricks flew everywhere, along with blood. That's right. Human blood shot from the hole like water through the dike. Red dots splattered on the table, on the floor, and on me.

Lego Me slumped forward, and his forehead rested on the table. He looked like he was napping. The smell of Polo drifted through the air. Its sweet aroma filled my nostrils, causing them to flare. It's funny what you remember in those situations.

After that, I couldn't hear a thing. It was like I had gone deaf. I saw movement in my peripheral vision and witnessed the terror on people's faces, and I imagined what my own terror-stricken face looked like. Without hesitation, I stood up, holstered my gun, and ran like my hair was on fire.

"You shot him?" Reverend Cole said.

"Yes. I got that fucker. I got that fucker good."

"Right there in Wegman's?"

"Yep. In the food court."

"Holy shit!"

"Yeah, I know."

"Did you kill him? I mean, can you kill him? Can Lego people die?"

"I don't know. I left. I just left him in a pool of blood."

"He bled?"

"That's what I just said." I rolled up my sleeves and pointed out the dark purple stains to the Reverend.

"Why, Lance? Why did you shoot him? Tell me why."

"Because I thought he was going to shoot me. When he reached into his pocket, I thought he was going for his gun. I wasn't about to wait for him to pull a weapon on me. I was scared, Reverend, and I reached for my gun, and that's how it went down."

"And the gun he was reaching for—did you see it?"

"No," I said, lowering my eyes. "It was the cash. When I shot him, the bills flew from his hand onto the table and all over the floor. I remember they floated like butterflies."

Reverend Cole nodded his head. His face turned ashen, and his eyes were big and dark. "I—I see," he said.

Despite his attempt to reassure me, he didn't look like a man who saw anything. He looked pale, and I wondered if I shared too much.

After a few seconds, the Reverend regained his composure. "Lance," he said. "I want you to stay with me tonight. It's going to take time to understand what you have told me. There are friends and colleagues I'll need to consult. You'll stay here tonight, and we'll sort this out."

I was grateful for the offer, but leery. "You're tricking me," I said. "You're going to call the police and get them involved."

"Not at all, Lance. If I wanted to call the authorities, I would have done so by now. I'm trying to help you. That's all. You need some rest and something to eat. I'll take care of you until we get some answers. And besides, if you fired a weapon in the Wegman's food court, the police are already involved. There are cameras all over the place."

The Reverend was right. I was a hunted man. I knew this much, if nothing else.

"I have no other place to go," I said. "Thank you so much, Reverend."

Reverend Cole nodded and smiled at me. "Good," he said. "It's settled then. And the gun, may I see it?"

"Why do you want to see my gun?" I said.

"I'll give it back to you. I just want to keep it in a safe place for now. That's all." I hesitated. "Look," he continued. "You just told me this incredible story, and I barely know you. It's as much for your protection as it is for mine. I have a safe. I'll keep it there and return it when you're ready to leave."

The Reverend held out his hand and implored me with his eyes.

"Ok," I said and handed him my Glock.

He took the pistol and rotated the handle to fit snugly in his right hand. Then he disengaged the safety.

"Careful, Reverend," I said. "You just switched the safety to the <u>off</u> position."

The Reverend raised the gun and took aim. I was calm, and I felt a sense of peace and even permitted a slight smile to wax over my face. I looked past the barrel to get a better look at the Reverend. He, too, was smiling—not a happy smile, but a tortured, grimaced one.

I never heard the gunshot. In fact, I heard nothing.

-Chapter 9-

Mrs. Cole shot straight up in bed. She thought she dreamt it, but it was real; it sounded like a gunshot. She ran downstairs, never bothering to put on her housecoat.

When she reached the bottom of the stairs, she saw her husband standing in the den. He looked dazed and held what appeared to be a toy gun in his right hand. She ran to him, but a sharp pain in her foot caused her to pull up lame.

"Ouch, ouch," she said, hopping on one foot while plucking the offending dagger from her arch.

"Are you alright?" said Reverend Cole.

"I'm alright. What about you? I thought I heard a gunshot."

"You did. I just shot a man."

"You did what?"

"Well, it wasn't really a man."

Mrs. Cole shook her head. "Robert," she said. "Have you been drinking again?"

"Well, yes I have, but I tell you it's true. He told me a story, some wild story."

"Well, where is this man now?"

The Reverend gestured towards the open front door. Mrs. Cole's eyes followed the plastic trail leading to the porch.

"Well, I'll be goddamned," she said.

Reverend Cole, still holding the gun, looked over at his wife. "What do you have there?" he said. "In your hand?"

Mrs. Cole rolled the plastic piece between her fingers. "Robert," she said in a hushed voice. "It's a Lego brick."

-Chapter 10-

My body chattered, and rattled against the metal bed as we traversed a bumpy, dark road toward an unknown destination. I gritted my teeth with every jostling blow, and I swore beneath my breath for the driver to slow down. The bad potholes sent stabbing pains through my arms, neck, and head. But it was the burning hole in my chest which caused the most concern.

I laid on my back and took deep breaths and stared up at a night sky because it was all I could do. The pain in my heart reminded me not to move. A billion eyes stared back at me, and I pondered the universe, its beauty, and its wonder; it was a subtle, but necessary distraction from the pain.

I reached for and found the hole in my chest, but I fought the urge to look. Instead, I focused on the stars and stemmed the flow with my hand. I was not religious, but I prayed for the first time in a long time. It was a prayer to the stars to keep me alive for one more night.

I was a captive, transported against my will. Passengers sit in the cab. Injured hostages lie bleeding in the back of a pickup. I didn't know who was driving the truck, or where we were heading, but it didn't matter. For the time being, I was alive, and I wasn't in a squad car, so that was good. I wouldn't do well in prison—I've heard stories.

My righteous rage dissipated as a feeling of regret washed over me. I thought I was defending myself against a Lego mannequin bent on harming me. You can't murder a Lego Man, but I was sorry for the mess it caused, the people I frightened, diving under tables with terror-stricken faces and my current calamity. I never intended to hurt anyone, but that's exactly what I did. What's happened to me? Where was that peaceful college professor, the decorated scientist whose aim was to advance society? Of course, they pushed me past my limit and desperate people do desperate things. This thought helped mitigate the guilt.

Recent events came to me as if recalling a fragmented dream. I was in Lily Dale and I remembered the Reverend's face; it made me smile. And then I remembered the gun, my gun. Oh, yes, he shot me, but why? He seemed like a nice man, and I meant him no harm. I must have sounded crazy, and he thought it the prudent course of action. What a pity. I liked the Reverend and trusted him. I should trust only myself from now on.

Curiosity took hold and with considerable effort, I attempted to sit up and sneak a peek through the rear window; however, this simple act made me wince, so I laid back down and sucked in a breath of cool, night air. Besides, it didn't matter who was driving. What mattered was where we were heading and what was waiting for me when we got there. I should enjoy the ride, stare at the blanket of stars, and take some consolation that I was still alive.

After about thirty minutes, we stopped, and the engine cut off. There were no streetlights it was coal dark except for the stars. I heard the truck door squeal open and the sound of my heart thumping heavy in my ears. Then I heard the second door open. Two sets of footsteps approached. The lump in my throat swelled to the size of an apple. *Time to meet my maker*, I thought.

The tailgate creaked down, and the first face I saw caused me to recoil. He was an older man in his sixties with a wild growth of stark white hair that sprouted from his head like a patch of overgrown brush. His eyes were wide and there was a hint of the mad scientist in them. He reminded me of Doctor Frankenstein's helper in the *Bride of Frankenstein*, not Igor but the other one, the crazed looking one with a wild-eyed, maniacal grimace permanently etched on his face. He looked at me with an enthusiasm that bordered on creepy. His smile raised goosebumps on my arms and made the hair on my neck stand on end. He looked like a slithering snake ready to strike its prey.

And then I noticed the second face behind him. It was Lego Me, bandaged and bleeding from the wound I had inflicted. He looked like a hurt puppy with sad, droopy eyes. I met his gaze briefly before I turned my head away. For the first time, I felt empathy toward my creation, and I was ashamed of my actions.

At that moment, I wished I was anywhere else, and though my aging body wasn't what it used to be, I thought about running to safety. I had darkness on my side and if I got a head start, I might have escaped. But the slightest movement lit my skin on fire; running was not an option. So, I just shrugged and smiled weakly at my captors. They were stoic and serious about their task. I looked around at the stars, the moon, anything I could fix my eyes on as it may be the last thing I see before I left this earth. I wanted my last memory to be a good one.

The old, white-haired man spoke first. "Look," he said. "There's quite a bit of damage."

The old man's brow furrowed, and I thought it was odd that he should care about my well-being. I didn't know him. I'm sure we never met and despite his concern, I didn't like him. It's just an impression I got, like a sixth sense, that told me he was no good.

Lego Me, the miserable wretch he was, also took pity on me. I saw it in his eyes.

"Let's get him inside," Lego Me said.

I looked up and off to my left and recognized the porch light and white siding in need of a power wash. I was home, a small measure of comfort, but I needed every win I could get.

I turned back to Lego me and our eyes locked. "He'll need help," he said to the old man.

"I can't climb up there," the old man protested.

"I'll go up and give him a hand. You just help him down to the ground."

The old man nodded and said, "Be careful."

Lego Me hoisted himself onto the flatbed. His blood-soaked bandage glistened in the moonlight. I shook my head in disbelief, but I reminded myself that bleeding Lego bots were my new normal, or another way of saying nothing was normal.

He crawled up to me on hands and knees, then steadied himself on my shoulder. "I'll get behind you," he said. "Can you help with your legs?"

I nodded my head. Lego Me slid between me and the cab and placed his hands under my armpits. I smelled the coffee on his breath and the Polo wafting in the night air. I wanted to make a crack, but decided against it. He was helping me, and I didn't want to spoil my luck by making him angry.

I managed—with Lego Me's help—to sit upright. From there, I rolled over and crawled to the edge of the truck bed where the old man was waiting for me. Lego Me escorted me with a gentle hand on my back. It was a compassionate gesture.

I needed help to get down from the truck, but the old man was useless. He offered his hand for support, but I spilled out and landed on the driveway with a clunk.

"Be careful," the old man said to me.

I shot him a glare. "Thanks," I said.

Lego Me and the old man each took an arm and with most of my weight resting on their shoulders, they assisted me into my house.

When we got inside, they led me to the sofa, where I folded myself into a heap at one end. The old man sat next to me and Lego Me sat in the chair across from me, and we all just sat in awkward silence for several minutes. I heard Lego Me's labored breathing, interspersed with an occasional gurgle. It sounded like he needed a respirator, or better still, a doctor, and I told him as much.

"I'll be alright," he said.

"It doesn't sound good," I said. Lego Me smiled, but he didn't reply.

I caught the old man staring at me, gawking, with that stupid grin wrapped around his face like a Cheshire cat. His presence annoyed me and all but told him so.

"Excuse me," I said.

"Look at him," he said, pointing to my face. From a distance, he traced my contour with his fingers as if illustrating a drawing. "Look, look."

Lego Me shrugged and said, "Yeah, I've seen him before."

The old man's expression bordered on maniacal. His eyes were black pits, filled with glazed-over wonderment. What did he see that was so astonishing? What was so special about me?

"Shall we have some tea?" I said.

The old man laughed. "And a sense of humor too," he said.

"Yes, well," Lego Me said. "Do I not have a sense of humor?"

"Yes, yes, of course. And so should he."

An excruciating minute passed while the two men talked about me as if I were not in the room.

"Perhaps someone should address the elephant in the room," I said, interrupting their conversation.

"And what might that be?" the old man said.

I looked at Lego Me for confirmation, but he was of no help. He was busy fixing his bandages, and I could see, for the first time, the extent of his injury. It was cringe worthy and the fact that I had inflicted the wound—a near fatal one—made it more difficult to stomach.

"Oh, I don't know," I said. "Perhaps one of you can explain what the fuck is going on."

The old man laughed; then he looked at me and said, "What would you like to know?"

There was a lot I wanted to know, but I thought I'd begin with a simple question. "Who are you?" I said.

The old man curled his lip into a smile and said, "I am Doctor H. H. Tavarius. You may call me Doctor T." The doctor held out a white, gloved hand. I stared at it for a moment before turning my nose up.

"Well, that tells me absolutely nothing," I said. "I mean, who are you? And why are you here, and how is Lego Me walking and talking and bleeding in my living room? That is blood, isn't it? Look. He's bleeding over my couch. Be careful there. Will you?"

Lego Me's eyes were soft and resigned, and I pitied the creature, the object of my genius. After all, this wasn't his fault—none of it was. Who was answerable for this malady, if not its architect? Am I not the creator and he the created? Am I not culpable... for everything? Should I not turn my rage inward and my reconciliation outward?

"I see an explanation is in order," Tavarius said. He and Lego Me exchanged glances; silently, the two decided Tavarius should speak. "Very well," Tavarius continued. "Look upon the eyes of your creator, your God, if you will. Well, one of your gods, at any rate. I being the other."

The Doctor motioned towards Lego Me as he spoke. "You're mistaken," I said. "It's the other way around. I am the reason for his being and as for you, well, I claim no credit. Someone else must bear that burden."

Tavarius looked unamused, which was fine, because I didn't say it to be funny. I was serious about the situation at hand—very serious. The doctor and Lego Me again exchanged knowing glances as if they were privy to a joke. It irritated me.

"I see the problem now," Tavarius said to Lego Me. "It's quite plain up close. I'm afraid I might be partially to blame—being the neuro specialist and all—or perhaps something went wrong on your end, Lance? Did you follow my instructions with due diligence? I think there was an error in your recursion. That must be it; Your code was faulty. Bits were lost, neurons dropped, memory impaired, and it created a fragmented reality similar to dementia. That's what he has, you know: dementia."

Lego Me's eyes narrowed in and focused on Tavarius. "I don't know," he said. "Perhaps, or perhaps, it was your shitty theory that's at fault. There are still a few rats running around with a severe case of dementia. Remember Egor? That poor thing chased its tail for hours on end. It still would had we not dismantled it and put it out of its misery. You were right, however. I should have reigned him in sooner."

Doctor Tavarius sat straight up at the edge of his seat. "Hey!" he said. "This was all new to me. The slices weren't thin enough. Once I discovered the mistake, I fixed it and the rest of the rats were just fine.

Besides, that was the destructive process. We couldn't use that, remember?"

I like to think of myself as a smart guy, with a keen awareness of many disciplines outside my own, but their conversation lost me. I was beginning to think it was gibberish akin to pig Latin, some construct made to not only confuse the listener but to irritate them as well. It worked well on both accounts.

"Fine," Lego Me said. "Let's just say it was my shitty code."

"I wasn't saying that, exactly," Tavarius said. "It's just the theory is so new, so unproven. Problems were bound to arise. Our research showed as much. We would lose neurons during the transfer; we knew this. And with lost neurons, there'd be memory loss and altered perceptions. All things considered, I think we did an excellent job. I only wish you had reigned him in when you discovered the problem, instead of letting him gallivant all over town like a senile old man."

"Hey!" I shouted. "I'm sitting right here. You know I can hear everything you're saying?"

Tavarius waved a dismissive hand in front of his face. "Yes, of course," he said.

"Maybe you're right," said Lego Me.

The old doctor cocked his nose toward the ceiling with an air of superiority. "Well, of course I'm right," he said. "You never listen."

"But we agreed he'd be autonomous. To live and function on his own. That was the whole point."

"That was the end goal, yes. But obviously he wasn't ready."

"Maybe if you were here to help. He's bigger and stronger than me. I could have used an extra pair of hands."

"I told you; my work at the university would not permit it. You're lucky I could get away tonight. Otherwise, you would have bled out in the Wegman's food court."

Tavarius's laugh shook the walls and my sensibilities at once.

"What's so funny?" I said.

"It's just that," he said. "It's just that you shot doctor Ziegel in the middle of Wegman's with a Lego gun you fashioned with your own hands. A perfect example of machine turning against its maker."

The Doctor's eyes welled up as he broke into hysterics.

"Oh, why don't you shut up for once?" Lego Me said.

"Oh, come on," Tavarius said. "You can appreciate the irony, can't you?"

The two prattled on like a cantankerous, old married couple while I tried to make sense of it all. I knew I was at the subject of their bickering, but the context was still a mystery. It was as though I arrived late to a murder whodunit. I couldn't tell the victim from the perpetrator, but I had an idea I was a little of both.

"Gentlemen, gentlemen," I interrupted. "May I?"

"Oh, yes, of course," Tavarius said.

"I'm not sure what you're going on about, but there is my creation," I said, pointing to Lego Me. "I call him Lego Me." The doctor and Lego Me exchanged knowing glances. "Would you cut that out?" I said in a raised voice.

"You're confused," Tavarius said. "You, my dear fellow, are Lego Me, the one and only. I wanted to name you Victor, but Doctor Ziegel insisted on Lego Me, a rather childish name, don't you think? I like Victor. It has more of an elegant ring to it. Would you not agree?"

I nodded my head to appease Doctor Jekyll. He was obviously delusional, and this madman had somehow intercepted my creation, programmed him, and turned him against me. For what reason, I do not know, but at least now, I could stare into the eye of my enemy, this doctor, if that's really what he was. How he made a humanoid Lego dummy come to life like an oversized Chucky doll, I do not know. Tavarius was an evil genius, if nothing else.

"Look, I'm tired," I said. "And I have a splitting headache. Would you be kind enough to take your leave now, Doctor Frankenstein? I mean, thank you for your help and all. And if you would take the Lego beast with you, that would be great too. He's yours, but I guess he's been yours all along. Do with him what you wish. He's become quite a handful; the likes of which I never imagined. All I ask is you leave me be. Go ahead, leave before I call the police or the FBI or whomever deals with such crimes. You'll have a running head start. Go on now."

"You're confused," the Doctor said. "I told you that—"

"Allow me," Lego Me said. "Doctor Tavarius is right. You're confused, but that's not your fault."

"Well, whose fault is it?" I said.

"It's ours." There was an awkward pause while Lego Me wrung his plastic hands and stared at the floor. "We were close," he continued. "You were nearly perfect. The hardware, robotics, software, operating system, chipset, power supply, everything. It was very complicated, and I didn't think we could pull it off. I mean, I knew it was possible. The theory was there, the science... It's just that it's never been done before, not like this. We couldn't anticipate every scenario, and we never predicted this outcome. Doctor Tavarius alluded to the missing neurons. They didn't transfer. Maybe it was the faulty code. I don't know. But there are some missing puzzle pieces. The integration between my personality, my memories, my thoughts, feelings, and emotions with your electronics— your electrical brain and nervous system as it were—failed. Well, I should say it wasn't a total failure. We did well, considering the pioneering nature of our work. We just need to take that last step."

"It's even messed with your optics," Tavarius said. "How you see the world. How you perceive objects and people, even your place in society." I must have looked as scared as I felt, because Tavarius told me not to be alarmed. "It's okay," he continued. "In this sense, you are no different from the rest of humanity and how we perceive the world in three dimensions when no such reality exists. We create the world envisioned in our minds. It's quite simple, actually. Quantum physics explains it all."

My ears rang and though I could hear well enough, it sounded like Tavarius was talking under water. I felt cold and my body shook.

"Is there a window open?" I said. "Someone, please close the damned window. It's freezing in here."

"See? See there?" The doctor said to Lego Me.

"See what?" I demanded.

"Your senses," the Doctor said. "You should not feel cold, nor heat, nor thirst, nor hunger. There is no reason to feel pain, hot, cold. Your emotions have transferred, and that's expected, but all the physical triggers that attach your feelings to a human body filled with nerve receptors should have been severed. Without nerve endings, there's no way to transmit those signals to your brain; and yet, as you sit before us, you perceive physical sensations just as any living organism would. Remarkable. Our experiment at once failed miserably and succeeded beyond our wildest expectations. We have reimagined life and stretched the limits of human consciousness on this earth. Hand over the Nobel Prize now. Of course, it was mostly my doing, but don't worry, Doctor Ziegel. I will not leave you out. I'll make sure you get credit, too."

"I'm not sure I want credit," Lego Me said. "Our experiment nearly killed me."

"Well, wouldn't that be convenient?" Tavarius said. "You download your thoughts, your personality into a machine and that machine disposes of you for the irrelevant being you are."

Lego Me said nothing. He simply stared at the Doctor.

"Okay, okay," Tavarius said. "Then you should have kept him under lock and key while we worked out the bugs. It was you that wanted him to run around, untethered."

"It was a social experiment."

"Yes, a failed one."

"He has rights."

"Yes of course he does."

This was absurd, I thought. They were speaking of me as if I were a robot, a science experiment gone horribly wrong. It would've been hilarious if not so preposterous.

"I am Lego Me? Is that what you're trying to tell me?" I said.

"Yes, yes. Now you got it," Tavarius said. "Is it clear to you now?"

"Oh, yes. Eminently clear."

The doctor looked at me suspiciously. "It is?" he said.

"Yes, of course. Very clear. You obviously got to Lego Me, cast some sort of black magic voodoo spell over him and turned an otherwise fine lump of Lego bricks into the monstrosity that sits before us now. That much is clear. Now you're gaslighting me for profit, or fun, or some other unknown reason."

Tavarius shook his head while making disapproving tsk, tsk sounds. "I see we have much work to do," he said. "But first, I need to use your bathroom. Can you tell me where it is?"

Lego Me, and I answered in perfect unison: "It's down the hall, to your left."

With Tavarius gone, Lego Me and I sat in awkward silence. He held a red-stained cloth over his chest. I knew it was impossible for him to bleed. Still, there was that damned red liquid oozing out of him like jam. I checked my arm for the dried, purple splotches. They were still there.

I heard pissing and coughing sounds coming from the hallway bathroom and I thought about what Tavarius and Lego Me told me. Their story, while theoretically plausible, was not practical from a scientific standpoint. There were too many holes. Namely, the science behind the theory was rudimentary. I've read books, research papers and seen documentaries which spoke of such aspirations—contriving, through mind transfer, to extend human life beyond physical death, perhaps maybe forever and thus, achieving a state of immortality. No more death, no more religion, no gods, no devil, no heaven, no hell. What purpose would they serve if man could download the bits and pieces of human consciousness into another vessel, one that did not whither and decay from age or disease?

As a scientist and as a person without religious affiliation, I thought the concept was brilliant. Despite my experiences with Aunt Sandy and her friends at Lily Dale, I've concluded there is no afterlife. Perhaps society and adulthood sucked all the innocence from me. I grew up and a new magic had taken over my life: science. Besides, if there is an afterlife and it is like the bible beaters describe, then I want no part of it; that we die and go to a place called heaven—for an eternity, no less—was repulsive. It was a contrived narrative to comfort the masses, and for many people, it had. But those people didn't ask the right questions; they never do. How do we know what heaven is really like? What if it's a big

Walmart in the sky, filled with that usual motley bunch? Imagine spending eternity in a Walmart filled with a bunch of pajama-wearing rednecks from rural America. I'd opt for Hell rather than suffer that fate.

I've placed my faith in science and scientific inquiry because they hold the actual keys to the afterlife. It's just a matter of time until we discover a cure for death. The theory is simple. Humans, like computers, have hardware (our bodies) and software (our mind, memories, feelings, and personalities). All we'd have to do is download our software onto a new storage device—a new suit made of plastic and metal and articulating parts, arms, and legs and, an electronic brain. It's exactly as Tavarius and Lego Me described. The brain works on electrical impulses. Those impulses are converted into a binary code, a set of zeros and ones that in combination represent just about anything, and explain everything in the universe, including ourselves. If humanity figures out how to take that energy, convert it to code and then store it on a disk, then we have found the cure for death. We'll live forever on a hard drive somewhere or in the cloud. How ironic is that? When we die, we'll live in the clouds just like man always said. It may have been a perverse imagining of heaven, but one I resonated with. Only we're not there yet. The technology, and the knowledge are fifty years in the future and the hubris to attempt the feat is another fifty years out.

Then there's the question of the soul. I don't believe in the afterlife, and by default, I don't believe we possess a soul. But what if I'm wrong? If humans have a soul, does that soul contain energy, and can that energy be converted to electrical impulses, and then copied and stored? And how can we separate the soul portion from the consciousness, or are they the same? These questions made my head pound. You would need a dozen or more Ph.D.'s with degrees in neuro and computer science and philosophy and perhaps religion to debate the concept, but even then, the answer would be nothing more than a haphazard, educated guess.

Lego Me's irregular, gurgling breath drew me back to the room. He held his hand over his bleeding heart, and he trained his eyes on his wound. He looked and sounded miserable. I would have let him be, but the inquisitive scientist in me had other ideas.

"There's a problem with your explanation," I said to him. "Actually, many problems." Lego Me raised a single eyebrow. "Well," I continued. "You say your personality, no, your very being, was downloaded into my—well, into my brain, and that I am you and you are me. Correct?"

Lego Me nodded his head.

"Well," I said. "Who is Tavarius? I should know him. If you know him, I should know him, right? And yet, he's a stranger."

"Well," Lego Me said. "There's where the problem lies. Some of your memories were jumbled. You're a copy, an image of me, but an imperfect one at that. Neurons were corrupted, some were displaced, and some were lost altogether. There's no telling how the bad bits organically melded with the good bits to create fresh memories that never existed or erase old ones that were perfectly accurate, or as accurate as any human memory could be."

I slammed my fist into the armrest of the chair. "What are you talking about, man?" I said. "I made you. I ordered the parts. I put you together."

"Don't be angry," Lego Me said.

I hadn't meant to lash out, but this was infuriating and my temper lived on a razor thin edge.

"I—I'm sorry," I said.

The toilet flushed, and in a few seconds, Tavarius rejoined us. "What did I miss?" he said.

"I was just explaining things," Lego Me said. He leaned forward and his eyes lifted and his defeated countenance gave way to hope as he spoke to me in a kind voice. "Perhaps," he said. "Perhaps if you looked into the mirror; you would see what we see."

"What do you mean?" I shot back. "I've looked at a mirror."

"You have?"

I paused and tried to remember the last time I saw my reflection. I couldn't recall, but that meant nothing. I couldn't remember what I had for breakfast yesterday; most people couldn't. And what of it? The mirror wouldn't dissuade me from my convictions. Tavarius was a scoundrel, a criminal at best and criminally insane at worse. And Lego Me was a puppet wired to mimic human consciousness.

"Of course," I finally said.

"And what do you see?" Tavarius said.

"Well, if you're implying I should see a humanoid form of interlocking Lego Bricks, I'm sorry to disappoint you."

"Go ahead," Tavarius goaded. "Look for yourself. Use the mirror in the bathroom, if you like."

This was preposterous, insulting even. I've seen myself in the mirror. I am Doctor Lance Ziegel, professor, or now former professor of robotics engineering. I'm an expert in robotics, artificial intelligence, and software engineering.

I looked down at my hands to appease my doubts and show the mad doctor that I was flesh and blood. I'd cut myself and bleed on his lap if need be. Then he could not argue with me, at least not with a straight face. I rotated my hands, first palms up and then palms down. The black gunpowder residue, which stood in stark contrast to my pale skin, startled me.

"There's the Lego Man," I said, pointing to Lego Me. "I see him plainly enough."

"Am I made from Legos?" Lego Me said.

I nodded my head.

"See," the Doctor said. "Those are his corrupted bits that were—"

"Oh, shove your corrupted bits up your ass," I told Tavarius. I half-expected him to erupt into his Hyena-like laugh, but he didn't find this amusing. He scowled at me and then turned his head in contempt.

"If you're right," Lego Me said. "Then how do you explain my wound, the blood, the fact I can bleed and talk and walk and do everything a human being can do?"

"I don't know," I said.

"Did you program me?"

"No, not to that extent."

"Where's my power supply?"

"I don't know."

"How about—"

"I don't know. I don't know. I don't know. Tavarius here is a Voodoo Witch doctor for all I know. You slipped LSD into my water supply. I'm having a hallucinogenic trip worthy of Alice in Wonderland. I don't know. Okay?"

There was an awkward silence before Lego Me spoke. "Calm down," he said.

"Look," I said. "You're the ones who need to be answering questions; not me. Like how I do the things I do. I eat, drink, piss, ejaculate. I shit and I'm pretty sure I'm not shitting fucking Lego Bricks in the toilet."

"What do you shit in the toilet?" Tavarius said with a smug and self-assured expression. "When you shit? What do you see in the toilet? I mean, before you flush. I do hope you flush and wash your hands afterwards."

Tavarius was a contemptuous little prick. Still, I felt obliged to answer, but I couldn't. I had no answer. My forehead felt warm, and I felt sweat forming around my temples despite the chilly draft.

"I have to use the bathroom," I said.

The two conspirators exchanged glances. I knew what they were thinking, but I didn't care. I stood up, hurried to the bathroom, and locked the door behind me. Once inside, I put the toilet seat down, had a seat and rested my chin in my hands. I thought about everything and nothing at once. My mind raced like a nest of bees swarming their hive. I could not stop it, nor slow it down; beating my hand repetitively against my temple was my only relief.

I felt things. I had urges, just as any normal being. I think, therefore, I am. A philosopher said that. I don't remember who. The point is, I must be human, because I walk and speak and sense the world as only a human can. I am not just a cache of memories. Memories don't feel. Microchips are not self-aware. Motherboards are not hearts and I know I have a heart because mine throbbed with pain.

I looked around the bathroom. When was I here last, in my house, sitting on this very toilet, or any toilet for that matter? How long was it since I had the urge to pee? I have to pee right now. I'm hungry too. I've been hungry for some time, ever since I ate those cookies at the Reverend's house. See there? I was hungry and ate cookies and drank Bourbon and coffee and that proves—

My mind spun uncontrollably. I placed both hands over my ears to muffle the high-pitched whining swirling in my head like magnet tape in rewind. I was searching, searching, searching for something. The Reverend brought me cookies on a platter. He placed the platter in front of me and then fetched the coffee.

But eating the cookies, placing them in my mouth and chewing and tasting... caressing my lips to the mug, the hot, steamy breath on my tongue, the bitter balanced with the sweet... this I had no memory of.

I bought breakfast from the McDonald's near my university. I carried the bag to my car where I could eat in privacy, away from prying eyes, but I don't remember eating. In fact, I don't remember eating or drinking anything in a month, only the urge to do so.

I thought about what Tavarius asked me a few minutes ago: *what do you see when you look in the toilet?*

What do I see?

I looked down at my hands again and they looked like, well, like hands—I mean, normal, human hands, with fingers and skin and nails. Nothing like the robotic claws of a Lego Robot. I fought the urge to look in the mirror. It was right there, just a few feet away, but why should I look? I've seen my face before. It was a normal face. Bearded, puffy cheeks, a friendly smile, not too bad looking. It was there. It was all there. My face wasn't made of Lego Bricks. If it were, I would have noticed and so would others. I would have gotten... I would have gotten strange looks.

Reverend Bob, the Girl at McDonalds, my students, Tracy and the people I passed on the street, they all looked at me; they stared. They had wide eyes and dark pupils as if they were seeing something strange. I chalked it up to my scruffiness, and a general unwell appearance contrasted against a jacket and bowtie.

I looked down at my chest where the bullet had ripped through my shirt and into my heart some time ago. I felt pain, to be sure, but not nearly as much as I should. In fact, I should be dead, a 9 mm bullet at that close range. I almost lifted my shirt, but I was afraid of what I might find, either a gapping, bloody wound, or something much worse. Instead, my fingers were my eyes; I prodded, probed, and jabbed until I found my answer. Afterwards, I held my fingers to my face. There was no blood. My hand should be covered in it. I should have bled profusely and required a compress to stem the flow, some pain meds, a doctor. I should have been in an emergency room, under anesthetic, and prepped for the surgeon's knife. But there was none of that. Instead, a greasy, lubricant-smelling substance covered my fingers.

I'll be damned.

Several minutes had passed and Lego Me had not returned. Doctor Ziegel was willing to wait. He was tired, hurting and wanted to nurse his wound. But Doctor Tavarius kept looking at his watch. His patience was thin, and he grew more-and-more agitated with each passing moment.

"Oh, for Christ's sake," Doctor Tavarius said. "Where is he?"

"Well," Doctor Ziegel said. "When you gotta go, you gotta go."

Tavarius shot his colleague a harsh look. "Oh, aren't you funny?" he said. "C'mon, help me fetch that plastic miscreant. The sooner we work on him, the sooner we can find out what's wrong and maybe fix him, or I'm just as happy to scrap him and try again."

Doctor Tavarius stood up and waited for Doctor Ziegel as he slowly rose to his feet.

"C'mon," Tavarius said.

"Excuse me. I've just had a bullet removed from my chest," Doctor Ziegel said. "By a mad Doctor friend of mine."

"Well, you're lucky to have me. I'll send you a bill."

"Yeah, real lucky."

"None of this would have happened if you had listened to me. Leaving him to his own devices. What'd you call it? A social experiment, that's it."

"He has feelings. My feelings. He has rights."

"Rights my ass. He's a thing, a piece of property. We own him and, more importantly, we're responsible for him. Lucky thing he shot you and not some innocent bystander. That's all I have to say."

The two men meandered down the hallway. Doctor Tavarius led the way, complaining all the time while Doctor Ziegel limped behind. When they reached the bathroom, Tavarius pressed his ear to the door to see if he could hear anything. He could not. He knocked and called out to Lego Me. "Hello," he said. "Is everything okay in there?"

There was no answer. The two men exchanged worried glances. Then Doctor Tavarius tried the knob. The door was locked.

"I'll get a butter knife," Doctor Ziegel said.

"No need."

Doctor Tavarius took a step back and raised his boot before sending it crashing through the door. The two men stepped cautiously into the empty bathroom. Dr. Tavarius shook his head and swore beneath his breath, while Doctor Ziegel's expression softened to a smile.

Dr. Tavarius walked to the open window and stuck his head out into the night air, but it was dark, and he couldn't see anything. He slammed the window shut and turned to his colleague. "This is all your fault," he said.

"How's it my fault?"

"Never mind that. We'll have to track him down again. This time, we'll do it my way."

Dr. Ziegel turned to exit the room but stopped when something caught his eye. "What's that?" he said, pointing to the toilet.

Doctor Tavarius saw a silvery glint sparkling in the bowl. He reached into the water, retrieved the object, and held it up to the light for closer inspection.

"What is it?" Doctor Ziegel said.

"It's a Lego brick."

"That's odd."

"It isn't odd at all," Tavarius smirked. "The GPS is attached."

END of PART I

Part II

-Chapter 1-

I stood approximately 6' 4" tall. I ascertained this based on my meeting with Doctor Ziegel. We were approximately the same height, which made sense if his intent was to build a creature in his own image; he would try to approximate his physical features as much as possible. And yet, I looked nothing like Doctor Ziegel or any other human being, for that matter. Though, I had all the requisite parts—legs, and arms, hands and feet, the general shape of a male body, a head, a face—I was a cyborg, a bizarre amalgamation of organic thought, computer chips, circuitry, wires, transistors, and actuators packed into a Lego brick frame.

I was not monstrous. On the contrary, judging by my reflection, I looked cool, distinguished, and elegant. I was a piece of technological art, a walking, talking, modern steampunk version of David, and a spectacular sight judging by the looks I received.

The kinder, or more oblivious people would toss me a passing glance and be on their way. Surprisingly, most acted in this manner. To them, I was nothing more than a robot cleaning the floors at Walmart, a technological spectacle lost on a jaded society.

Then, there were those who stopped and stared and cocked their heads to the side and asked annoying questions with their eyes. I saw the gears spinning in their heads; that was my cue to hurry off in the opposite direction while stealing glances over my shoulder. I called them the paparazzi because they'd reach for their cell phones for a photo op. The paparazzi seemed harmless enough, but I knew it was a small step from snapping a photo to placing a phone call. Where would I be then: in a prison cell, or a laboratory being examined as a freak, or worse, returned to my handlers?

I hadn't seen them, but I knew they were out there. Call it intuition or a sixth sense. Maybe I was paranoid. Every snap or rustle made me jerk my head around, half-expecting to see my tormentors. God only knew what they'd do if they found me; nothing good, I guessed. I'd rust and power down like the Tin Man before I surrendered. I trusted Tavarius like I trusted a ravenous wolf to stand watch over a lamb, and I was that lamb.

So, I sat in my leaky tent, and listened to the raindrops plop like marbles against the canvas and I wondered if it was worth it.

Yes, I lived and experienced life just as any living creature would. The damp forest bed and the warm breeze sifting through the pine trees smelled like spring. The sun against my plastic shell was warm and comforting, just as the snow pelting my cheeks made me shiver and hunker down for the evening. An anxious, bounding deer gave me goosebumps. I felt the roughness of rock, the wetness of water, the sting of mosquito's bite, and the burn of a prickly bush. My stomach ached with hunger, and my throat scratched from thirst. I lamented for things I did not have and fussed over my few possessions. In this way, I was human.

And yet, it was peculiar because I had no olfactory, no mechanical means by which to inhale and distinguish one scent from another. I could not measure ambient temperature; I had no nerve endings, nor sensors to experience my world. My heart wasn't really a heart. It was simply a clock that delivered a series of electrical impulses, marching bits throughout my electronic nervous system at a predetermined rate. And my brain, well, it was a CPU working in tandem with a 5d optical drive to house and retrieve memories: taste, site, sound, touch, passion, pain, love, hate, anger, loneliness, fear, loathing, joy, hot, and cold. The same feelings I had as a human, I now had as a Lego man.

I could have been the Tin Man, a mechanical automaton, chopping wood in the forest until that fateful day when he froze in mid chop. That's not completely accurate. I was a human personality housed inside a mechanical apparatus. I was Lego Me, a copy of Professor Lance Ziegel. My mind was a computer file that was transferred from one storage device to another. That's all the human body is, you know, a storage device, a piece of hardware to store the software—our consciousness. But our hardware has an expiration date of around a hundred years. The mind, well, that's limitless. Transfer our memories and experiences from one device to another, and when that device expires, rinse and repeat and there you have the cure for death. No fear. No worries. Heaven, hell, God, they are obsolete, rendered useless by science. Erased. It was ironic and brilliant at once. The scientist in me rejoiced. My humanity, well, not so much.

It never entered our thinking. There was the science, the theory and, well, let's see if we can do it; we'll worry about the consequences later. We were brilliant scientists, but we exercised the care of children playing with their father's gun. Bang, and now, well, here I am, alive but emotionally ill-prepared to deal with the aftermath: all these feelings, emotions, and self-loathing.

It wasn't all bad. There were moments: a hawk would swoop overhead from a clearing and cast her shadow over me and the earth below. An angry Blue Jay barked its displeasure at my presence, or a hungry squirrel would chatter from its tree branch perch. These things made me happy, and I was grateful to experience them at least one more time.

But there were dark and lonely stretches that enveloped me like a black cloud. I could suppress physical discomfort, but the emotional pain sapped my hope. I spent long hours sitting, reflecting, and feeling sorry for myself. It was the loneliness that hurt the most.

Logically, a mind housed inside a plastic, mechanical body is the best of both worlds, the perfect blend of human consciousness, physical, metaphysical, and technological realms melded together in a single piece of living, functional art. It's where humans were headed anyway, and I simply arrived before everyone else, a passenger on a train that wasn't yet built. I was fine with that, but I had miscalculated the intangibles, the soul, the part so easily wounded and prone to erroneous thoughts, fear, depression, and self-loathing. I had trouble with these soft skills. What made me think changing suits would make things better? Problems didn't go away. They multiplied and took new forms.

I hid in the woods during the day (it was safer), and traveled by night, when people slept. The small town in the valley below was ideal for scavenging. Yes, I scavenged and stole as needed. I wasn't proud of it, but I was a machine and, like other machines, I needed maintenance and care. Backyards and garbage cans held all kinds of currency. I found a roll of duct tape and I used that to patch the hole in my chest. I would have left it because it looked like a cool war wound, but I was afraid the elements would find their way in and cause havoc.

Someone left a tent on the side of the road for the garbage pickup. It was worn, ragged and missing parts, but I carried it back to the forest and jury-rigged it in a small clearing. I missed my two thousand square foot house, but the tent was shelter, a place to rest, and take long naps. I called it home.

When I got bored, I played chess in my head—my electronic brain was well suited for the task. I could project a board and all the pieces into my mind's eye. I played both sides equally well, calculated thirty moves ahead, and I always won.

When I grew tired of chess, I adopted a new pastime called self-torture. I made up wild narratives and cast myself as the main and pathetic character. In one story, my body peeled away at the seams and crumbled to rubble while my electronic brain continued to function as normal. I was a mind detached from its body, yet fully aware of its fate. Then, a group of stoned teens found my mangled body, covered, and entangled amidst the foliage. They mounted my head as a grisly hood ornament on their Ford F-150. I spent the rest of my days flying down a back-country road at a hundred miles per hour, the blurred scenery racing past while the wind whistled in my ears: "hey, stupid. I bet you never counted on this." It was at once a frightful and amusing image.

In the cooler, quieter times, when it was dark and the daytime noise gave way to peepers, I'd wrestle with and try to find peace with my being. I'd close my eyes and surrender to nature and my reason for living and that's when I reminded myself: the goal was to be fully human, to experience the good, the bad and every shade in between. Anything less would render me a glorified, walking, talking, hard drive, a cyborg without feeling or sentience. There was a downside, of course, mainly pain and longing, and the usual problems associated with human consciousness. But there was no other way, and so I tried to remain grateful.

When spring arrived, and the weather was fine, I left my tent more often and walked. I called it motion therapy because it kept me from fixating on negative thoughts, which only raised my anxiety. I felt most alive when I moved.

I chose remote trails, away from casual hikers but not too overgrown for navigation, and not so far from civilization. The wooded canopies provided shade from the sun. More importantly, they hid me from the prying eyes of judgmental and distrustful people. I needed people, but I never liked them. And in my present state, they were more than just a pain; they were my greatest threat.

Dreams haunted me; yes, I slept, and I dreamt. Often, I'd awake in a cold sweat and lay in my tent for hours. I'd hear a snap or a crack and go outside to investigate and though I strained my eyes against the dark canopy, I never saw the culprit, just two glowing eyes staring back. I had to guess what or whom was out there.

And then the over-thinking would start all over again. The questions kept spinning-and-spinning in my brain like a vinyl record skipping, repeating the same phrase over-and-over. I'd beat my palm repetitively against my temple until the narrative eventually changed, and then I'd have peace and accept the fact. Despite this Lego suit, the processor, hard drive, and actuators, I was human. I needed sleep and shelter like any man. I needed love. I needed companionship.

Humanity had a promise—as dubious as it was—of an afterlife, heaven and clouds and eternal bliss with God (whichever God you wish). Some believed they'd come back for another crack at this world, to take the lessons from their past lives and apply them to a new incarnation in a cosmic video game. Those ideas were fine for normal beings, but what did I have? I had no such promise, only the dark specter of an unknown abyss hanging over me. I wasn't sure I could die, not in any proper sense. Of course, I could crack myself open, pull a few wires and power down, but would I be dead? Wires could be reconnected. Machines could be restarted. I'd awaken in a hundred years and announce, *Happy New Year*, like Frosty after donning the magic hat.

The thought of immortality, the reason for my being, weighed like a brick in my stomach. Who wants to live forever? What was I thinking? But I've decided it is better to stay alive for now, as wretched as this life may be. I'll go on, I'll exist until I figure things out.

Of course, I miss my old life, or should I say my memories of a life known as Dr. Lance Ziegel. What I wouldn't give for a cup of coffee. I could practically smell the earthy scent of a fresh-brewed pot wafting into my nostrils. I couldn't drink it, of course, but I craved its notes and the rush of caffeine. How many people were drinking their first cup in the neighborhoods in the valley down below? I wondered what it was like to be them.

I craved a women's touch. Sometimes, I thought of Tracy. She was bitchy and anal at times. She'd lose her mind over a misplaced hair and picked on me constantly, criticizing every flaw, real or imagined, as if the earth depended on it. I don't miss that. Still, there were good times. She was kind and generous. We had contemplated marriage once. How absurd. I wondered what she was doing, how she was feeling. Does she know of me, or what I've become? I remembered our life together. She was alive within me, her smile, her touch. I saw her in my mind's eye. That's where she lived.

I pulled my coat tight to my shoulders. As ragged as it was, it kept me warm and served as my security blanket. I felt lucky that morning. I had everything I needed for the time being. Barring traumatic injury, or poor self-maintenance, I should be fine. Starvation was not an issue, nor sickness. Just like other machines, I'll stop working one day and maybe that's not a bad thing. I possessed something most other machines don't, a kind steward, someone vested at the most intimate level. I had me.

I'll be okay. It was morning again. The birds were singing in the trees—my pets, as I referred to them; their chirpy serenade made me happy. It felt good to be alive. I sensed all was right in the world. There was nothing pressing, no work, no classes to teach, nor anyplace to be. It was a pleasant feeling. I could be me, whomever I was. I had a long time to figure it out.

Of course, this pleasantness won't last. Angst and worry will set in. But on that morning, the morning dew on my lips was like nectar dripping from a bird's tongue. I was at peace.

-Chapter 2-

He was sitting, leaning against a tree, when I first stumbled upon him. He looked at me with an unremarkable expression, as if I were as normal as the flora surrounding us. His eyes were blue, glazed over and unquestioning. I think I was more shocked by him than he was by me. He said nothing but offered me a hit of his joint. I looked over my shoulder. No one else was around. I smiled nervously at him.

I considered explaining my unfortunate circumstance—how I couldn't breathe let alone inhale the smoke and as far as getting high, well, that wasn't a possibility. But I decided it was too difficult to explain, especially when I didn't have all the answers, and so I kept quiet. I considered turning around and walking or running back to my camp, but my curiosity made me stay. He handed me the joint. It was about the size of a matchstick, but my thick fingers were surprisingly nimble, and I took it easily from him. I never noticed my Lego hands before now. They were hands I used for grasping, but I realized they were technological marvels. Each digit moved independently. I could pick up a grain of rice or punch holes through walls, whichever I preferred.

The young man seemed amiable, so I smiled, and held the joint for a moment; I stared at it while I took in its pungent aroma. I remembered I loved smoking and missed it as much as I missed human companionship.

"Go ahead," he urged in a soft voice.

I placed the joint in my mouth and did my best pot-smoking impression, tilting my head back and making my eyes grow wide while sucking my chest in. Though I did not, could not inhale, I recalled the sensation and felt the burn in my lungs and throat and I even hacked out a few coughs in sympathy with these memories.

"Thanks, man," I said in a gruff voice. "That's some dank weed."

He took his joint back and said, "Righteous."

I felt safe. He was clearly lit and didn't seem to notice or care about my unusual appearance. I was about to bid him farewell and leave, but he stopped me.

"Say, man," he said. "What are you?"

"What am I?" I said, hoping my casual tone would throw him off. Sadly, it did not.

"Yeah, man. Like what are you?"

Given my appearance, it was a perfectly reasonable question which deserved a perfectly reasonable response, but I was reticent to share. He was, after all, a stranger, and I could never predict how people might react; experience proved it was rarely good. I began with something simple.

"They call me Lego Me," I said.

The stoner looked unimpressed and took another hit off his joint. "Far out," he said. "They call me Lenny."

Lenny passed me the joint, and I took another pretend hit. I felt the perma-grin wax across my face; my mind detached and floated across the tree line. I was mellow, more relaxed than I had been in recent memory. I handed the joint back to Lenny. His face appeared blurry, and his body swayed even though he was sitting still.

"What are you doing out here?" I said. "Alone in the woods?"

"I'm smoking weed," he said, as if this were the most obvious thing in the world.

"Yes, of course. But... oh, never mind."

"What are you doing here?" he said.

I liked Lenny and wanted to tell him everything, like regurgitate my history onto his boots. Experience taught me restraint and caution.

"I like it here," I said honestly.

"That's cool, man," he said. "I like it here too. The birds, the trees, the wildlife, and no one here to hassle you, man. You can just sit here and smoke your ganja and be free. Right, man?"

"Yes, that's right."

Lenny made room for me. "C'mon, man. Sit down and have a seat," he said.

I decided it was safe. I could run if need be. I could outrun any man or take him in a fight if it came to that. So, I slowly descended to a seated position next to him. Then Lenny took another hit and stared off into space as if deeply contemplating the universe and all its wonders. I was at ease because he seemed unaffected by my being. I could have been a human, a Lego man, or a tree, judging by his expression. I don't know if he was really stoned or if this was his normal personality, but he treated me like any ordinary person, and I liked that.

Lenny was silent for several minutes, and it made me wonder if he had forgotten about me. I called out his name, and this stirred him.

"Oh, yeah, man," Lenny said. "I was bogarting the joint. My bad."

Lenny and I passed the joint back and forth until it burnt out. I don't know how it was possible, but I was higher than a kite, or that's how I felt. Lenny was stoned too, and we spent a glorious time sitting and saying nothing most of the time. I enjoyed his company, and I believed he enjoyed mine. When we spoke, we talked about crazy, philosophical shit that only stoned people think about.

"UFOs are real, you know?" Lenny said.

"Well, I suppose. Scientist can predict the number of possible civilizations capable of communication by using the Drake equation. You simply take the average rate of star formation in our galaxy, multiply that by the fraction of those stars that have planets, times that by the average number of planets that might support life per stars that have planets, times the fraction of planets that could support life that actually develop life, times the fraction of planets with life that actually develop intelligent life, what we would know as civilizations, times the fraction of civilizations that develop a technology that releases detectable signs of their existence into space, times the length of time for which such civilizations release detectable signals into space. Now the estimated values for several of the variables are based on conjecture, but I believe the equation underestimates the number of intelligent civilizations, and well, there you have it."

Lenny's eyes glazed over. I couldn't tell if it was from the pot or amount of data downloaded into his brain.

"Wow," he said. "You're wicked smart."

"Well, yes."

"But It's more than that, man. I mean the government released videos and said they're real."

"Oh, they have?"

"Yeah, haven't you seen them? They're tic-tac shaped objects that fly at supersonic speeds. It's technology far beyond this earth, man."

"Well, I guess I haven't watched too much TV lately."

"The thing is, the government said yeah, they're real, but no one cared. That's how crazy 2020 has been."

I nodded my head as if I understood, but I was too embarrassed to admit the truth. I thought it might be the ramblings of a stoned hippie, but my curiosity was piqued, and so I dug deeper.

"2020?" I said.

"Yep."

"What about it?"

"Well, all the crazy shit that's been happening, the COVID, the politics, social unrest. UFOs didn't seem that big of a deal after that."

Lenny thought I was a genius, and I didn't want to say anything to dissuade him, so I continued to nod my head.

"Yeah, 2020 sure is crazy," I said.

I knew about the politics; that's been going on for the past three years, but the other stuff, the COVID and social unrest, meant nothing to me. I've been preoccupied for the past several months, namely my identity, living in the woods while trying to avoid detection. I had checked no news sources recently, but I didn't want to sound ignorant in front of Lenny, so I dropped the topic. Besides, extraterrestrials were way more fun.

"So, where do you think the aliens are from?" I said.

Lenny took a hit from the joint before handing it back to me. He blew a long plume from his mouth and then told me everything he knew about aliens, which was a lot more than me and most humans combined. According to Lenny, aliens are interdimensional beings who have mastered anti-gravitation, worm holes, time travel, cloaking and interdimensional travel, among other things. They traveled great distances by taking shortcuts through the fabric of space and time. I was really stoned by this time and didn't know if he was feeding me a line of bullshit, but it was fascinating, and so I really didn't care.

"Yeah, man," he said. "They're beings like you or me, but they're just more evolved, maybe a billion years ahead of us. You know; they figured things out."

"I'm sorry," I said. "I'm afraid I finished the joint."

"No worries. There's more where that came from. Just make sure you put it out. We wouldn't want to start any forest fires. It's been pretty damp out but still."

"So, are they friendly?" I said.

"Yeah, most of them are. They're spiritual beings who don't have time for petty fights and arguments and wars. They figured out what's important."

"And what's that?"

Lenny smiled and nodded his head. "Love," he said. "Love is all that counts."

Lenny and I locked eyes, and I nodded my head in agreement. Maybe he was a stoned-out hippie regurgitating a bunch of ideas he read in a new age book, but it sounded... well, it just sounded right. I don't know; I've spent my life pursuing things: jobs, money, possessions, women, all the things society tells us we need to be happy. Yet, I had it all and more, and I was never happy.

"I wonder if they're just us," I said. "You know, like our future selves who have mastered time travel and are coming back to help us."

"That could be," Lenny said, pointing a finger at me. "That could be. Now you're thinking, man."

I zoned out after that, and I think Lenny did too; neither one of us spoke for a long time. We sat at the base of the tree and stared off into space and it was pleasant, like I felt good to be there and have a companion. After a while, Lenny stirred and gave me a resigned look.

"You have to go?" I said.

"Yeah, I'm afraid so, man." I tried to hide my disappointment, but I think I made poor work of it. "I can come back," he said.

"Can you?"

"Yeah. I'm between jobs right now."

"Yes, of course you are. That would be fantastic. How about tomorrow?"

"Can't do tomorrow. I need to get my shit together, send out some resumes, make some phone calls."

"Yes, of course."

"How about this weekend? Saturday?" he said.

"Okay," I said, trying to sound nonchalant.

Lenny and I stood up, and he started to walk away.

"Wait a minute," I said. "Do you play chess?"

"Chess?"

"Yeah, I've been dying for a game, like an actual game with another opponent."

Lenny shrugged. "I'm not very good, but I know how to play."

"Would you like to play Saturday?"

"Yeah, I can do that. Do you have a chess set?"

"No. I just play in my head against myself."

"I could probably get us a chessboard," Lenny said.

"Where?"

"From the Walmart in town."

"Well, I don't have any money."

"That's okay. They're probably only ten bucks. I could get it. I mean, if you really want to play."

I lowered my eyes. "I wouldn't want you to go to any trouble," I said.

"No worries. Well, I better be going."

"Lenny? What's today?"

"Today is Thursday."

"I'll see you in two days then. Good."

Lenny walked away, and I deliberately walked in the opposite direction of my camp. Every so often, I looked over my shoulder to see if he was following me. He was not.

That evening, I sat in my camp and made a fire. The flames were hypnotic, and the loud cracks reminded me of the cap guns I used to play with as a boy. Every so often, I stirred the logs with a branch, causing sparks to flare and flames to lick the night air. I wondered if I had made a mistake. Would Lenny come Saturday with a chess set or a bunch of curious friends or the media or the authorities? I made the mistake before. I trusted the Reverend and had a 9 mm slug deposited in my chest because of it.

And yet I needed someone, a friend, a companion, someone I could converse with, to play chess with. We spent an hour sitting, talking, smoking, and he didn't bat an eyelash. To Lenny, Lego Men, walking and talking in the middle of the woods was as normal as UFOs and aliens. Lenny seemed alright, and he made me think I was alright too.

Of course, I could survive alone. I was used to solitude and often preferred it to the company of my so-called peers. I was the smartest guy in the room and smart people were alienated from society and cast into the role of an outsider, or weirdo, as I was not-so-affectionately called. It's something I've dealt with from an early age. Computers, robots, electronics, code, comics, books, tv—they kept me company, and a few, like-minded individuals filled in the gaps.

Besides, we bonded over a joint, the ceremonial peace pipe. Lenny would not turn on me. He wouldn't turn me in or bring gawking eyes. He was just a cool guy, unbothered by my appearance, my origin, or my being. Of course, he was stoned out of his mind, so there was that, but I had a feeling I had made a friend during our brief encounter. He was a regular dude, and he could play chess. I'm sure he wasn't a highly rated player, but that didn't matter. I'd go easy on him and maybe we'd talk, shoot the bull. Maybe he could help me; we'd help each other out. I could teach him chess, and he could bring me things I couldn't get on my own, like books and magazines, stuff like that. I wasn't Polly Anish enough to believe in miracles, but it could happen. It could.

I spent the next two days moving between elation and panic, joy, and fear. Every twig snap or leaf rustle caused me to jerk my head in anticipation of a strange face emerging from the shadows. There were none, just a passing squirrel or deer. Still, I needed to be vigilant. I may have brought a calamity on my head. I don't know.

Two days felt more like two decades. On Saturday, I headed toward the tree where Lenny and I first met. He said he would be there in the morning, around eleven, and that he would bring the chess set. I judged the time by the rising sun, but I'm sure I was early. I was excited and anxious, and I felt a cold sweat run down the back of my neck. Of course, there was no cold sweat, but I felt it none the less. I wanted to make sure he was alone, so I parked myself a distance away from the big oak and hid behind some brush, obscured from view but still in sight of the trail. I waited for what seemed like forever and then a terrible thought entered my mind. He wasn't coming. I counted on him being here, alone or with friends, but he was pretty stoned. I wondered if he even remembered our meeting or if he actually believed what he had remembered. Perhaps something came up, and he couldn't make it.

I was losing hope, but then I heard leaves rustling. Lenny's long, golden hair appeared out of the green, speckled light; it reflected the shafts of sunlight streaming through the branches. He stepped with the youthful enthusiasm of a teenager, and his eyes were bright and sober. He smiled and carried a box under his arm. I watched him take a seat on the ground next to the big oak. He placed the box next to him, crossed his legs, and looked around. I remained hidden and looked and listened for any unwelcomed guests. After a few minutes, I summoned the courage to approach.

"You came," I said.

"Yeah, I brought the chess set."

"Were you followed?"

Lenny wrinkled his forehead and said, "Just the cops, but I gave them the slip a mile back."

"Funny."

"Relax man. No one followed me."

"Did you bring weed, my good lad?"

Lenny smiled, then he produced a bag filled with dark green flower from his pocket. We spent the next twenty minutes rolling joints. He was an expert, and he tried showing me the proper technique, but I made a real mess of things. My fingers, while good enough to grasp things, struggled with the complexities of joint rolling. Besides, I had no spit to wet the gum's edge and secure it. My joints looked like deranged elf fingers compared to his miniature doobie masterpieces. Since mine were useless, we smoked his.

"What kind is this?" I asked after taking a hit.

"It's Big Buddha Cheese."

The name made me laugh. "I like it," I said.

We passed the joint back and forth and talked. He was a good talker, floating in and out of topics with ease. We talked mostly about weird shit again, UFOs, ghosts. I asked him if he believed in Sasquatch and if we might see one today. He said he believed in them and they were probably related to UFOs, but he said the area was too small to hide a breeding population. I was disappointed, but relieved at the same time. The last thing I needed was to be torn apart by a mythical biped. The irony wasn't lost on me. I could see the *National Enquirer* headline in my head:

LEGO MAN TORN APART BY SASQUATCH.

Enquiring minds want to know.

Lenny and I talked and smoked, and the more we did, the more relaxed and higher I became. Lego man or not, I was lit. I felt lit anyway. Talking with Lenny made me feel like everything was right in the world, like I was a regular person and not some odd mix of wires and emotions, just two dudes passing time in the woods, sharing a spliff and talking about everything and nothing at once.

I could tell a lot about Lenny in our brief time together. He was young and bright and, judging by his vocabulary, highly educated. Yeah, he was a stoner, but there was more to him. He was a sensitive being, and curious about the world, the seen, and unseen. He taught me a lot, things I never thought about, nor imagined. I'm not sure I believed everything he told me—he told me some fantastical stories—but he had a lot of facts and scientific tidbits to back his claims, and I liked that. I shared with him my knowledge of science, art, and technology. It may have been the weed, but Lenny listened to me with an unwavering eye and asked questions and offered his insight where appropriate. We learned a lot from each other.

I appreciated his sharp wit and our shared sense of humor. We had the same liberal, political views. It would have been awkward otherwise. So, we spent an hour bitching about the current administration and the sorry state of conservative politics. We were both saddened by it. He told me he was out of work by design. He never told me what his trade was, and I never asked. I imagined he was a graphic designer or in some other artsy, touchy-feely field. He said that he wanted to travel the country and eventually see the Far East. I pictured him in an ashram in India, dancing and chanting, *Hare Krishna, Hare Krishna, Hare, Hare.* He loved nature, and he knew a lot about the flora and fauna that surrounded us. He was a hippie nut, but I liked him.

"Do you hear that?" he said.

"Hear what?"

"Drink your tea. Drink your tea," he said in a high-pitched, singsong voice. "It's the drink your tea bird, also known as the Rufous-sided Towhee."

"Oh, yes. I hear it."

"You should wear long sleeve shirts."

I looked at my mechanical arms, an amalgamation of Legos, data lines, power lines, and actuators. I wondered if he was offended, or worse, freaked out.

"Deer ticks," he said. "Lyme disease is a bitch. I've had it. You don't want it. I never got COVID, but a friend of mine had both Lyme Disease and the COVID and he said they sucked equally hard."

There was that word again: COVID.

"So, he had the COVID?" I said, trying to sound nonchalant.

"Yep."

"And they both sucked?"

"Yep. Equally hard."

I nodded my head and said, "Wow. Imagine that."

"Yeah. Oh, by the way, I hope you don't mind the maskless look. But I thought because of your, well, your condition, there's no chance of spreading the virus. I mean, I have it in my pocket if you need me to put it on."

"Oh, no," I said, waving him off with my hand. "No need for that; and thank you for the tip on long sleeves. I'll try to remember that next time."

"I think I have some extra shirts at home. You look to be my size, maybe thicker around the midsection; no offense."

"None taken, and yes, I'd like that. Thank you."

Lenny told me about his dreams and aspirations, and I enjoyed listening to him; his voice had a Bob Ross quality, hypnotic and soothing at once. Maybe it was the lack of human companionship all these months that made me latch onto him; but he was the most interesting person I had ever met and the most compassionate too. He was the younger brother I never had. I felt guilty. I should have been the one teaching him and offering advice. But despite my advance years and many advanced degrees, he was more worldly than I. And out here, in the middle of nowhere, my formal education was useless. Lenny's knowledge of earth and heaven, all things spiritual and metaphysical, was well suited for a nature living being like me.

It was inevitable. The conversation turned back to me and my story; I didn't mind. The questions were the normal questions you might ask any other new person: What do you do? How long have you been here? Where to next? Have you ever been West? Lenny was cool, or oblivious, or stoned; I couldn't decide which, and I didn't care. His laid-back manner put me at ease, and that feeling was like God to me. His calm seemed to radiate from him, and my circuitry seemed to resonate with it.

I answered his questions dutifully, but I didn't fill in the gaps and he never did question me about my origins. It was as though a Lego man, walking and conversing, was the most normal thing in the world. *Of course*, I thought. There were millions of us Lego bots with organic, human consciousness walking around. What's one more?

"You ready to play?" I said.

"I'm not that good of a chess player," he said.

"I know. I figured as much. But I'm tired of playing myself, so any opponent will do."

"How do you play against yourself?"

"I play both sides equally."

"But how do you play without a board or pieces?"

"I play in my head?"

Lenny's eyes lit up, and he jerked his head back. "You can do that?" he said.

"Yes. I have a photographic memory. Well, I should say I had a photographic memory. I suppose I still do, but I'm missing some pieces of it before I was reborn as a Lego Man. I can still project the board, and pieces in my mind's eye, and my once-human brain is now jacked by the power of Intel's finest eight core processor, clocking 5.3 Gigahertz, that's approximately 5.3 billion instruction sets per second." Lenny blinked repeatedly; his eyes were wide and glazed over and he wasn't even that high yet. "I'm really smart," I continued. "I can teach you how to play if you'd like."

"Yeah, that'd be cool, man."

He removed a black pawn and white pawn from the box and placed them behind his back. Then he held out his fists. I chose the right hand, which held the white pawn. I liked white because I could be aggressive and attack from the opening move.

"Now," go easy on me Lenny said as we set up the pieces. "I haven't played in a while."

He didn't have to tell me. I could tell by his misplaced queen he was no Bobby Fischer.

"Queen takes her own color," I said.

"What?"

"The black queen goes on the black square."

Lenny smiled and fixed his queen. "See?" he said.

I told him it was alright, and that I was just happy to play against someone other than myself. I played E4, a standard opening, nothing too crazy, and Lenny opened with C5.

"The Sicilian," I said. "See? You know more than what you let on."

The look in Lenny's eyes told me he no idea what I was talking about, and his subsequent play confirmed his self-assessment. He was in chess parlance, a potzer—someone who stunk at chess. As I mounted an attack on his king pawn file, Lenny played moves which completely ignored my offensive, like moving his rook pawn to the middle of the board, a beginner move that defended or attacked anything. Lenny clearly didn't understand the most basic concept of chess strategy, that you must defend your king while attacking the opposing king. I trounced him in the first game. He left major pieces hanging, but I didn't bother taking them. Instead, I went for the jugular and mated him in eight moves. He was good-natured about it, but I was afraid, deep down, I may have crushed his spirit and that he may not want to play anymore. I suggested we play again, and that he should take white; I'd suggest moves and that it would be more of a learning experience than a competition. He agreed and with my help, and a great deal of compassion, he seemed to enjoy our next game more. There was a sparkle of hope in his eye, but of course, even with practice, he'd never challenge me. I wasn't arrogant; it was a fact. I learned something, playing games in my mind and now with Lenny. I was special. Whereas a skilful chess player could see three or four moves ahead, and grandmaster could see eight to twelve moves deep, I saw thirty moves in advance and calculated the best moves for both black and white considering all the interchanges based on an initial move. Against Lenny, I wasted my computational engine because he rarely played his best move. I quickly discovered I didn't even have to focus on the game at hand. I could instead play other games in my mind; sometimes, they'd be new games, black vs. white, me vs. me. And sometimes I'd replay games by the masters that I recalled from old books: Fischer vs. Spassky, Kasparov vs.

Topalov, or my favorite, Deep Blue vs. Kasparov. Besides chess, I watched old, black and white films from memory or re-read books, or solved quadratic equations, or anything else I put my mind to. I hadn't reached my limits because I didn't know what they were. I was child-like, learning about me, the world in which I lived and my place in it. It gave new meaning to born-again.

What Lenny lacked in chess acumen, he made up in congeniality and humanity, something I've been sorely missing for a long time, even before the transformation. I valued his company. It gave me a sense of peace, an internal warmth I hadn't felt in forever. When I was alone, I was cold, lost, broken, and Lenny made me feel whole again. He wasn't trying. He was just being Lenny.

"See there?" I said. "You're doing better already."

"I think I'd do better if I weren't so stoned."

"On the contrary," I assured him. "I think the weed helps you play better?"

"Really?"

"Well, I don't know for sure, but I like the weed. Will you bring it next time? There'll be a next time, right?"

"Yeah sure. You want to plan on next Saturday again, same time, same place?"

"Yes. We can make it a regular date."

I thrashed Lenny in twenty moves. I could have mated him in six, but I resisted. After that, he stood up, and packed up his weed and the chessboard. He smiled before turning and strolling off. As I watched him disappear into the thicket, I started counting the moments until Saturday.

-Chapter 3-

Every Saturday, Lenny showed up to the big oak, wearing his boyish grin and carrying his chess set—oh, and his weed, too. He always had great weed. I told him I felt guilty for smoking his pot and offering nothing in return, but in typical Lenny fashion, he told me not to sweat it. He told me he grew his pot—many strains for different effects: Purple Haze, Girl Scout Cookies, Big Buddha Cheese, Matanuska Thunderfuck. The man was a cannabis encyclopedia.

"Do you have trouble sleeping?" he said.

"Sometimes. Yes."

"I have a nice Indica for you. I'll leave you with some joints. It will knock you the fuck out," he said, laughing.

"That would be nice."

Lenny and I spent hours beneath the big Oak, smoking and talking; we played chess when we got around to it, but our conversations were more interesting. After a while, we dropped chess altogether and just talked. He had an easy manner that made the craziest things sound normal. I tried holding up my end of the bargain by sharing the wisdom that comes with age. He wasn't the least bit interested in computer science and, aside from chess, I had little else to offer. He asked me about relationships. I laughed and told him he was asking the wrong person, but I shared other things. I told him to find his purpose in life; the whole know thyself bit. I told him to forget about money and find something he loves or really likes, even if it was growing and smoking pot.

However, I think Lenny already knew the wisdom I was trying to impart, and it made me feel guilty. While I shared trite clichés, Lenny blew my mind with weed and metaphysical ideology that seemed to originate from another world. I had grown up around a similar mindset at Lily Dale and with my aunt, but I never paid much attention back then. To a precocious boy, it was just superstition, lacking scientific evidence to support the wild claims. It was another religion—with different gods and rules—to ignore. But with Lenny holding court beneath a tree-lined cathedral, I was intoxicated. This wasn't church talk. It was something deeper and more meaningful to the human condition, and that's what I needed, a master's level course in what it means to be human in mind, body and spirit. Lenny talked about life and death, and he said this wasn't his first time on this planet; he lived before.

"You mean you believe in reincarnation?" I said. "So, you believe you've had a past life?"

"Oh, many lives."

I nodded my head and took a long drag from the joint. "I see," I said. "So how do you know this?"

"I take nothing on faith. It's all evidentiary."

"And what evidence supports past lives?"

"All the major religions have a belief in past lives. It was in the Bible before they took it out."

"Reincarnation was in the Bible?" I said.

"Yep. That's before the church sterilized the Bible. See, the church spins a narrative. They tell you a story and they only tell you the part that supports their conclusions, and they leave out the parts that go against their preconceived ideology."

"Who's they?" I said, passing the joint to Lenny.

"They, the church. You know, the man, the people in charge. Men in white collars who control all the money. Well, they control the narrative too and they spun one that gave them control and money."

Lenny's explanation was wonderfully blasphemous and refreshing and it lured me in like a siren's song.

"How do you know all this stuff?" I said.

Lenny shrugged. "I don't know," he said. "I just read a lot."

"Okay, so tell me more about this reincarnation. Besides the religions and the Bible, what other evidence exists?"

Lenny stared into space for a long time. He looked like he was meditating or had fallen asleep with his eyes half-open.

"Lenny?" I said.

"Oh yeah, man," Lenny said. "There have been these kids, man."

"Kids?"

"Yeah. They have memories of past lives and have knowledge that a child couldn't possess, things about who they were and where they lived and how they died, things they couldn't Google even with help from an adult. And then researchers would come in and track down their story and verify it with people who knew the deceased."

"I see."

"And there are past life regressions. Have you ever had a past life regression?"

"I'm familiar with them, but I never had one. I had an aunt that lived in Lily Dale, so I was surrounded by that kind of stuff."

Lenny's eyes lit up. "Oh man," he said. "Your aunt lived in Lily Dale? Was she a psychic?"

"Yeah, sort of. She read Tarot cards and gave people readings. Aunt Sandy was the black sheep of the family. Mom called her and her friends devil worshipers, but she let me stay with my aunt every summer."

Lenny laughed. "So, your mom let you stay with a community of devil worshipers?"

"She didn't approve of the devil worshipers, but it was her sister, and I think she wanted me out of her hair for a month."

"Oh, that's far out, man. So, you already know about this stuff."

"No, not really. I mean, I was surrounded by psychics and palm readers and reiki healers, but they never preached, and I never paid much attention to them."

"Oh, that's crazy. I need to get back there sometime."

"You've been?"

"Yeah. I used to make a pilgrimage every summer."

"Small world."

"Who was your aunt?"

"Sandy Candy. Are you familiar with her?"

"No. I never heard of her."

"Well, she may have been before your time. That seemed like forever ago."

"Ever get back there?"

I closed my eyes, and in an instant, I was back with the Reverend, his faded smile and the gun pointed at my chest. There was a blast, the impact, the pain, and I saw myself slumped over the table, thinking it was over; but I was alive, so I stood up and ran out of the house and then darkness, emptiness like I went to sleep. I woke up in the back of a pickup truck.

I reached for my chest and poked the hole through my shirt. "Several months ago," I said, snapping back to present time.

I tried to avoid the question ever since I met Lenny and had been doing a good job of it. Lenny never pried, but I knew I was treading water and needed to broach the topic before I was burned again.

"Lenny," I said. "I'd like to address the elephant in the room."

"What's that?"

"You know I'm not human, right? You can see I'm made of Lego bricks and wires and actuators? My eyes see, but they're not real eyes. My hands grasp, but they're not real either."

"Yeah. You're called Lego Me for a reason; right?"

"Well, okay, but don't you find this the least bit, well, the least bit disturbing? I mean, you talk to me as if I were a regular Joe you met in the forest. I know you're stoned, but how high are you?"

Lenny laughed. "Well, I'm pretty lit," he said. "But you _are_ a regular Joe I met in the forest."

"I don't understand."

"It's just that I don't think of you as a Lego man. I think of you as a person, a person not in a human suit, but in a Lego suit."

My chest expanded, and I felt a rush of energy in my body. "Do you really?" I said. "But aren't you curious about how I got this way?"

"Now that you mention it. I thought it was some weird voodoo shit, but I didn't want to pry."

"That was nice of you."

I sat for a moment in silence. I wanted to share, to spew everything I knew into a cathartic heap on the forest floor, but a persistent voice warned me: *ignorance is bliss. Sharing could get you killed or worse.*

"I guess I don't feel comfortable telling you my life story," I said.

"No worries, man."

Lenny and I finished the joint and started another. I closed my eyes and melted into the forest floor. Colors exploded like fireworks in my mind's eye, red, greens, blues. Old faces turned and morphed like a kaleidoscope. I saw mom, Aunt Sandy, myself as a boy, as Lance and as Lego Me, then a disturbing face from the past—Tavarius.

"What is this shit?" I said.

"Crack." I raised a single eyebrow, and Lenny flashed an impish grin. "It's Girl Scout Cookie," he said.

"I like Girl Scout Cookie."

Lenny smiled. "Yeah, man," he said. "I had some real nice Maui Waui, but the racoons got to it."

"The racoons ate your weed?"

"Yeah. They piss me off."

"Did they get high?"

"Yeah, man. I caught them in the act. I was like, hey you fuckin' wood rats. Get away from my weed. And they were like chill man, we're just having a taste. This shit is amazing. Do you have any nachos? Crank some Floyd, man."

Lenny's stoned racoon story made me laugh. We both laughed until tears ran down our faces. Lenny's tears were real. Mine were a figment.

"Aren't you the least bit curious?" I said after we settled down.

"About what?"

"My name," I said. "My real name."

"Yeah, sure."

"I'm Doctor Lance Ziegel. I mean, that's who I was, or that's who I am now. To tell you the truth, I'm not sure anymore."

Lenny turned his head slowly. He said nothing, but his eyes said everything. They were soft, blue, and compassionate and they asked for more.

"I was a professor," I said. "My discipline was robotics and artificial intelligence. I was an expert in machine learning, natural language processing, and deep learning."

"So, you're a programmer?"

"Not to brag, but I was probably the best programmer in the country by the time I was fifteen."

Lenny nodded his head. "Far out," he said.

"At any rate, I wanted to put my skills towards a cause, to see if I could cure the greatest malady humanity has ever known."

"And what would that be?"

"Death."

Lenny's high-pitched cackle startled me. "What the fuck, man," he said. "Death is not a malady."

"It's not?"

"Fuck no. It's a transition. It's the natural order of things."

Lenny started singing: "To everything (turn, turn, turn) There is a season (turn, turn, turn) And a time to every purpose, under heaven. A time to be born, a time to die, a time to plant, a time to reap. A time to kill, a time to heal. I swear it's not too late... or something like that."

"You have a nice singing voice," I said. "Why did you stop?"

"I forget the fucking words, man," he said. "At any rate, you don't have to fear death. It's like getting out of one car and into another."

"Be that as it may, I did fear death, and I still do."

"Didn't Lily Dale teach you anything, hanging out with your aunt and all those psychics?"

"My aunt was a wonderful woman, and I liked her psychic friends, but I thought they were kooks."

"You must think I'm a kook."

"Well, yes, but I love your pot."

"At least you're honest."

"I don't know, Lenny. If I were as confident as you, I wouldn't have bothered. But I was scared, like it was the scariest thing in the world. It wasn't always that way. I was like most young people. I felt invincible, and I'd live forever. As I got older, I realized there was a clock, and it was ticking, and it sped up with each passing year. I didn't have all the time in the world. And then when I looked back on my life, I realized I had accomplished nothing of substance, not for someone of my ability. Teaching at a university might be fine for the average person, but for me... Well, I was supposed to be more; I wanted more. I felt like I had wasted time, my talent, and I needed to do something magnificent before it was too late. Is any of this making sense?"

"Yeah, man. It makes perfect sense. You let your ego and your fears dominate your thinking."

Our eyes met and he must have sensed my hurt feelings, so he softened the blow by saying this was normal and that he was guilty, too.

"Yes," I said. "I suppose you're right. I've been accused of being egotistical, and I have lived my life in fear; still do."

"Okay, so you were afraid of dying and you wanted to do something great; what's up with the Legos?"

"Yes, well, I had a plan that would solve both problems. I'd transfer my thoughts, my ideas, my personality, my likes, my dislikes, my insanely enormous ego, in fact, everything that was me onto a computer chip housed inside a cyborg body partly made from the humble Lego brick. And, well, I was born."

I looked at Lenny and he stared at me with huge, glazed over eyes. "Fucking el," he said. "So, you're like an actual human inside of an artificial body?"

"I'm not so sure how human I really am. I have memories, some of them are jumbled, but I have them. I feel things. I feel everything Doctor Ziegel felt: happiness, sadness, joy, sorrow, loneliness, and well, there it is."

"There it is. You're human then."

"But I feel like the tinman in the Wizard of Oz. Yes, I walk and talk, and pot makes me feel high, but do I have a heart, a soul, and can I be fully human without one?"

Lenny didn't answer right away. He leaned his head back against the tree. I could tell he was thinking, searching for a deep philosophical reply that would satisfy the question.

"Yes," he said, finally.

"How do you know?"

"I can see it."

"You can see my soul? Is that even a thing? How high are you?"

"Well, let's just say I can sense it." I implored Lenny with my eyes. "When I talk to you," he continued. "I'm not talking to a machine that's running a pre-programmed set of instructions like some glorified Lost in Space robot. Like you said, you have feelings and emotions; they're written on your face. It's in your eyes and how you carry yourself, your body language."

"Yes, but how do you know that's my soul and not some illusion created by the magic of technology?"

Once again, Lenny went deep inside for the answer. "I just know," he said.

Lenny spoke with quiet conviction. I wanted to believe him. I thought transitioning from human to machine would spare me from physical death, but I realized I was wrong. Machines can outlive men, but they die too, and then what? Humans had their cute stories about God and heaven and an eternity of bliss, but what did I have? Without a soul, I didn't have those stories.

"You know, I never even thought about the soul when I was making me," I said. "I was more concerned with the neurons transferring, the memories, the personality... I had no concept of a soul or the afterlife. I didn't think I needed one."

"So, you made yourself?"

"Me and another chap. I call him Dr. Frankenstein. I was mainly robotics and software. He helped with the neurology, the mind transfer."

"Man, this is really interesting. You guys must be really smart."

"Really?"

"Well, yeah."

"I don't feel smart."

I could tell Lenny was excited and so was I. Lenny had provided all the magic and fairy dust, and now I had something for him.

"So, wait a minute," Lenny said. "If your Doctor Ziegel in Lego form, where's the real, I mean the human Doctor Ziegel?"

"Probably dead."

"Why dead?"

"Well, because—because he was sick," I said.

"Yes, of course."

"What do you mean, of course?"

"That would make sense. If he was sick like terminally ill, that's why he wanted to transfer his personality to a robot."

"What did you say, Lenny?"

"I said if Doctor Ziegel was terminally ill, he'd want to transfer his personality to a machine before he died. Make sense?"

"Yes. It makes complete sense."

"Don't you know? Weren't you him and he's you and wouldn't you know if you were terminally ill and that's why you made a Lego version of you, to cheat death?"

"I—I don't know," I said. "Not all the memories copied over. There were corrupted bits and missing neurons. It's an inexact science; we made it up as we went."

"I wouldn't worry. Wherever Doctor Ziegel is, he has a soul, and the soul never dies."

"Yes, but what about me?"

-Chapter 4-

I waited for a long time near the big Oak. I amused myself by playing chess in my head and replaying old black and white horror movies I had seen as a boy. Frankenstein and The Mummy (the original Mummy, not the shitty remake with Brandon Frazier). It was fun for a while, but then I realized Lenny was late and not just by a few minutes. I had so much to talk about, and I wanted to pick his brain to see what new treasures he had for me. Lenny had wonderful ideas that made me see things in a new light. I was smart, but in an academic sense. I had an impeccable memory (not counting memory fragmentation after the transfer), and I could code like the Devil. But Lenny was thoughtful and spiritually wise.

Another few minutes passed. I picked up some stones and hurled them aimlessly into the thicket. Then I picked at some grass blades, pulled them up by their roots, and flung them into the wind. Damn it, where was he? I didn't like waiting. I was never patient.

Finally, I heard the crunch of feet and saw Lenny's face emerge. His usual soft and friendly face was absent. He looked bland and was missing his normal glow.

"Where have you been?" I said. "I've been waiting here like an hour."

"An hour?" he said, looking at his watch. "It's only five past ten."

I realized I sounded like a dick. "Sorry," I said. "I really need to get a watch. Maybe you can get me one, just something cheap so that I can tell time."

There was something about Lenny that morning. It was more than the absence of a smile. It was deeper than that. His body drooped. His spirit was down; I sensed it.

"What's wrong?" I said.

"Nothing's wrong."

"You're lying."

"I have news," he said.

"Oh. Nothing bad I hope."

"Nothing bad. In fact, it's good news. I got a job."

"Oh. Is that all? Well, congratulations. I thought by the way you were acting, you'd lost your best friend. What job?"

Lenny looked at the ground and kicked the dirt with his feet as he spoke. "The University of Wisconsin," he said.

It took a moment to process; I didn't respond right away, and when I did, I pushed out a thin syllable. "Oh?" I said.

"Yeah. I'm going to be a college professor," he said enthusiastically. "Just like you."

I was confused. Lenny? A college professor? I asked him to explain, and that's when he opened up and told me things I never knew. I found out he had a PhD and had been teaching as an adjunct at a local community college.

"You're Doctor Sageman?" I said. "What's your degree in?"

"I have a Ph.D. in philosophy. I'm going to be a philosophy prof. at Wisconsin Green Bay."

I played Bg5; mate in three moves. I set the black king down.

"Lance?" Lenny said.

"Oh, yes. Congratulations. Tenure Track?"

"Yes. Tenure Track."

"Oh, wow."

"Isn't that something?"

"Yes. That's something alright. When do you leave?"

"Not until August, so we still have another couple of weeks."

"Oh, August. When were you going to tell me?"

"I'm telling you now. I just found out yesterday. They made an offer, and I accepted."

"But you must have known this for a while. You went on interviews, visited the campus, right?"

"It was all on Zoom. I even did my presentation on Zoom."

"Zoom?"

"Yes. You know video conferencing because of the pandemic."

"Oh, yes, of course, video conferencing. The pandemic."

"I didn't want to say anything until I was sure."

"I suppose congratulations are in order. Well, congratulations, then."

"You seem upset."

"Do I?"

"You know, with the COVID, it's getting hard to find jobs, especially at universities. I was lucky to land this gig."

"Oh yes," I said. "The COVID."

"We can still hang out. I have to drive out maybe one weekend to find a place to stay and get settled, but I can visit until I leave for good. I mean, if you want."

Warmth spread across the back of my ears, over my cheeks and forehead. I was like a child separated from his parents at the store.

"Yes," I said behind a forced smile. "But my God, Lenny. You have a terminal degree and ambitions to become a college professor. Why didn't you tell me? I could have helped you, or at least share my experiences."

"You never asked."

"There's that I suppose, but I assumed you were a stoner hippy dude. I didn't know you had ambitions other than to grow and smoke pot and maybe gaze at the stars and talk about the metaphysical realm with a middle-aged college professor dressed in a Lego suit."

"I am a stoner hippy dude," Lenny said. "But there's more to me than that."

"Did you bring pot?"

"Of course."

"And snacks? I get the munchies terrible when I smoke."

"You make me laugh, Lance."

Lenny and I settled into our routine. The lump in my throat gradually faded, and I relaxed; I talked. The weed helped. There was so much I wanted to ask, so much still to learn from Lenny; the clock was ticking. In a few weeks, Lenny would leave, and I didn't know when I would ever see him again. Wisconsin was a long way away. Probably never, I thought. And I'd lose the best friend I had or ever had.

"I'm afraid," I said.

"Afraid of what?"

"Lots of things. Dying. What about you?"

"No," he said with conviction.

"Why not?" I said.

Lenny shrugged. "I don't know," he said. "I guess I don't believe in death. Like I said, it's like getting out of one car and into another. We shed our physical bodies, but our spirit lives on and then we meet with our spirit guides and decide what to come back as. Death is a lie. We never die."

"That's what I'm afraid of. I believe there's no death for humans, but I am no longer human. I'm a thing, a piece of machinery with human thoughts and feelings, but I'm an imitation, a copy of a soul but not the soul itself. It's ironic. I wanted to cheat death and now I'm afraid I've cheated myself out of an afterlife. Lance, the human Lance, has a soul. He'll have a wonderful afterlife and reincarnate long after I'm a steaming pile in a metal graveyard."

Lenny reached out his hand; I lowered my head, and he rubbed it. "If it means anything to you," he said. "I believe you have more soul than most humans."

I smiled. "Well, yes," I said.

"Look at it this way. Your lifespan will far exceed a human's. Just think of all the wonderful lessons you'll learn, all the adventures you'll have, long after we're gone."

"Well, that was the plan. Live forever, or as close as I can get."

"See? You've been given a wonderful opportunity. Just think of the great books you can read, the art you can see and all the music and film."

I lost myself in a blissful daydream until I remembered where I was.

"Out here?" I said. "I'm living in the middle of the woods like a homeless man. In fact, not <u>like</u> a homeless man. I <u>am</u> homeless."

Lenny's eyes lit up. "Make a list," he said. "Books, tools, clothing, anything else you can think of."

"That's kind of you, Lenny, but I don't have money. I could never repay you. I've already smoked your weed and gave you nothing in return."

"You've returned plenty. Besides, I'm a university professor now. I'm rich."

"You forget, I was a professor too. I know you're not rich."

"Books are cheap. I have a bunch lying around the house that I've already read. I have a bunch of old clothes that will fit you. We're the same size."

"That's very kind."

Lenny was a good friend and true to his word. Every weekend, he showed up at the big oak and brought me things: books, magazines, clothes, a watch and a big knapsack to carry everything in. It was a small gesture, but it lifted my heart; it gave me hope and made me feel human.

"Thank you so much," I said. "For everything. I devoured the books. Next week, can you bring more Deepak Chopra and Michael Beckwith? And maybe bring some more Hemmingway, perhaps a collection of his short stories? I finished *The Sun Also Rises* and—"

Lenny lowered his eyes.

"What's wrong?" I said.

"There won't be a next week."

"What? Why not?"

"I have to leave for Madison on Monday."

"Okay, when will you be back?"

Lenny did not respond. His eyes were grey and misty.

"I see," I said. "But I thought you had several more weeks. You told me."

"I know, man, but I have to get there early; get moved in and settled."

"Didn't you know you had to leave early to get settled in? You could have told me. We could have planned better."

"I'm sorry, man. I'm not used to moving. I guess I didn't think that far ahead."

"I see," I said, trying to sound understanding

"You're mad?"

"I'm not mad. It's just that it's so sudden. I'm sad."

For the first time, there was a long, awkward silence between us. I raised my hand to my eye and wiped away an imaginary tear. I swore it was there, hanging just off the corner, ready to cascade down my cheek before depositing its salty taste into my mouth. After a few moments, Lenny stepped forward and the two of us embraced.

Lenny whispered into my ear. "Goodbye, my friend."

He wasn't gone yet, but I already missed Lenny.

-Chapter 5-

I was a hypochondriac and swore I had the bloody virus several times over. Every upset stomach or mild fever triggered a mild panic attack. *I'll got the COVID, and I'll die alone in the woods*, I thought.

"This is it," I said, while clutching my heart like Fred Sanford. "This is the big one. I'm coming to join you, Elizabeth."

I had to remind myself I was fine and even better than fine. While COVID ravaged the human population, I was unscathed. COVID killed people, but it saved me. At first, I did not know what it was. It's like that old saying: *were you living under a rock?* Well, yes, I just about lived under a rock. Lenny talked about it frequently, but I didn't ask for fear of sounding ignorant. I never guessed that such a thing could or would happen. I was too young for the Spanish flu or the plague, or any other pandemic. Yes, I knew these things existed, but unless you've experienced a thing, you don't really know it. It never entered my consciousness and besides, I had my own problems.

The first clue came from the traffic or the lack thereof. One evening, I looked out over the valley, from my vantage point high in a clearing. It was early summer, yet there were very few cars out. Even late at night, there was usually some traffic. But on this day, there was nothing, not a single car on the road for hours at a time. Then I might see one, and then nothing again for a long time. It was strange for a car obsessed nation.

Then, on a late-night foray into town for supplies, I found masks laying on the ground; they were the surgical kind that doctors and nurses wore. I ignored the first few, but after seeing three and four, I knew it was too much to be a coincidence; it piqued my curiosity, and I wanted to know more. Then I found a discarded newspaper, which spelled it out for me:

PANDEMIC. BUSINESSES CLOSED. PEOPLE DEAD

The world was living out a scene from one of those pandemic movies and I walked in on the third act, bewildered but intrigued.

It must have sucked for society, but then an idea came to me in a light bulb moment: the mask. It covered the face. I could hide behind it. If I found a pair of gloves and maybe some dark glasses, I could pass for, well, I could pass for a human being. That would buy me some freedom. I could roam around like any other man, even in the daylight, and perhaps rejoin society as messed up as it was. I'm not sure I wanted that, but at least I'd have the option. Even though I valued privacy, living like a hermit was getting old.

I picked up a discarded mask, and while it didn't cover my entire face, it concealed my mouth, nose, and jawline. One of Lenny's old turtlenecks covered up my neck and muffled the sound of my actuators. As for my plastic skull and bulging eyes, I found a remedy in an old baseball cap I foraged from a dumpster and a pair of dark sunglasses that were fortuitously left on a park bench. Lenny told me to set my intentions, pursue my heart and the Universe will come to my aid. "It will provide everything you need to realize your dreams," he said. Lenny was right.

Parked car windows provided an exaggerated, funhouse reflection that made me look bloated and about thirty pounds overweight, but they told me what I needed to know. I looked like any other dork walking around with a mask.

The gloves were harder to find. I ended up stealing a pair from a small convenience store in the sticks. I wasn't proud, but I did what I had to, and it was a relatively simple task. I walked in with my hands in my pockets, nodded to the clerk—she didn't react oddly, a good sign—and I walked out wearing a fine pair of tan, brushed leather work gloves. I looked back over my shoulder to see if anyone was following me. Nobody was. Then I took off at a dead gallop and didn't stop until I reached the safety of my camp in the woods.

The last puzzle piece was in place. I looked like them, and for better or worse, I could rejoin society. All I needed was a job, and a paycheck, then I could rent a place, buy some creature comforts, maybe get a radio or a tv and perhaps save for a computer. Then I'd feel human again. Humans had jobs, and they owned things, so why not I?

It wouldn't be easy. Millions of people were out of work, mostly in the food and service industries, so if I wanted to wash dishes or bus tables, I'd be out of luck. I didn't want either and fortunately, other places were hiring. One day, I saw an ad in a discarded newspaper: Mail Carriers Wanted.

-Chapter 6-

I tried to convince Dick to let me take the company car home so I could get here on time. I walked to work every morning, a distance of 3.4 miles, and so I had to get up early to be on time, and this was difficult because I valued my sleep.

"Hank!" Dick said to me. "You're late... again!"

Dick was my supervisor at the post office. His real name is Richard Grady. Most employees called him The Dick. I'm the only one who called him Dick. He's a short, self-important man with a receding hairline and a foul disposition that thinly veiled an occasional hint of compassion. He acted like he hadn't been laid in years, and that was probably true. I know I shouldn't, but I couldn't help having fun at his expense. Low hanging fruit as he was.

"Sorry, Dick." I said. "I got stoned and drunk and I was up half the night watching porn."

Dick stared at me through squinted eyes while deep furrows formed on his forehead.

"Jesus fucking Christ," he said. "If I thought you were serious, I'd call the police on you."

"The police? What the fuck for?"

"I don't know. There has to be a law against watching porn."

"Naw, there ain't no law against it. They were of legal age and all."

"Jesus Christ! That just ain't Christian."

Dick walked over to his desk and scrawled something on a piece of paper. I knew what it was before I saw it. He handed it to me and waited for my response.

"What the fuck is this for?" I said.

"I'm writing you up."

"What for? Watching porn?"

"No, for coming in late and hung over and smoking pot."

"Aw shit, Dick. I was just kidding—"

"Hank, if you fail one more drug test, I'm going to can your sorry ass."

"Alright, alright, Dick."

Yes, they drug tested at the post office. I befriended a homeless man sleeping in the park. His name was Tony, and I told Tony I'd buy him wine if I got the job. He agreed to give me a urine sample and, by some miracle, he was sober that day. I snuck the sample in, passed the test, and got hired. I think Tony had mental issues, but I counted him as my only friend since Lenny left. Tony was more of an acquaintance than a friend, but I felt sorry for him, and since I didn't need food, I bought him groceries occasionally. I begged him to stay clean in case I needed his piss again; he said he would try, but he hadn't been sober since our first meeting.

I could have and should have been fired many times over, but I think Dick, despite his gruff nature, liked me. He scolded me a lot, but it was always with a nod and wink like he was sort of serious but not. We kibitzed back and forth, and I pretended to be an uncouth, redneck from Dumbfuck Pennsylvania. I looked and played up the part by wearing lots of plaid and speaking like one of them.

Dick was a Trumpster, and we bonded over our disdain for the left-wing liberals or libertards as Dick called them. Actually, I hated the fascist ape. His name evoked a sensation of creepy, crawly cockroaches slithering from every orifice in my body. A trained monkey would have made a better president. In fact, the monkey wouldn't have to be trained. It could've been one of those wild monkeys that defecates in its hands and throws its shit at you. One of those miscreants would make a better president. However, Dick thinks I'm his people, a conservative from small-town America. In my past life, I wouldn't give Dick Grady the time of day. But my past life was, well, past, and so I swallowed my pride. It wasn't much different from before when I stooped to bosses and administration at the University, individuals with half my intellect and talent. We all did it. I told myself it wasn't a big deal—just job security.

Dick thought my name was Hank. That's the name I gave him when I applied. He was desperate for mail carriers, and I don't think he bothered doing a background check. If he had, I wouldn't have the job. He knows me as Hank Potter. I made up the first name, and I borrowed the last name from the famous book. He should have seen Hank Potter had no link to the social security number I gave him. The social security number belonged to Lance Ziegel. So did my driver's license and every other legal document I owned. It was, after all, Lance's wallet. However, the post office was small, and tucked away in a tiny building in a forgotten town. I'm not even sure it qualified as an official post office anymore. I'm pretty sure the government shut it down years ago, and they just forgot to tell Dick, or they told him, and he ignored them and continued to deliver the U.S. mail as usual. Dick had been working there for years and wasn't much for following rules or protocols, even though he demanded strict adherence from his workers. All of this worked in my favor. I could have been an escaped felon wanted for mass murder in several states for all he knew. I'm pretty sure we had a couple of escaped felons working for us now. That's how loose things were.

"Dick," I said. "If you'd just let me take the company car home with me, I wouldn't be late."

Dick grumbled and told me I was late for my route. I took that to mean he'd consider it.

Mail delivery wasn't a bad gig. The benefits were great; I got all the major holidays off, and the pay was good too. When I was sick or sick of work, I called in and Dick would get a sub.

You meet a lot of people too—mostly women. I learned there were a lot of lonely housewives out there. Some didn't have jobs, and many worked from home because of the pandemic. And it didn't matter whether they were single or married or whatever. They were home and alone, and they hated their lives; they sat around, bored senseless, or they worked from their kitchen tables, or watched TV, or babysat the kids; I came along and they liked to chat me up.

"Mr. Mailman. Mr. Mailman. Do you have a letter for me?"

"No Ma'am. No letter for you today."

"Are you sure? Maybe you should check."

"Ma'am, I do this for a fucking living. Don't you think I'd know if there was a letter for you?"

"Well, you better check. You know that sack of yours is big. Maybe it's stuck on the bottom."

"No, Ma'am there's no letter for you today, maybe tomorrow."

"Wait a minute. Where are you going? Come back here. Would you like some lemonade?"

My route took me to the outskirts, where the houses stood farther apart, and the income levels soared. Eagle Ridge—I don't know why they named it Eagle Ridge, because I was sure an eagle hadn't lived there in the past hundred years—was airy compared to the poorer neighborhoods in town. Dog walkers smiled and waved as I passed them, and no one stared. They were maskless, but I kept mine on; they must have assumed postal workers were required to wear masks all the time. And the sunglasses, hat and gloves didn't seem to bother anyone. I felt normal being around people again, working, delivering the mail. I was never so happy to be normal.

One customer stood out above the rest, partly because she had a cool-sounding name: Kasia Kozlova. And partly because she made me nervous in a good way. I didn't know what she did for a living, but she was home a lot and often greeted me at the door.

Kasia had a slight paunch that was thinly veiled by thin fabric. I called her pleasingly plump, and those soft, female curves invited me in like warm apple pie. She wore no makeup. Instead, she had a natural beauty that didn't need it. Her hair was fiery red—I presumed from a bottle— and she wore a matching red housecoat with the top button undone so I could see her cleavage. She was blessed and so was I to bear witness to this site. Oh, I tried not to stare, but I was grateful my sunglasses concealed my prying eyes. Her housecoat came down just above the knees, revealing a silky pair of chubby legs. She was an older woman, but she looked sweet, someone I wanted to be with. I could tell she was smart; maybe it was her blue, cold, studious eyes magnified through dark-rimmed glasses. She just looked smart.

"Hello," she said. "Do you have something for me?"

"Kasia Kozlova?"

"That's me."

"Did I say it right?"

"It's Russian and yes, your pronunciation is perfect. My friends call me Kat."

I handed her the mail. "Here you go, Kat."

The protocol for social distancing was six feet, but I didn't care. I couldn't get sick, and I couldn't transmit COVID. Kat was maskless, and she didn't seem concerned either. She took the mail from me, and that's when I caught a whiff of perfume. It was Lilac, or some other pleasant, flowery scent. Of course, I couldn't smell a thing, so I relied on memories to create images in my brain. I literally saw what Kat smelled like; I could almost taste her.

I smiled at her and wished her a nice day, but she stopped me as I was about to leave.

"Wait," she said.

"What is it?"

She grabbed a strand of her long red hair and twirled it between her fingers. "I was wondering..."

"Yes?"

"I just made some tea, some cold, iced tea. I was wondering..."

She smiled, and the devil sparkled in her blue eyes. There was a pandemic, and she looked lonely, and I wanted to take her up on her offer. Instead, I panicked and told her I couldn't, that it was against policy. She nodded and said she understood. I walked away, exhilarated, and sad at once. Later, I was angry with myself. But then again, there was the business about drinking tea. How would I explain that?

"Excuse me, Kat, while I pretend to drink your tea and then spit it out when you're not looking."

I lived in a fifteen-hundred-dollar trailer home on the outskirts of town. My neighbors' front yards were littered with broken, rusted-out cars and trucks, old bathtubs, and Trump signs, lots of Trump signs. As far as the eye could see, Trump signs littered the ground, growing wild like weeds on the side of the road. If there was any doubt who put him in office, my neighborhood and the thousand others just like it, should lay those doubts to rest. I ignored the neighbors, but they gave me funny looks. Maybe it was the mask. I was the only one wearing one outdoors. Many people refused to wear them indoors and in public places: "The last time I checked, America was still a free country." God, their southern Pennsylvania drawls grated like nails on a chalkboard.

Okay, whatever; they knew I wasn't their kind, which suited me. I had to live amongst them, but I didn't want to be mistaken for one of them.

My trailer looked like what you'd expect a fifteen-hundred-dollar trailer to look like. It was a piece of shit. I beg your pardon; a piece of shit would have been a step up. The ceiling leaked and I'm sure something or someone died in the living room. There was a big, reddish-colored spot on the carpet that looked faintly reminiscent of blood. It could have been cherry Kool-Aid for all I knew. Thoughts of my old house made me queasy. I missed it. I thought about Lance, the human Lance, nice and comfy, no doubt watching TV and boning Tracy when he got the chance. It pissed me off, but I took comfort in being indoors and sheltered from the elements. Besides, I planned to fix the place up once I saved enough. It was home and would have to do for a Lego Man starting from scratch. I was lucky to have a job and a place to live.

One of my neighbors was friendly, actually a little too friendly. I called him Elmer because he looked like an Elmer—I think his real name was Dave. He liked to visit and stick his nose in my business. His outgoing, busybody attitude made me want to run for cover—*more eyes, more problems*, I thought. I was at my mailbox by the road when he spotted me.

"Howdy, neighbor," Elmer said to me. "Do you like tomatoes and zucchini?"

He held out a plastic bag filled with more tomatoes and zucchini than I could eat if I could eat <u>any</u> tomatoes or zucchini. I wanted to tell him as much, but I didn't.

"These came from my garden," he said while handing the bag to me. "I thought you might like them."

It was a friendly gesture. I thanked him and accepted the bag and then I wanted to turn and run back to my trailer; but Elmer was one of those talkative types—as in he talks a lot but says nothing—and he yakked incessantly about something. I'm not sure what he said because I stopped listening after the first few words because I thought my ears would melt off listening to his jabber. But I stood there while aimless drivel spewed from his mouth and then I answered a bunch of mindless questions about who I was and where I was from and what I did. I wasn't a good liar, so I told him everything. Well, almost everything. I told him I was a mailman, and that I was originally from Upstate New York. I left out all the crazy shit about being a Lego man. Maybe I should have confessed everything. It's like telling someone you're married to a Bigfoot; they'd think you're crazy and probably stay clear after that.

Finally, I made an excuse and hurried back to the safety of my trailer. I wondered what I would do with all the tomatoes and zucchinis. I could cut them up, toss them in a nice salad and serve them with a juicy, rare steak and then reminisce about the memories of food, its taste and texture. The pleasant feelings would come after that.

After tossing the bag aside, I said hello to my babies, Herby and Melinda, two cannabis plants I grew from Lenny's seeds. I'd tell you they were stinking up the place, but I liked the weedy smell and they did a good job of covering the putrid death odor from the recent homicide. I couldn't smoke them, but I could light a joint and pretend to inhale, and get high, just like I did with Lenny. Ah, Lenny—those wonderful weed-fueled conversations I had with him always made me smile. I should forget about him, live in the present, be mindful and pay attention to what was happening in the now. Get your head out of your past, Hank or Lance, or whatever my name was. But based on the state of my living quarters, the now was shitty. I thought about my little makeshift tent in the woods, and I wondered how Lenny was doing.

Herby, the Sativa, looked well. However, Melinda, the Indica, looked worn out. I wasn't sure if it was the light or the water. I got a book: Growing Weed for Dummies. Yes, that's a real thing. Hopefully, I'll figure it out. I'll need something to calm my nerves.

-Chapter 7-

I pulled on my clothes and headed to work. I jogged some of the way and ran the rest. My cyborg legs covered ground quickly.

"Hank," Dick said when I arrived. "You're late."

"Yes, Dick," I said. "I know. Just write me up."

"What's wrong with you, Hank? Were you smoking dope and watching porn again?"

"Well, yes, on both accounts."

Dick shook his head and twisted his mouth into a distressed grin. "Jesus Christ," he said.

"Oh, what's wrong, Dick. Don't you smoke dope and watch porn?"

"I'm a Christian."

I was dubious. I believed he didn't smoke because he needed weed in the worst way. But whenever a man professes to be a Christian and sexually pure, that usually meant they were a certified sex-fiend.

"So, you never watch porn?" I said.

Dick tossed a pen on his desk. "No," he said. "That's just—well, that's just weird."

"Weird? What's so fucking weird about it?"

"Jesus Christ, Hank. Come to my church this Sunday. You can sit with me and my wife."

I'd eat shit before I stepped foot in a church, but I didn't tell him that.

"Is your wife pretty?" I said.

Dick ran his thumb and forefinger against the side of his jaw. "Well, she is kind of pretty; sorta."

"Sorta?"

"Yeah, sorta, for her age. Why are you asking?"

"Just curious."

Dick grumbled something inaudible. Then he told me to deliver the mail.

"Aren't you forgetting something, Dick?"

"What's that?"

"My write up."

"Aw, get outta here, Hank. You'd just end up tearing it to pieces, anyway."

"You know I'm just messing with you? I don't really smoke pot or watch porn. I have a long walk and it's brutal to get here on time."

Dick said he believed me, but I'm not sure he did. Then, he started in on about how he worried about me and how he thought of me as a son. It was a nice, saccharin sweet sentiment that made me wish I was somewhere else.

"The wife and me are going to a Trump rally this weekend in Beaver," Dick said. "You're welcome to come."

I felt my ears burn like the fires of bloody hell, and those creepy cockroaches crawling out of my orifices.

"Thanks, Dick, but I made other plans."

"Well, if you change your mind."

I gave Dick a military salute. "I'm off to deliver the U.S. mail," I said.

The rain fell like marbles against my windshield. I couldn't see the road ten feet in front of me. School kids were probably smashed like bugs against my grill, and I would have never known except for their tortured cries. I thought about my poor trailer at home; its leaky roof, soaked carpeting, black mold sprouting like moss on a stone, and the smell of death intermingling with the pungent aroma of cannabis. No matter, the U.S. mail doesn't stop, through rain and snow and all of that.

I hated the rain. Snow was almost as bad because it made the driving treacherous, but rain was especially miserable. I could dress for freezing temperatures and the more layers I wore, the better it covered my secret. But the rain soaked me through. My pants, my shoes, socks, and hat were drenched by the end of a rainy shift. Lubed joints kept my moving parts articulating, but I worried about my electronics. A short circuit could render me a very smart paperweight—able to think clearly but unable to move. I'd be a lucid mind in a frozen body like I saw in those old black and white documentaries they showed in health class, otherwise healthy minds trapped inside a paralyzed body and held together by an iron lung. That's all I needed.

Despite the weather, my route went smoothly. Several regulars didn't have mail, so I made good time. I hoped to be done in time and make it home at a decent hour. Today was Tuesday. My favorite night for TV.

I arrived at Kat's house in the late afternoon. She had a registered letter, which meant she had to sign for it. She wasn't waiting for me; I presumed because of the bad weather. So, I rang her doorbell. There was no answer. Normally, I would leave a note in her mailbox, but as I peeked through the window, I thought I saw movement in a dark corner of the kitchen. I rang the doorbell again and again, but there was no answer.

"Ms. Kozlova," I called through the door. "I have a registered letter for you. You need to sign for it."

The transformation revealed my character, or lack thereof. I realized I was an asshole, but there was a nice guy in me that wanted to do better. The nice guy wanted to deliver the letter and save her a trip to the post office. At least that's what I told myself. It had nothing to do with her red hair, her smile, or the invitation to tea. I tried the door. It was open.

I stepped inside and called out into an empty kitchen. "Ms. Kozlova," I said. "It's Hank from the U.S. Postal Service. I have a registered letter for you. Hello?"

I heard nothing, so I went inside. I stepped gingerly through the kitchen and into the living area. It looked typical: sofa, chair, television, end tables. But sitting on the coffee table was a chessboard, black versus white, frozen in mid-game. This wasn't a random position set up for decoration by an unwitting person. This was the board of a learned player practicing the intricacies of the endgame. *Kat must be a strong player*, I thought.

I looked up from the board and peered down a hallway.

"Ms. Kozlova?" I said. "Kat?"

There was no reply. I should have left, but I was damp and shivering. Besides, black's position was caving in; with its bishop and knight on the same rank and separated by one square, white was in position to drop a pawn fork. I did the calculation; mate in six moves. I moved the black knight back (Nf3) to break the symmetry and protect the king. It was a temporary fix, however. Laying the black king down in resignation was the more prudent choice.

I looked once more down the empty hallway, and all I heard was the rain pounding on the roof. I was alone in the house and the right thing to do was to leave the note and try again tomorrow. The weather should clear by then.

But I didn't leave. Instead, I looked around and lost myself in the décor. Several paintings hung on the walls, dark, original oils of elaborately dressed combatants sporting cartoonish-sized mustaches and brandishing swords atop of their huge steeds. They looked like they belonged in an art gallery, rather than a private collection. Then I noticed the Russian dolls lined up on the mantle above the fireplace. Their colorful, elaborately painted faces made me smile. I realized something: Kozlova, the chessboard, military battle scenes and Russian dolls—Kat was really Anastasia, the youngest daughter of Czar Nicholas II. She was alive and well and living in rural Pennsylvania.

"Ms. Kozlova? Are you home? It's Hank from the post office."

I made my way further into the house, edging my way down the hall. My wet sneakers squeaked like mice with each step. In the empty, quiet hall, it sounded much louder than it probably was.

"Ms. Kozlova. It's Hank from the U.S. Postal Service. I have a registered letter. You need to sign for it."

I was alone in a woman's house, free to peruse as I wished and in violation of just about every policy in the postal worker's handbook. But there was something scary and wonderful about being in Kat's home. The house looked happy and well-kept, nothing like my dingy trailer. I kept walking; my heart rate slowed, and her story grew bigger and more elaborate with each step. Yes, Kat really was the Grand Duchess Anastasia Nikolaevna from Russia. She escaped her captors, much like I did, and then hopped a cargo ship headed for the states. Now, she leads a quiet life in this rural subdivision, playing chess and carving Russian dolls to remind her of home.

I walked gingerly, but my baby steps only exacerbated the squeaky sound. There was a bathroom on my left. It was dark and empty, so I walked past and saw a bedroom that was converted into an art studio. I peered inside. In the center of the room was a large, paint-splattered table filled with dirty brushes and colorful tubes oozing from their caps. I walked up to the table and saw miniature images painted on postcard stock. They were good if you liked Bob Ross scenic landscapes filled with happy trees and happy clouds; I liked Bob Ross, and I liked Kat, or at least the image of a chess playing artist with Russian ties. What was her real story, I wondered? And how did she come to be here at Eagle Ridge? She was smart and cultured; this much was obvious. This woman could hold her own with me.

I left the studio and stepped into a second room further down the hall. Inside was a queen-sized bed covered in a white quilted comforter. The comforter was adorned in a pattern of red, geometric shapes reminiscent of a folk-art painting. At the head of the bed sat six pillows, piled on top of each other. They looked nice, but I wondered why she needed so many. Then I closed my eyes and saw Kat nestled in her bed, surrounded by pillows and wrapped in the blanket. I was lying next to her, spooning her curvaceous body and caressing her breasts like a security blanket. I opened my eyes, laughed and shook my head; it was a crazy thought, but it was all I had.

I quickly exited the bedroom, but I couldn't resist one last stop. I was wet and there were towels hanging in the bathroom, so I helped myself. Kat wouldn't mind. I just wanted to dry myself off and wipe the steam from my sunglasses before I left. The biblical rain was still falling.

As I was toweling off, I saw brightly colored lipsticks on the counter. They reminded me of the watercolor pans I used to play with as a boy. There was other makeup too, mascara and rouge. One flesh colored bottle caught my attention: *Maybelline Coverage Foundation*. A feeling came over me like a come to Jesus moment. Perhaps I could lose the dark glasses if I covered the seams with a flesh toned makeup. Okay, it was a long shot, but I thought I'd try. I took off my glasses and placed them in my pocket. Then I dabbed a bit of the foundation on my finger and spread it across the bricks around my eye socket. Well, Brad Pitt wasn't staring back at me from the mirror, but I'll be damned if it didn't work. The makeup covered the Lego bricks, hid the seams and colored the white Legos a flesh tone that made it look almost-skin-like.

"I like it," I said to my reflection.

I was like a spellbound boy engrossed in his finger-paint art. I lost track of time, of what I was doing and where I was. It was fun applying makeup, layering, sculpting, adjusting. And then I had that electric feeling like you do when someone's watching you; the hairs bristled on the back of my neck. I was hesitant, but I had to look.

Yes, my worst nightmare had come to fruition. Standing in the doorway was Kat; the look on her face, well, it was the expression of a woman who just caught a stranger applying makeup in her bathroom. Her jaw dropped; her eyes turned black and round, and her already pale skin turned several shades whiter. I was afraid she would have a heart attack.

"Oh, good afternoon Ms. Kozlova," I said, trying to sound casual. "I guess you caught me in a rather compromising—"

"What the fuck?" she said in a surprisingly calm voice.

"Yes," I said in a resigned tone. "What the fuck indeed."

She stood there for a moment, like she was trying to figure out what to do next. Then she pointed at the counter and told me there was an applicator brush I could use.

"Oh, yes," I said, as she turned to leave. "Thank you."

They knew me around campus as the absent-minded professor, but you could add stupid-professor to that list. My intelligence, combined with my lack of common sense, made me a dangerous character; mostly to myself. Now I had to explain to a customer why I was applying makeup in her bathroom and pray my story would stop her from calling the police. The trespassing was bad enough, but the makeup thing, well, that just added to the absurdity.

I looked around for something to wipe the makeup off with, but there was only an empty roll of toilet paper mocking me.

"Ms. Kozlova?" I yelled out to her.

"What is it?" she yelled back.

"You've run out of toilet paper. Do you have any more?"

"What in God's name do you need toilet paper for?"

"Uh, it's not what you think. I just wanted to wipe the makeup off my face."

"Check the cupboard under the sink."

I found the roll and cleaned the makeup off as best I could. Clumps were embedded deep within the cracks, but I'd have to dig those out later with a toothpick.

Still, without a plan, I walked into the living room, where I found Kat huddled on the sofa with a pillow clutched tightly to her chest. She seemed calm under the circumstances.

"Ms. Kozlova?" I said.

"Yes?"

I pulled the letter out of my mailbag and held it out to her with a shaky hand. She looked past the letter and straight at me. Her eyes locked onto mine and I had to look away.

"I have a registered letter for you," I said. "If you'll sign it, I'll give you the letter and I'll be on my way."

"Oh," she said in a soft voice. "What were you doing in my bathroom?"

"I was—I had to use the bathroom."

"Do you normally use bathrooms in stranger's houses?"

"No," I said. "I don't normally. But I had this sudden urge to go, and I didn't think you were home. I didn't think it would do any harm."

Kat's jaw fell open as if she were about to say something, but she didn't. Instead, she looked at my eyes.

"It's a registered letter," I said, reaching for the pen in my shirt pocket. "You'll have to sign for it."

Kat took the pen and signed. I handed the letter to her, and for a moment, I thought I dodged a massive bullet. I promised myself I would never be that stupid again.

"Well, goodbye," I said.

"Wait a minute."

"Shit," I whispered.

"What are—I mean, what's your name?"

I nearly made the mistake of giving her my fake name, the name the post office knew me by. It was probably too late. Dick will find out what had happened, and I'd be looking for a new job, maybe stocking shelves at a grocery store.

"I'm Lance," I said.

"Lance," Kat repeated. She smiled at me, and her eyes softened into dark, liquid mirrors. "I like Lance. It's strong."

"Please, Ms. Kozlova. Please accept my apologies. I didn't mean to frighten you. I don't know what got into me. I behaved badly. I should have never entered your house. I–I need this job."

Kat smiled; she closed her eyes and shook her head as if to indicate it wasn't a problem.

"But I frightened you," I said.

"I wasn't frightened."

"Yes, but I didn't follow protocol. You see, I had a registered letter and if you don't answer your door, I'm required to leave a note and then you'd have to make a trip to the post office to pick up the letter. I thought

I saw movement through the window, so I stepped inside and called out to you to sign for the letter, and when I didn't see you, I wandered inside and it's rainy out, and so I thought I'd just towel off before going back out. I hate the rain and it's awfully rainy out."

I sounded like Charles Manson strung out on coke. I wasn't helping my cause.

"Well," I said. "I'm sorry to have bothered you. I'll be on my way."

"Wait," she said.

"What?"

"Why don't you stay?"

"Why? What for?"

Kat slunk into the couch and made herself small like a child. "I'm lonely," she whispered.

Those two words, vulnerable and spoken gently, melted my heart. She was lonely, just like me, and I was instantly drawn to her. I was a misfit because of my physical predicament, but she was perhaps a misfit too because of her age and isolation. We shared this in common, and I haven't felt so close to a human being in some time, not since Lenny and never with a woman. Besides, she asked me to stay. She wanted my company.

I looked at Kat as a man would look at a woman. Though she was older than me, she wasn't unattractive. She had an hour-glass figure, well endowed, with a muffin top hanging over her beltline. I didn't mind. She was soft and curvy, and I liked that.

She had wrinkles, but her face was soft and kind and pleasing to the eye. I held her gaze with mine and her eyes sparkled with a youthful soul that belied her age. I closed my eyes momentarily and pictured her as a young woman, and I imagined she must have been beautiful at one time. My spine tingled like it was the first cold, fall day.

I wanted to stay, but I was anxious and leery. I told her I had mail to deliver and had to leave. Well, it was the truth, but perhaps the real truth was I was afraid she'd find out what I really was.

She flashed me an understanding smile, rose to her feet and stepped towards me. Then she leaned in as if she was about to share a secret.

Kat whispered into my ear, "What are you?"

I stepped back; my body went rigid. I immediately checked my mask; it was secure and covered my nose, mouth, and jawline. But then I realized something: I was indoors, and it was bright; the colors were natural. My sunglasses—I had taken them off and placed them in my pocket and forgot to put them back on. Kat could see my eyes.

I stood there, panicked and frozen, hoping my stillness and silence would somehow fool her into thinking I wasn't really there.

"I mean," she continued. "Are you like one of those Amazon drones that deliver the packages? Are you like a high tech, secret, government prototype?"

The idea seemed plausible and actually more believable than the real story, so I nodded my head in agreement.

Her eyes lit up like a Christmas tree. "Oh, wow," she said.

"Yes, well, I guess I still have a few bugs that need to be worked out. Goodbye Ms. Kozlova."

"Are you sure you can't stay?"

"I'd like to, but I have to deliver the mail. That's how I'm programmed."

I did a little robot dance, but this only made her laugh. I turned to leave, but the chessboard caught my eye and I couldn't resist.

"Oh, Ms. Kozlova," I said. "I'm sorry, but I moved your black night to E4."

Kat studied the board. "I see that," she said. "Why?"

"Well, black is getting slaughtered. White will promote the bishop's pawn and it will be all over. It's a band aide, I'm afraid. Black has a losing hand and should resign."

"No," she said emphatically. "Black has mate in four moves. Look at the board."

"I have looked at the board. You look at it. White has mate in three."

Kat looked at the board with a worried expression. Then she expelled a single syllable. "Huh."

I tipped my cap to her and wished her a good day.

The rain turned to a slow drizzle, but the sky was dreary and grey. I sat in the car and pounded the steering wheel for a solid minute, then I gave myself a few good whacks to the side of my head for good measure. It provided some relief.

How could I be so stupid? The pandemic, the economy, not to mention the fact I wasn't a real person—not in any legal sense of the word—made it nearly impossible to find work. Even real folks struggled. I took a big chance entering her home and applying makeup in her bathroom. She was convinced I was some sort of postal bot. However, she may come to her senses and call the post office and file a complaint against me. The thought of that conversation brought a smile to my face and a sense of relief.

"Hello? I'd like to file a complaint against one of your robot mail carriers."

"Yes, ma'am. Are you drunk?"

I quickly finished my route and returned to the post office to drop the car off and to learn my fate. I trembled and could barely walk straight as I made the long approach to Dick's desk. He greeted me in a friendly manner. It was a good sign that Kat hadn't notified the police or the post office, and Dick didn't seem to have any problems with me.

Still, I was nervous. Losing a job was bad enough, but for me, there were greater consequences. What if the authorities discovered me? What would happen then? They couldn't arrest me. You cannot arrest a machine and I was, technically, a machine. Yet, I was fully human in every other sense, a human filled with memories, emotions, and feelings, just as any other being who came before me. What of that part? What would happen to that part of my being?

My real crime was being different. Different colors, nationalities, and religions were victimized. I could only imagine how a collection of electronic impulses stored on a hard drive and housed in a ridiculous Lego body would fare. Not well, I'm afraid. Death was a better fate, if I weren't so terrified of it. I remember Lenny telling me not to fret; that it was like getting out of one car and into another, but I'm not sure I believed him and even if I did, I'm not sure I could die in any human sense.

"Dick?" I said.

"Yeah?"

"Have you received any complaints about me?"

Dick laughed. "Yeah, I complain about you all the time," he said. "Why? What have you done?"

"Nothing. Have a good evening."

I put my head down and walked away, but Dick stopped me.

"Hey, Hank," he said. "Hold up. I'll give you a ride home."

I didn't want Dick to see where I lived, so I refused.

"C'mon," he said. "It's wet outside."

I shivered inside my damp, cold clothes, and I didn't want to listen to Dick any more than I had to, but it was a short drive and besides, I could earn some brownie points in case I needed them. I accepted his offer.

"You can take your mask off," Dick said after we entered his pickup truck.

I had a bunch of ready-made replies for this situation. "If it's all the same, Dick, I'm cold and I'll just keep it on."

"Cold? It's freaking August. How can you be cold?"

"It's the damp," I said.

"I could turn the heat on."

"I'm okay. Thank you."

"Why don't you take those stupid sunglasses off for once?"

"I told you, Dick."

"Yeah, yeah. You have that stigmatism or something."

"Yes. I'm going to need surgery."

"Well, I hope you get it soon. You know you look like a character out of a goddamned horror movie. Did you ever see the Invisible Man? You look like the Invisible Man in that getup."

I was grateful for the ride, but my punishment was listening to Dick cackle like a chicken at his own stupid jokes. That was bad enough, but then he segued effortlessly to bitching about politics. I fantasized about the damage I'd sustain if I jumped out of a moving truck. I decided against it.

Dick was the boss, so I continued the ruse and pretended I was a good ol' boy like him. It was all I could do to keep from wrapping my Lego paws around his neck. It wouldn't take much. My grip strength would make quick work of him.

"Well, I pray Trump wins in November," Dick said. I just nodded my head and hoped he'd change the subject. "Otherwise, our taxes are going to go up and they're going to take our cars away."

I did a double-take when I heard that. I understood the taxes part; the republican party was filled with crazy conspiracy theories and as far as crazy conspiracy theories go, higher taxes was one of the saner ones. But the car thing baffled me. I should have dropped it, but I was curious, and my curiosity got the best of me.

"The Democrats are going to take our cars away?" I said.

"Sure."

I waited for an explanation, but when none was forthcoming, I asked him to expound.

"It's all them emission standards," he explained. "Our cars are dangerous to the environment, so he's going to take them away."

"Then how will we get around?"

"I don't know. They'll probably make us ride donkeys," he said, exploding into laughter.

"Do you watch a lot of Fox news?" I said.

"Sure. Don't you?"

"Uh, yeah, of course, but I was flipping through the channels one day, and I turned on CNN."

Dick gave me a stern look. "Oh, fake news," he said, shaking his head. "Fake news."

"Yes, of course, but I'm just saying it ain't all fake. It could give you a different perspective."

Dick grunted. We were from different worlds, but I sensed he looked at me like a son. To me, he was like a dysfunctional father.

"Hey, Dick. How's the wife?"

Dick thought carefully before he answered. "Yeah, she can be a real pain in the ass," he said.

"I hear a but in there."

"Yeah?"

"But you love her. Don't you?"

Dick stared straight ahead and wiped his eye with the back of his hand. "Me and Michelle have been together for thirty-one years," he said. "We were high school sweethearts. She's a good woman."

"That's fantastic, Dick. Congratulations."

"What about you? Do you have someone?"

"Sort of. Turn left here. Mine is the next house down."

Dick slowed his car to a stop; he looked out his window and stared at my trailer. Then he turned to me and asked if I was alright and if I needed money. I thanked him and told him I was fine.

"Are you sure?" he said. "I know it takes time to get settled and save money. You have enough to eat, right?"

I stepped out of the car and told him I was good. Then I thanked him and walked into my trailer while he drove off. Dick was an idiot, and I couldn't stand his politics, but he was kindhearted for a Republican.

I sat in my recliner and rocked myself to the rhythm of raindrops plopping into a bucket. The light outside had faded and I could barely see a foot in front of me. It was a blessing given the mess that was my living room. God, how could I bring a woman here? What about a friend, if I ever found a friend? Lenny came to mind. I wondered how he was, what he was doing. I really should fix this place up. Be ready for good things, Mom used to say, and good things will come.

-Chapter 8-

I tossed and turned and dreamt strange dreams about work, worried dreams, sick dreams that left me cold despite the mild temperature. They were fragments of images and stories, disjointed and bizarre, as most dreams are. Dick was there. I remembered that much.

I got up and spent five minutes looking for my mask until I realized I was wearing it. The absent-minded professor strikes again; the thought made me smile and wince at once. I was proud of my professor title, and I still had one fantasy left: maybe I could teach again. But I quickly dismissed the idea for the madness it was. I was fortunate just to climb this far back into society, and I needed to make peace with my current plight if I was to be happy.

There was no need to get dressed or put on my shoes. I slept in the clothes from yesterday. I had no odor, so I took shortcuts where I could. Baths were unnecessary and out of the question; water would render me a smart paper weight. Besides, I was never a slave to fashion, not even when my mind inhabited a human body. Clothing covered my Lego body, and that was good enough for me.

I normally took time to watch CNN before heading to work, but I was in a hurry this morning and besides, the news made me angrier and more frustrated than I already was. It was best to keep the TV off and be on my way; to see what fate held for me.

I kept my head down and trudged through the morning fog; I tried not to obsess? Kat promised not to tell, and I believed her. Even so, the indiscretions, like entering her house and using her bathroom? For the life of me, why would I do such a thing? I knew better. The old Lance would never do such a thing. Old Lance was shy and reserved and never so bold as to enter a residence and use the bathroom without permission. The new Lance disturbed me. How many other differences existed between old and new?

I was a copy, but an imperfect one at that. I was like a song that was digitized and compressed from its original analog version. The listener thinks they're hearing continuous sound, but what they're really hearing are zeros and ones filled with gaps where music should be. Most people can't tell the difference. My mind had those gaps; I could tell.

I wouldn't blame Kat if she had filed a complaint with the police. She had every right. That's what I would've done. Perhaps she called Dick. He was probably lying in wait and ready to pounce with my final notice. Dick liked me, but this transgression was too much for him to ignore. He would have to fire me.

Yet, Kat seemed so kind, cool, and clever. She believed I was a technological advancement within the United States Postal System. I was nothing but a drone to her delivering mail like a bot with a lot of personality and an ego the size of New Hampshire.

She could call the post office and complain about their buggy android that didn't know enough to keep out of people's homes—I'd love to eavesdrop on that conversation. I smiled at the thought. Someone would drop a net over her head before I got into trouble.

Still, I needed an alibi, just in case. I did nothing illegal, did I? I was trying to be helpful. You know, an exemplary employee, and well, I got sidetracked. I could apologize to Dick, agree that it was wrong, and promise not to do it again. Maybe I'd get away with another write-up.

When I arrived at the post office, Dick was in a cheerful mood. There was no sign of anguish, just his smiling face greeting me like an old friend.

Dick looked at his watch. "Well, what's this?" he said.

"What's wrong?"

"You're early. Usually, you come sauntering into work like a damned alley cat who couldn't be bothered; ten minutes late on a good day."

"Well, I want to change my ways. You know, I really like my job and I want to do better."

I was scared, scared out of my mind. I couldn't wait to get into work and see how much trouble I was in.

"Say, Richard," I said. "Did you get any bad reports on me?"

Dick said he heard nothing, but wanted to know why I kept asking and why I was calling him Richard.

"Well, that's your name, isn't it?" I said.

"I told you to call me Dick. Everyone calls me Dick."

"Yes, of course, uh, Dick. There's a crazy, old woman named Ms. Kozlova, and she has this dog, and it was bothering me, and I yelled at it and then she started yelling at me."

"Did he bite you?"

"Nah. It just grabbed my pant leg. That's all."

"Well, you really should file a report."

"Nah, Dick. It was nothing. Just tugged on my pant leg. That's all."

"Well, she hasn't called in a complaint. I'll let you know if she does. You should really file a report."

"No. It's nothing, Richard, I mean Dick. It didn't even break the skin. I really have to get to work."

Dick stared at me. I didn't like lying, but it was a necessary evil. I was thankful Dick couldn't see my eyes or the smirk I always wore when I fibbed.

It was warm and humid from yesterday's rain, a perfect summer day filled with the sounds of chirping birds and leaves rustling behind the weight of a light breeze. Lenny taught me to be grateful for the simple things.

I liked my job even though I didn't always act like it. It was beneath me, but it had its benefits. The paycheck was a lifesaver, and I wasn't chained to a desk. I hated offices and cubicles and the soul-sucking florescent lights beating down on my head like a cursed sun. That's why I became a teacher in my first incarnation. Teachers don't sit for long periods and are not constrained by traditional workplace norms and hours. They have more freedom than most people.

That's why I was well suited for postal delivery. Postmen have more freedom, and the job's not hard. It was mindless and gave me time to think, to conjure warm memories like the smell of spring hanging in the air like perfume and images of a boy stepping onto a baseball diamond with his new glove; the smell of oiled leather mingling with freshly mowed grass was intoxicating. I was alive then and blissfully ignorant of the future. It was a splendid memory, tranquilizing like an opioid. I wish I could return to those simpler times for a week or even a day.

Tracy appeared occasionally—her perfect smile and feminine curves. I missed a woman's touch. All the good times we had, the great sex and those tender moments—afterglow—lying awake in bed, snuggling, and talking late into the evening, or for a few minutes until I fell asleep.

Her image eventually faded, and I was left with a hollow feeling gnawing at my gut. Tracy was a ghost. All my relationships had dissolved. Finding love before the transformation seemed like a monumental task. Now it seemed impossible.

Yes, I was alive, but at what cost? I thought and felt as a flesh and blood human would think and feel. Yet, I was sequestered from society, still part of it, but not belonging. Family, friends, they were absent. I was like that child viewing the birthday party behind a pane of glass, an outsider longing to get in. I yearned for the company of contemporaries, to share their laughter, to feel the sensation of finger scrolling down my naked back. But there was no flesh, only an amalgamation of plastic, wires, and transistors housing a human spirit.

Sometimes the loneliness made me so crazy. Dick's offer to hang out looked more palatable with each passing day. I thought about buying a parrot. I could teach it to talk, and we'd have coherent conversations; it would be some consolation. Birds make an awful mess, however, and the thought of cleaning up parrot shit turned my stomach. Besides, a bird isn't a person; it isn't a woman.

I thought about Kat. I thought about her a lot. She hadn't turned me in or made any phone calls. I would have heard something by now. Still, my obsession with her frightened me. She was older than me, but what does that matter in my physical state? She had a devilish wit and charm. I could tell in our short time together, call it a vibe or her spirit or whatever, but I picked up on it and not with my intellect, but something else, something I couldn't describe or articulate, but was there.

Her chess acumen captivated me. Unlike Lenny, she wasn't a potzer. She could give me a game. And she didn't balk at my machine works. Instead, she seemed impressed by my appearance. I couldn't wait to deliver her mail. Maybe she was waiting for me and I could talk to her and get to know her better. I shook my head and laughed. Nothing could come of this, so why did I think these crazy thoughts?

It was late in the afternoon when I parked in my usual spot on Pleasantview Drive. I got out of my car and made my usual rounds, Then I arrived at Kat's house. I ascended her driveway, slowly and casually, as if this was just another delivery; business as usual. But when I stepped onto her porch, I saw a plain, nondescript shoebox laying there and it was addressed to me. I saw it marked clearly on top with black marker.

To: Lance:

A million things went through my mind, none of which were any good. Was it a bomb? A stack of legal notices, bundled so thick, they had to be served in a box? I didn't want to look. I thought about leaving it and pretending I didn't see it. But the kid on Christmas morning couldn't resist. So, I removed the lid and peered inside.

I nearly dropped the box.

It wasn't anything I guessed, nor could have guessed, because it was so fiendishly clever, and disturbing. It was creepy in a way that could only come from an evil genius. Kat wasn't Anastasia. She was a demented mastermind who liked to fuck with people's mind. A chill ran down my spine, and I felt like I was being watched. I looked up and to my right, and I saw Kat smiling down at me through the window. I smiled back sheepishly and wiggled my fingers at her; she disappeared and reappeared a second later at the front door. Her face was warm and welcoming, and I felt relieved.

"What's this?" I said, while holding the box in front of me.

"Makeup," she said.

"Why?"

"I saw you trying some on yesterday."

My eyes begged her to expound. "It's okay," she said. "My husband used to wear my make-up and tried on my clothes. He was a good guy, and I loved him."

I didn't know whether to thank her or feel humiliated.

"Well, won't you need them?" I said.

"No. I don't wear makeup anymore, so I don't know why I kept them. I figured maybe you'd like to have them."

For the longest time, I stared into the box and was transfixed by the wonderful colors staring back at me. It was a nice gesture, and I realized there was no malevolence behind her actions, no evil genius, only a kind person who seemed to care. My cheeks felt warm and red, but I thanked her.

"Ms. Kozlova," I said. "I hope I wasn't out of line yesterday. I mean, about everything. If I upset you, please accept my apologies."

"I wasn't upset at all."

"Indeed. It's just highly irregular walking into your house and you know, trying on your makeup, and you know—"

"It's okay."

There was a long, awkward pause before she asked me for her mail. I handed over two envelopes, and she thanked me.

"You're not a postal drone, are you?" she said.

Her face was sweet, so tender and relaxed. It conveyed the confidence of a woman completely assured of herself. She knew. All I could do was stare at my feet and shake my head.

"May I ask?" she said.

"I'm afraid the real story is so incredible you might not believe me."

"Try me."

"It's long."

"Are you working tomorrow? Come over around lunch and we can play chess."

I nodded my head and thanked her again for the makeup.

-Chapter 9-

Kat's perfect, blue eyes scanned the pieces with the intensity of a bulldog contemplating its next meal. Behind her eyes was the mind of a chess master, capable of picking apart most opponents and reducing them to dust with a few brilliant strokes. On this day, she was overmatched.

Every so often, she'd catch me sneaking a peek at her. She'd smile, shake her head slightly and then returned her worried gaze back to the board. After a particularly devastating move, she winced and squirmed in her seat. She was not used to losing. It was a foregone conclusion in my mind, but she was too stubborn to admit defeat; deep down, however, I knew she had that sinking feeling. I could tell by the deep furrows that lined her forehead.

"I'm made of Legos," I said while she studied the board.

"I see that."

After ten minutes of contemplation, her eyes grew wide and then narrowed to two black slits. She saw the brilliantly laid trap that ended with her lost queen. Kat mercifully set down her king and flashed a contrite smile as if to say she was sorry for disgracing my presence with her inept play. I smiled back and winked to say it was okay.

"Where'd you learn to play so well?" she said.

"I was born this way."

She believed me for half a second before I revealed the ruse with an unapologetic laugh. Then she laughed, and I felt my cheeks grow warm.

She told me she had studied under her Russian-born father, who was supposed to be a fair chess player back in the old country. If her father was a fair, Russian player, that means he'd kick just about everyone's ass in the states. He taught her well, and she'd trounce any normal person, but I was not normal. With my organic brain, I was good, but with my electronic brain and quartz memory, I was unbeatable. Pity I couldn't show the rest of the world.

"I hate losing," she said. "I'm pissed off and beguiled at once."

"You did well."

I offered my congratulations, and she stared at my hand for a moment before accepting.

"Wow," she said. "I watched you move the pieces. They look clumsy, but they're not."

I avoided her eyes and sucked in a deep breath.

"What was that opening?" she said. "I've never seen that before."

"It's a variation on Ruy Lopez. Something I came up with in my free time."

She nodded her head as if she understood. I smiled and pretended not to notice her bewilderment. Then I asked her if she wanted to play again.

"Why?" she said. "So you can kick my ass again, and I can feel worse about myself?"

I laughed. "Well, yes," I said. "I can kick most people's ass if it makes you feel any better."

She squinted and studied my face before declaring I was a cheater. I just laughed and agreed with her.

"It's true," I said. "I'm not most people."

"I can see that."

"You're an outstanding player. Much better than Lenny."

"Whose Lenny?"

"Just a friend of mine, a potzer I met in the woods."

"I see."

"Ms. Kozlova, I'd—"

"Stop calling me that," she said. "My name is Kat. Call me Kat."

"Yes, of course, Kat. Can we talk? I don't get much chance to talk to people anymore. Well, at least not interesting people like you."

Kat blushed. "Yes," she said. "I'd like that."

Within minutes, we fell into a familiar rhythm like Lenny and I had. She was like him in many ways—smart and funny. I suspected she could dole out a lashing with her sharp wit; I kept my distance, remaining at arm's length from her rapier tongue. She was nothing like Tracy. Instead, she was me in drag and I liked that. I could have let myself go, to share my dreams, my fears, but I held back. Lenny left me and there was always a chance of getting hurt again. I couldn't handle another disappointment; not now. We spent the next several hours talking and exploring common interests. I discovered we shared a similar taste in music. She loved Steely Dan and was a self-described Dead Head.

"I was a twirler," she said.

"Oh, so you were one of those hippie chicks that twirled around for the entire concert." She nodded her head. "I always wondered how you kept from getting dizzy."

Kat shrugged. "I don't know," she said. "We were so high, it really didn't matter."

We both laughed, and then she described her drug-infused, hippy lifestyle, listening to rock and roll, dancing, twirling, and living freely. But her description didn't match her vast home filled with art and textbooks.

"I can't picture you dancing at a Dead concert wearing tie dye and twirling like a top."

"Oh, I didn't wear tie dye. I usually went topless."

I was hooked. The image of a young, topless Kat dancing and gyrating to the Dead's hypnotic rhythms made me feel warm and fuzzy. Kat's laughter shook me from my daydream, and I started laughing too. I'm not sure what we were laughing at; probably me, I guessed; I didn't mind. Kat was new and exciting, and she made me feel good.

Before now, my days were filled with work, routine and long hours spent alone at home, playing chess or watching reruns of Three's Company—I can't think of a bigger loser pastime than to watch reruns of Three's Company. My time with Kat was like a cold drink to a desert traveler. I was lonely, and she was lonely, and inside this Lego shell beat the heart of a relatively young man, with all the young man's angst and longing.

When the room fell silent again, I looked into her eyes and smiled.

"Yes. I was a big hippie in those days," she said.

"Yes, I'm sure you were, but I can't picture a hippy living in the burbs on Eagle Drive in such a beautiful home."

"I guess I'm not most hippies. Me and my late husband weren't. We met at Penn State and we both had engineering degrees and good jobs and, you know, we smoked pot on weekends. Well, I got high on weekends and Ralphie got high pretty much every day. He used to tell me he only got high two days out of the week: weekends and weeknights. It was so corny, but it made me laugh."

I suspected she was a pot smoker; she looked like an older version of Velma from Scooby Doo and all those cartoon characters were all stoned as fuck, even the dog.

"Do you still smoke?" I said.

"Yeah. I have a medical card."

"We should smoke sometime."

Kat's face dropped, and she gave me *a what the fuck are you talking about* look?

"I'm sorry," I said. "I don't mean to imply I'll smoke up all your weed. I'll gladly pay. It's just that Lenny gave me seeds, but they haven't matured yet and—"

"No. It's not that. I was thinking, how is that even possible? No offense, but you're not, well, you're not real. I mean, are you a pot-smoking machine?"

"Well, I've never really thought of it that way. I don't actually smoke the pot. I hold the joint in my mouth and pretend to inhale and I have the memories of getting high and so I feel high."

Kat blinked her eyes repeatedly and said, "No shit?"

"Yeah. No shit."

"Jesus. That's amazing."

"Well, yes."

Kat's eyes demanded an explanation, and I did my best to explain the complexities through oversimplification.

I told her we could summarize human consciousness into a series of electrical impulses comparable to binary code. Our minds—memories, personality traits, talents, likes, dislikes—act as the software which controls the hardware (our bodies). All I did was upload my software to another piece of hardware—my Lego body.

"You're blowing my mind," she said.

"You believe me?" I said.

"I do, but…"

"But what?"

"… so, you're not a robot?"

"I am not."

"But the way you play chess."

"What does that have to do with anything?"

"You play like a computer. You're three moves ahead of me."

"By my estimation, more like thirty."

"Yeah, okay, whatever."

"I am a human," I said, emphatically. "A human stored in a mechanical body."

"So, you're like a human conscience inside a Lego body?"

"That sums it up."

"Why Legos?"

"Why not Legos? They're cheap, sturdy, interlocking, easy to assemble. A child could do it."

"But aren't you afraid you'll come apart and crumble into nothingness?"

I was tempted to show off my scar where the bullet had put a hole in my chest, but it wasn't time for scars and it wasn't time for the story and questions behind it.

"Loctite," I said.

"What?"

"Loctite is an adhesive used in the automotive industry to secure nuts and bolts. My bricks were glued in with Loctite, so I don't crumble into nothingness, as you so eloquently stated."

"Jesus. But how do you move so fluidly? Legos aren't flexible?"

"Well, the Legos are a kind of exoskeleton. I'm also made up of ball and socket joints, actuators, wires and computer chips and a quartz crystal, 5d memory drive; let's just say there's more to me than meets the eye."

"Jesus," she said, shaking her head.

"Can you hear my actuators when I move?" I said.

Kat turned an ear towards me, and I moved my arms and head to accommodate her.

"No," she said. "I don't hear anything."

"Good," I said. "They're whisper quiet, and my clothing helps dampen any sound they make."

I knew what she was thinking. Her sparkling eyes and open mouth gave her away. But I asked anyway.

"I don't know what to think," she said. "It's a little overwhelming. You're like a human soul in a Lego body, and I'm not even high."

"You believe I have a soul, and that I'm not simply an amalgamation of human thought and memory and electronics?"

Kat thought for a moment and then answered. "Yes," she said.

"How do you know? In all my calculations, in all my algorithms, and code, I never accounted for the soul. I was an atheist, still am, and so I never believed in a soul or an afterlife."

"So, why are you concerned now?"

"Who says I'm concerned?"

"You asked about a soul, didn't you?"

"I suppose I did."

I looked at the chessboard and Kat's downed white king lying horizontal and impotent on the squares. "What if I'm wrong?" I said.

"And what if you are?"

"Well, that changes everything, doesn't it?"

Kat shrugged. "Oh, I don't know," she said.

"I've had a lot of time to think about these things."

"Sometimes, thinking too much is a bad thing."

I looked up and into her eyes. They were warm and soft.

I smiled and said, "I'm not so sure. I wish I had thought things through before I started this bloody mess."

Suddenly, I felt her hand slip effortlessly into mine. "Maybe it's better that you didn't," she said. "Otherwise, you might not be here now with me."

I felt myself blush, and I mouthed the words, "Thank you."

"Can I ask you a question?" she said.

"Really? Just one?"

"What were you doing with my makeup? I thought you enjoyed wearing makeup like my late husband, but now I'm not so sure."

I placed my hand on my cheek and told her I was I was trying to cover up. "All the seams," I said. "I wanted to look human."

"But I like the way you look."

"Thanks, but not everyone shares your opinion. Besides, if I feel human, I should look human too. Right?"

"I don't think so. What's so great about looking human, or feeling human for that matter? There's many people wishing they weren't so human right about now."

"Well, it comes in handy when you're trying to fit in and find work."

Kat's eyes narrowed. "Why do you even need to work?" she said. "<u>Not</u> working is one perk of being a Lego man. I would never work if I didn't have to."

"It's not that simple. I still need things, shelter to feel warm and safe, books to entertain, art, music... The inside of me is still very human and needs nurturing, just like any other person. Maslow's hierarchy of needs, I'm still bound by them."

"And the mask, the sunglasses and gloves cover you up? That's how you got the job at the post office?" I nodded my head. "That's amazing," she said.

"Yes, well, it pays the bills."

Kat looked at me for what seemed like a long time. She wore a bemused smile and slowly shook her head from side-to-side.

"What is it?" I asked.

"Why?"

"Why not?" Kat smiled and shook her head as if to reject my dismissive response. "I thought I could cheat death," I said. "I thought I found a cure for death. Maybe I just wanted to see if I could do it. I don't know. There were many reasons. They all seemed so wonderful, so righteous at the time."

"And now?"

I smiled, picked up a pawn, and twirled it like a baton between my fingers. "I don't know," I said. "I'm here. I'm alive. I'm sitting here talking with you, so it can't be all bad."

"But it's not all good?"

"I suppose it was never meant to be all good. To live is to struggle. That's the price we pay for checking into this world. The price we pay for checking out is the unknown. I know this now."

"And where is the real Dr. Lance Ziegel?"

"What do you mean?" I demanded. "I am the real Dr. Ziegel."

"Don't get upset," she said. "All I meant—"

"I know what you meant, and I'm sorry. I'm not upset. I'm having trouble with the concept, and I'm living it. There's me and there's another me walking around with a normal body and a somewhat normal life. It's hard for me to grasp. I can't expect anyone else to understand."

Kat lowered her eyes and began pulling on an imaginary thread from the sofa. I felt bad about the turn our conversation had taken.

"Look," I said. "Lance could be alive, sipping Mai Tais on a beach somewhere for all I know. All I know for sure is that I'm here. I am the real Lance Ziegel."

"Why wouldn't he be alive?"

I fell silent and looked down again at the fallen king again. I blocked out the events leading up to my freedom. I hadn't meant to dismiss them, but I did.

After a few moments, I blurted something out. "COVID," I said. "You know, COVID killed many people and Lance—the human version was at risk. He had a heart condition that made him more vulnerable."

"I'm sorry to hear that."

"Don't be. I mean, it's okay."

"Wasn't that part of the plan, anyway?" I looked at Kat and questioned her with my eyes. "I meant by transferring your personality to another body, and cheating death," she said.

"Yes. That was the plan; to cheat death."

-Chapter 10-

We were supposed to pay to get in, but Rock City was closed because of the pandemic. However, Kat discovered a crack in the chain-link fence, and I pried it open wide enough for me to slip past. Then I leaned back to create a bigger hole for Kat to crawl through. I could hear my actuators strain and protest from the effort.

"Ah," she said. "I'm stuck."

"It's your purse. It's hung up."

Kat freed herself and joined me inside the park, where we stood like two fugitives from justice. Then she laughed and called me the six-million-dollar man referring to my fence-bending strength.

"More like the eighty-thousand-dollar man," I said.

"Really? That's how much you cost?"

"Give or take a few bob," I said in a British accent.

"That's the worst British accent I ever heard," she said.

"The dickens, you say."

"I would have pegged you at six figures, easy."

"Maybe it was more. I don't know, really. I didn't pay for it, because I couldn't afford it."

"Did you do crowd funding?"

I looked at her and just as I expected, she had that eat-shit grin on her face, the same one she flashed whenever she was messing with me, which she seemed to do with more frequency as our relationship developed. I didn't mind. It made me feel normal.

"You love mocking me," I said. "Don't you?"

She pleaded her innocence with a straight face and raised hands, but I knew better.

"I had a friend," I told her. "Well, a colleague is more like it. He wasn't much of a friend. I detested him, actually, but he was an expert in neuroscience and, well, he had money too and so I enlisted him in the Ziegel army."

"Where's this detestable friend now?"

I didn't answer her. Instead, we started down a gravel path leading into the park. I was deep in my head, staring off into space, when I felt Kat's hand slip into mine.

"It seems like a long time ago," I said.

"Have you talked to him lately?"

"No. I had to get away from him."

"Why?"

"He wanted to poke and prod me and treat me like a sideshow freak for his enrichment."

"Like the Elephant Man?"

I looked at her to see if she was teasing me again, but her expression was serious. "The who?" I said.

"You know. John Merrick. The Elephant Man. He had that disease that made him deformed."

"Oh yes. I saw the movie, but what does that have to do with me?"

"Well, the doctors wanted to study him for their edification, but they really didn't care about him as a person or offer any real medical help. Your story reminded me of that."

I touched my hand to the side of my face. "Oh, God," I said. "I hope you don't think I'm as hideous as the Elephant Man."

"Of course not," she said. "I think you're quite pleasing to the eye. I like looking at you."

"I like the way you look too, Kat."

We stopped walking, and Kat turned toward me. She blushed, and I knew it was the right time, but I couldn't bring myself to do it. Fortunately, Kat had courage for both of us. She rose to her tiptoes, and I leaned over to meet her halfway. The kiss was warm and moist and touched down with the weight of a feather. I grabbed my cheek and smiled; she smiled back.

"C'mon," she said. "This place is really neat."

A sign near the entrance described the park's history and we read about how the local Indians lived here and used the rock formations and caves for shelter. I imagined what it was like back then, a hundred or more years ago, and thought about how their lives differed from ours. It was a hard life, I imagined, alone, no grocery stores, motor vehicles, internet, or other technology, but then again, I wondered if it wasn't far superior to modern living. They had no psychiatrists, no Prozac or OxyContin. They didn't need it. When they got depressed, their families would cheer them up. And when they got injured, or the pain was too much, they simply died. There was something elegant, even poetic to it—something we modern humans have a hard time grasping.

"It's nice," Kat said. "I'd bring my kids here when they were young, and we'd explore the nooks and crannies for hours. Too bad the gift store is closed."

"Yeah, but then we'd have to pay to get in. I wonder what the native Americans would think of me?"

Kat's eyes scanned my body and then she told me I'd be worshipped as a God. I laughed and assured her I'd be sacrificed to their real gods or simply killed as a devil.

Kat flicked her hair with the back of her hand and said, "What about me, with my red hair and cutoff jean shorts?"

"Oh, you would have been their sex slave for sure," I said.

Kat smiled. She grabbed my hand and led me down a path and deeper into our adventure.

Rock City consisted of, well, rocks, or more specifically, large rock formations with narrow corridors between them in which two bodies— and sometimes just a single body—could squeeze through. It was fun traversing the narrow lanes with Kat, looking up at the clouds and feeling the cool stone on my fingertips. Sometimes, I'd let Kat walk ahead so I could snap pictures of her. She looked so tiny against the massive rock cathedrals.

The path led us to the top of a large, flat rock formation that looked out over the forest-covered valley below; that's when my vertigo kicked in. I crept forward, taking baby steps toward a one-hundred-foot sheer drop. I couldn't get closer than ten feet, but Kat was fearless. She walked up to the edge, looked down and commented how beautiful it was; she said I should join her, but my feet were cemented to the ground, and they wouldn't budge.

"You should stay back," I said. "You have the car keys, and if you fall, I'll really have a hard time trying to get back home."

"C'mon," she said. "I'll hold your hand."

"I'm good."

"Are you afraid of heights?"

"No," I lied.

Kat was persistent. She held out her hand and urged me forward with her eyes. Well, I wouldn't have done it for just anyone, but she was a woman, and I liked her and so I inched forward and squeezed her hand.

"Look down," she said. "It's beautiful."

I took her advice and immediately regretted it. My knees trembled and my body wobbled. I imagined myself falling, smashing up against the rocks below—a pile of Lego bricks and computer parts lying in disarray like an abandoned child's toy. All the technology, all the man hours, all the knowledge undone in a momentary lapse of balance. I recalled a sermon I heard as a little boy: *you are dust and to dust you shall return.* I didn't believe it then. I believed it now.

"You okay?" Kat said.

"I'm not really immortal; am I?"

Kat shrugged. "Welcome to the club," she said.

"I thought I'd live forever, but that's not really true, is it? Machines break. Computers get old, parts need to be replaced. This idea we can live forever in body form is a fallacy. Isn't it?"

Kat placed her hand and my elbow. "Let's have a seat," she said. "You'll feel safer."

Kat removed her purse and placed it on the ground. Then she took my hand and guided me to a seated position while she sat next to me. Kat wanted to hang her legs over the edge, but I insisted we sit further back. She was about to protest, but she sensed my anxiety and agreed to sit a safer distance away.

"You really don't like heights, do you?" she said.

"No. In fact, just watching you stand so close to the edge made me nervous."

Kat smiled and shook her head. After a few minutes, I slowed my heart rate and scanned the horizon. It was a spectacular panorama of the countryside, its treelined hills and a luscious, grassy valley. Sitting with Kat, enjoying the view and listening to the birds, made me feel one with the infinite. I missed nature, the solitude, but not the loneliness. I never wanted to be lonely again.

We sat for a long time in silence. The sun reflected off Kat's face and she appeared to glow from within. I basked in her spirit. Our shoulders touched and our torsos swayed with a light breeze. This was the closest we've been since I started coming over and playing chess. This was the closest I've been to a woman in over a year. I forgot how wonderful the feeling was. I pressed closer to her and sniffed the air.

"What's that perfume you're wearing?"

She laughed and said she wasn't wearing any.

"I smell something," I insisted.

"You're smelling a memory," she said.

"Yes," I said. "I'm afraid I am. It's a sweet memory."

"I used to bring my kids here."

"Where are your kids?"

"There all grown up now, live in different states."

"Weren't you afraid they'd fall and get hurt on the rocks?"

"Meh. I always thought I had too many kids, anyway."

"Mother of the year."

"I know, right?"

We laughed and kibitzed like an old married couple; that's when I knew. The feelings were real and mutual. I was sure.

"What?" she said, startling me out of a daydream.

"What?" I said.

"You're staring."

"Well, so are you."

"I have a right."

"Well, so do I."

Kat rubbed my shoulder and asked if I wanted to walk.

"No," I said. "Let's stay. The view is marvellous and I'm okay now."

We sat silently, transfixed by the landscape reminiscent of a Bob Ross oil painting. I stole glances at her every so often and I caught her looking at me once or twice. Then I spoke absentmindedly.

"I'm not immortal," I said.

"Who is?"

"I thought I was, or as close as one can get."

"I think immortality is highly overrated."

"You do?"

"Yes. Why would you want to live forever?"

I didn't know what to say at first. I thought everyone wanted to live forever, but I remembered those miserable souls that checked out before their time. Japan had an entire forest named after them: *the suicide forest.* The wealthy and famous—those with everything to live for—were not immune. But even with life's hardships, death didn't sound fun, and I told Kat so.

"I'm going to die sometime," she said.

She was right. Kat will die and I'll be alone again. I'll have to cycle through relationships, and friends until... until what? Until I meet my end? Perhaps death wasn't so bad. I never embraced the Christian belief in Heaven, but Lenny's idea of reincarnation appealed to me; it was the most believable narrative.

I looked at my hands and rotated them three hundred and sixty degrees. *They were brilliant,* my entire being was brilliant, but what about my soul?

"Maybe I should create my own heaven," I muttered

"What?" Kat said.

"I don't know. I was just thinking out loud."

"Tell me."

"Well, you know I'm a software engineer. I was thinking I could create a digital version of heaven and then I really could live forever, an actual place of my creation, my imagination."

Kat looked at me; her mouth hung open, and she slowly shook her head from side-to-side.

"You think it's a crazy idea?" I said.

Kat shrugged and said I was a crazy idea. I agreed with her and then I explained my plans as quickly as I could think of them. I told her about the different worlds I'd create and the wonderful things I could see and do there.

"When I have enough money saved, I'll buy a computer and start programming it. For now, I'll sketch the design, all the different layers and powerups."

Kat stared at me while I talked. Then she told me it was a crazy idea.

"Yes," I countered. "But you want to go with me."

"Well yeah. It sounds fucking amazing."

"It's going to be. We'll live in pure consciousness, as pure energy beings, no bodies to worry about, no disasters, no catastrophes. We can drop from the tallest buildings and simply regenerate. It will be pure bliss." Kat was quiet and looked down at her hands. "What's wrong?" I said.

"I don't know," she said, while scanning the horizon. "Do you think you'll be happy?"

"Happy?" I said in a surprised tone. "Of course, I'll be happy. That's what bliss means." Kat laughed. "Are you laughing at me or with me?" I said.

"I think I'm laughing at you this time."

"Yes. That's what I was afraid of."

"I don't know. I think I want to take my chances."

"You mustn't say that, Kat."

Kat questioned me with her eyes, and I had to look away.

"Then what will become of me?" I said.

I looked at the setting sun and the soft pink horizon. I felt Kat's hand on my shoulder, and I instinctively placed my hand on hers. Our eyes met, and we smiled.

"When will you finish making heaven?" she said.

"It will be awhile. I haven't even started yet. I'll have to make preliminary sketches."

"I want to see them."

"I'll get started and bring them over next time."

"How about if I come over to your house some time?"

"My house?"

"Yes. You have a house, right? You visit me all the time, but you never invite me over to your place."

"You wouldn't like it. It's not as nice as yours."

"I'd still like to see it someday."

I smiled and shook my head. "C'mon," I said. "We should get going. You must be starved."

"Yeah, that's kind of a thing with us organic life forms. Eating is such a pain in the ass. Do you miss it?"

"Of course not," I lied. "It's such a pain in the ass. I save so much money on groceries."

Kat stood up and extended her hand toward me. "C'mon," she said. "It's getting late."

I nodded my head and then she helped me to my feet. "You good?" she said.

"Yes, I think so. I'm not as wobbly."

She smiled and patted my chest. "Hand me my purse," she said.

I knelt down and picked up her purse. It felt like it had bricks inside.

"You got rocks in this thing?" I said.

"My nine."

Kat's face was placid.

"Ha," I said.

"No joke."

She opened her purse and pulled the gun out. "SIG P320," she said.

I stepped back and asked her if it was loaded.

"Of course. What good is an unloaded gun?"

"Is the safety on?"

"Yes, of course the safety's on."

Kat pushed a button on the grip and removed the clip, then she racked the barrel and a bullet fell to the ground: *tink.*

She turned the gun around and tried to hand it to me, barrel down, but I held my hands up and refused.

"What's wrong?" she said. "Haven't you ever seen a gun before?"

"I—I have. I just never thought of you as a gun owner. You don't seem the type."

"What's the type?"

"I don't know. Plaid-wearing Republican?"

Kat laughed and told me liberals owned guns too.

"A single woman," she said. "Living alone during the pandemic. You never know."

"Yes, well, I know. Guns are dangerous."

Kat retrieved the bullet. She placed it back into the clip and popped the clip back into the gun. Then she chambered the first round.

"Jesus," I said. "You're ready for combat."

"Zombies," Kat said with a straight face. "You can never be too careful."

Kat put the gun in the purse. "All better?" she said.

"All better."

I took Kat's hand, and we walked towards the exit.

It was the summer of 2020, and the world had lost its collective mind. There was some good in the insanity, however. I felt normal by comparison. Better than normal, actually, because I couldn't get sick.

Before COVID, I felt lost and alone. After COVID, I was just one of many lost souls rethinking everything, searching for answers, finding hope in the madness. Kat helped. She grounded me and just like Lenny had; she accepted me for who I was, and she never judged, nor questioned my being. Before Kat, I survived, but I didn't live. She made this world a little brighter. She brought me joy.

-Chapter 11-

I was alive, and life meant hope. I remembered what Lenny said about reincarnation. It was the best explanation of the afterlife I ever heard. But I was still a man of science. Death held more holes than answers, and so I remained dubious. Besides, all the spirituality smacked of traditional religion. Science was my religion. My God was a CPU. My passion was fueled by knowledge and a quest to unravel the mysteries of the universe for the betterment of humanity and for my own benefit.

People thought butterflies and rainbows came shooting out your nose and mouth when you discover your passion, but that's not accurate. Finding your passion is only the first step, and it leads to more steps, all fraught with more problems. I wished I hadn't ventured so far from shore. I wished I had been more complacent, to go quietly into that good night without so much as a whimper. But I remembered who I was and the impossibility of taking any other course of action. We think we have a choice, but there's no choice. We're simply acting on the behest of our programming, our genetics, our family, our history, where we grew up and when. Our so-called choices are a billion and one different prompts that caused us to go down one path and not another. We had no choice. I understood I had no recourse but to become a Lego Man. It was written, as they say, in the stars.

And so, it forced me to come to terms with my new life; slowly, I adapted and there were long stretches when things felt normal. Still, I reminisced about my professor days. I missed my research at the university, my title, my status. I free fell from the mountain top of university professor to the valley known as the United States Postal Service. Yet, every time I considered slitting Dick's throat—I thought about this often when he talked about politics—I reminded myself I was lucky to have a job. And then Dick would do something nice for me or say something nice that belied his conservative political views. Republicans weren't supposed to be caring or have feelings for anyone but themselves, but Dick showed me another side. I learned his son was killed in combat. Maybe that was it. I was his replacement son. I didn't want to be, and didn't ask to be, but I was cast into the role; it wasn't all bad. When Dick wasn't talking politics, he was kind and we could talk, hold a conversation, even though we had little in common. Inevitably, he would talk about one of his crazy conspiracy theories and it would ruin it for me; but it was nice while it lasted.

Dick was excited to hear I found someone, like real excited, as if he was the one in love. I didn't mean to say anything. It just slipped one day when he asked about my plans for the weekend, and I told him I was playing chess with Kat. That's when the questions started. I didn't tell him Kat was my girlfriend because I wasn't sure myself.

"Good," he said. "I was beginning to think you were a fag or something."

Dick started laughing, but stopped after he saw I wasn't joining in.

"I mean, I have nothing against those people even if you were," he said.

"Sure, Dick."

He looked worried and walked his statement back.

"I mean, I shouldn't have used that word," he said. "I was just joking, you know that?"

"Of course, Dick."

"You know, like a couple of buddies, right?"

"Yes, of course."

"But I shouldn't have said that at work, and I don't want you using words like that either. You hear?"

Dick pointed an accusatory finger at me.

"I won't Dick. I promise."

"Yeah, let's just keep this between us. Okay?"

"Sure, Dick. Sure."

"Maybe you can invite her over to my place for dinner. The wife will cook up something real nice."

I smiled at the image: a Lego man and his girlfriend having dinner at the boss's house. Dick would insist I remove my mask and my stupid sunglasses, as he liked to call them. I could picture the slacked-jaw faces staring at the Lego freak sitting at the dinner table. Mrs. Dick would stare at me for a while and then at her husband. Dick would bear the brunt of her bewilderment. Kat, in her deadpan manner, would ask to pass the butter and I would lose my shit. It would have been hilarious, but I still needed the job.

"Well, I'd love to," I said. "But you know with this pandemic, we're not supposed to gather and keep six feet apart and all of that."

"Bah," he said, waving me off. "You don't believe in all that crazy libertard shit. Do you?"

"Yeah, Dick. I kind of do. The science—"

"Aw, that science is a bunch of B. S."

I was tempted to take my mask and sunglasses off and reveal my true scientific self, but I refrained. Instead, I entered a philosophical debate that I regretted as soon as the words had left my mouth.

"But you believe in other science, don't you?" I said. "Gravity. You believe in gravity, right? The earth is round, not flat. Your car doesn't run by fairy power. There's an engine in it and that's engineering and that's science."

"You're talking like a goddamned liberal."

"I'm just saying Dick."

"Do you know anyone who actually contracted COVID?"

"Yes," I lied.

"Who?"

"Kat. She had the COVID."

"Kat had the COVID?"

"Yes, and believe me, you don't want it."

Dick stood there with his hands on his hips and worked his jaw like he was chewing on cud. "Huh," he said.

"Okay, Dick. Gotta go deliver the mail."

We were in the habit of meeting at her front door every afternoon. I'd bring her mail, and she always had a smile for me. She tried to cajole and then shame me into coming inside, and I'd refuse at first, but then I'd break down and visit for a while. Her air-conditioned house felt so good, and we'd sometimes play speed chess. I'd always win, but I felt bad and told her so.

"If you feel so bad, why are you smiling?" she'd say.

"Well, I guess I don't feel that bad."

On this day she didn't have mail, but I stopped anyway.

"No mail," I said.

"That's okay. You usually bring me bills. Try to do better next time."

Her voice was thin, and her paper-white skin appeared two shades paler than normal.

"You seem off," I said.

"I have a doctor's appointment."

I placed my hand on her forehead. "Oh no. It's not the COVID," I said.

"It's nothing like that. Do you want to stop in?"

"I have to deliver the mail."

"Just come in. You know you're going to anyway, so you might as well just do it."

"You're very self-assured, aren't you?"

"Well, yeah."

"Some would say cocky."

"Some would, I suppose."

It took little arm twisting. I quickly stepped inside and placed my bag down.

"I feel like a pack mule," I said.

"One of the job hazards," she replied.

"I suppose. You feel like getting your ass whooped in chess?"

"Not today."

"Are you sure you're okay? Why are you going to the doctors?"

"I'm old."

"You're spunky."

She smiled weakly and pointed to the kitchen chair. I took a seat, and she sat across from me and questioned me with her eyes.

"What?" I said.

"What's it like?"

"What's what like?"

"You know. Being you; living in your skin?"

I shrugged. "I don't know. It's a bit like anyone else, I suppose."

"Are you in pain?"

I lifted my sunglasses up and lowered my mask. Kat averted her gaze. "Only when I stub my toe," I said.

Kat stared at me for a long time, then she asked if I was fucking with her, and I told her I was.

"Why are you asking?" I said.

"I guess I don't know that much about you. You could be a Russian spy for all I know."

"Wasn't your dad a Russian?"

"Yeah, and he warned me about Russian spies."

"Oh, now you're fucking with me."

Kat shrugged; her impish smile gave her away. "I want to know more," she continued. "Do you have any regrets?"

It was the first time the question was posed. I asked myself several times and decided there were regrets, some at least. It was inevitable. We all have them, so why shouldn't I? Yet, I was here, and I was still me with a few notable exceptions and I liked me. Oh, I was still an arrogant prick. There was still that, but I was less so. This past year, homeless and outcast, brought a newfound appreciation for life and its frailty. I learned no matter how smart I thought I was, I was no match for the collective intellect of the universe and all its diverse intelligence. Lenny taught me spiritually and Kat taught me kindness and how not to take myself so seriously. I appreciated life like I never did before.

"How do you regret something like this?" I said. "I'm alive, and that's what matters. If life were so bad, I could exit early if I wished. But life seems good now."

Kat and I locked eyes, and her cheeks turned red. "Well, I'm glad you're here," she said.

I winked at her and said, "Yeah, you are."

-Chapter 12-

Moving in freed the money and time I needed to move forward, to purchase the equipment, the best hardware, the best software. Kat's deceased husband had provided well for her, and we could live comfortably off her income. Dick looked a little hurt when I told him I was leaving, and despite our differences, I was sad to tell him goodbye.

"Kat isn't well," I told him. "I'll have more time to take care of her. You understand, right?"

"How long have you known this Kat?" he said.

"About six months or enough time to know that, well, we're fond of each other."

"Uh, huh." Dick took off his hat and scratched his head; then held out his hand. "Okay," he said. "If you say so. I wish you luck."

I stared at his hand for a moment, then shook it.

"Oh, for fuck's sake," he groaned. "Why don't you take the goddamned gloves off and your sunglasses and your mask for once? You look like the goddamned invisible man."

"Well, I was badly burned. It's not pretty, Dick."

Dick's eyes popped and his jaw dropped, and I almost wished I hadn't lied.

"Jesus Christ," he said. "Why didn't you say something before. Jesus Christ, you're like a fucking enigma wrapped in a goddamned mystery."

"You don't know the half of it," I said. "Well, goodbye, Dick."

"Hey, you take care of yourself; you hear?"

"I will, Dick."

"And take care of that woman of yours," he said, pointing a finger at me. "That's what a man does. He takes care of his woman and his..." Dick's eyes swelled with tears, but he finally finished his sentence. "... and his kids."

"I know," I said. "I plan on it."

"And if you need anything, just let me know. You'll always have a friend here."

"Yes sir. I know. And thank you for everything."

Dick and I hugged. My eyes stung, and I felt a lump in my throat. When we pulled apart, Dick looked surprised.

"Goddamn," he said, feeling my right bicep. "You're built like an anvil."

"I've been spending a lot of time at the gym, Dick. Take care."

It wasn't just economics; Kat and I had something, a connection. She was older than me, but her spirit was young and that never grows old. We finished each other's sentence, and she kibitzed me mercilessly. I suppose I was an easy target for her rapier tongue. I tried to give back as much as I received, but I was a rank amateur by comparison.

We worked well together. I gave her chess lessons. She still couldn't beat me, but she got better. I helped around the house whenever I could. She liked my cooking. Most of my original recipes were cannabis-fueled creations conjured around midnight after smoking a joint. Nutella and butter spread over marbled pumpernickel toast was one of my specialties. Kat wasn't picky, and I enjoyed cooking up new concoctions even though I couldn't eat.

We shared the same bed, and that made me feel more human than anything else. Holding a woman, her hair tickling the nape of my neck, and breathing her scent. It was heaven. Sometimes, I'd rub her back, and she'd moan with pleasure. It was innocent and yet exhilarating at the same time.

We sat on the back porch in the mornings—she with her coffee and toast and me with a joint hanging sideways out of my mouth while I sketched.

"Show me," she said. I tilted the drawing pad so she could see. "Jesus. My boobs aren't that big."

I compared my drawing to Kat and told her it was an accurate depiction of her boobs.

"I think there's something wrong with your eyes," she said, looking down at her bosom.

"No. I think the proportions are accurate. Perhaps the hips could be wider."

"Are you saying I have big hips?"

"No. I'm just saying…"

I stopped in mid-sentence; she was laughing at me.

"Okay," I said. "Can you stop using your ability to speak?"

"Did you just tell me to shut up?" she said in mock anger.

"Me? Never."

"Cause it kinda sounded like you did."

Kat stood up and placed her hands on her hips.

"Can you please sit?" I said. "We're not through. I'll need to make more sketches."

Kat looked like an angry school marm. "Stand up," she said. Her voice was cool and stern.

I slowly rose to my feet, and though I towered above her, I was nervous. Her eyes were piercing as she studied me like a chessboard; she took a step forward and slipped her arms around my waist, then she drew me in close and pressed her breasts against my torso. Our eyes met.

"Feel that?" she said.

"Uh—I feel something," I stammered.

"What's it feel like?"

"It feels like—it feels like heaven."

"How?"

"What do you mean, how?"

"I mean, how is it you feel that? Do you have tiny sensors? And how do you get high when you smoke or feel pain when you stub your toe?"

"It's the rubber hand experiment."

"What's that?"

"After the mind transfer, I had to assimilate the Lego body as my own so I could experience the world based on my memories."

Kat was smart, smarter than me in many respects, but her eyes glazed over, and she kept staring, waiting for me to expound.

"It's like this," I said. "You can't just build a robot and transfer thoughts and feelings into it and expect it to act like a human in Lego drag. There's no artificial intelligence, no matter how clever it is, that can replicate human consciousness and achieve sentience. If we did that, you wouldn't have me, Doctor Lance Ziegel. You'd have a really smart robot that acts like me and possesses the same memories."

"Okay. That makes sense, but what does a rubber arm have to do with it?"

"The rubber arm is an experiment that shows how humans can assimilate other limbs as part of their consciousness. If I were to place a rubber arm next to yours, and then use a feather to tickle your arm and the rubber arm simultaneously, then your mind will believe the rubber arm is part of your body. After that, I can stop tickling your real arm, but you'll still feel the feather through the fake arm. I can even stab the rubber arm and you'll feel the pain."

"Jesus," she said. "How'd you figure all that out?"

"Oh, I didn't figure that out. Other scientists from different disciplines had worked that out before me. I merely read their papers, and stood on their shoulders."

"So, you used this principle in making you? I mean the Lego you?"

"Well, that was one principle, that along with mind transfer, or the ability to transplant the mind to a computer drive. Mind blowing, isn't it?"

"A little creepy, too."

"Do you think I'm creepy?"

"Not at all. I'm glad you did it. Otherwise, I wouldn't have you."

Kat closed her eyes. I lowered my head and placed a kiss on her lips.

"Take your clothes off," I said. Kat cocked her head to the side and smiled. "I want to sketch you."

"Naked?"

"Yes, of course. I want to get it right; every detail, all the nuances."

"Here, on the porch?"

"The hedges will block the view. No one will see."

"Sure. Why not?"

I watched Kat disrobe. Her casual, matter-of-fact attitude—as if she were going to shower—made it more tantalizing than a striptease. It was the first time I had seen her naked; the memories poured back, and I felt a tingle, first on a surface level and then more deeply in my core. My breaths came shallower; my pulse quickened, and a feeling of bliss washed over me like sunshine on a warm summer day.

I pulled up a chair for her and faced it toward the sun. "Have a seat," I said.

Kat sat down and crossed her legs. "How's this?" she said.

She didn't look nervous, but she wasn't exactly comfortable. "It will do for now," I said.

I pulled up a chair in front of her, and I drew. My hand moved awkwardly at first and all I could manage were amateurish, stiff marks. But after a few minutes, I warmed up. The lines flowed and loosened, and Kat emerged onto the paper, big boobs and all. It was amazing to think she was in her seventies. Perhaps the wrinkles and sagging jowls gave her age away, but her body was trapped in a time capsule from the seventies.

As I drew, Kat appeared more relaxed. She smiled and threw her head back and then she raised her hand over her head in a dramatic pose reminiscent of a renaissance cherub. With my encouragement, she stood up and tried out unique poses and angles. After an hour, I had several full body illustrations showing her front, back and sides, along with details of her face.

"Is that how you see me?" she said while flipping through my drawing pad.

"It's how you are. I don't want to change you. I want you as you are, Kat."

Kat looked at me with her blue puppy eyes; there was an unspoken communication between us. I placed my hand on the back of her neck and pulled her in close. She closed her eyes and accepted the kiss. I was about to apologize—for what, I did not know. Kat was smart enough to interrupt.

"Again," she said.

The summer ended too soon. I dreaded the cold, winter weather and long nights, but autumn was always nice in Western Pennsylvania. I especially liked Halloween. Kat liked it too. We couldn't pass out candy at the door because of COVID restrictions, but we decorated the house with skeletons and ghosts, and left out a candy-filled-bowl for the kids. I wanted to hide behind a bush and scare the little bastards. I'd pop out, shirtless and maskless, and wave my hands above my head and scream like a wild banshee—oh, the terror in their eyes, what fun. Kat liked the idea but said I shouldn't, and I reluctantly agreed.

I thought about driving to the grocery store without my disguise to see if I could pass as a trick or treater, but then I remembered the risks. I had to be vigilant, and take care, not only for my sake, but for Kat's.

Shortly after Halloween, and after the preliminary sketches were complete, I set up a lab in Kat's basement. I equipped it with computers, motherboards, hard drives, actuators, tools and an operating table, which was an old picnic table I painted white. It was everything a mad scientist could hope for. It reminded me of my old lab, but nicer, better lit, and more spacious.

Getting back to work, my scientific work, felt good. I was a problem solver, and I liked puzzles and, though the task was daunting, I was eager to begin. I woke up around seven every morning and put the coffee on for Kat. Then I'd go into the bedroom and kiss the still-groggy Kat on the forehead before going downstairs to work.

"How far are you?" she asked one morning.

"Oh, I barely started. I devoted the first few weeks to design on the computer screen. You know, pixels."

"Can I see what you've done so far?"

"Well, there's not much to see yet. Come visit me later. I get lonely down there by myself."

The coding came naturally to me. Everything else was a problem. I never thought I'd miss Doctor Tavarius, but he was an exceptional neuroscientist. He did the heavy lifting with the brain. But he worked alone, and never shared what he was doing. Instead, he spoke unscientific terms, designed to keep me in the dark. I think he liked it that way because, well, he was a smart prick who wanted to guard his secrets. I was okay with it because I learned you must work with pricks to get something accomplished. He had his job; I had mine, and we didn't collaborate unless it was necessary.

"Just do your thing," I told Tavarius. "Make it good."

I regretted that decision. Without his notes, I was navigating blindly. Imagine playing a symphony, alone and with no printed score. That's what I faced. I was okay with the design and software stage, but I'll hit a wall shortly, and I'll have no clue how to scale it. I was smart, creative, and resourceful, but my confidence ebbed and flowed with the wind. One moment, I felt like superman, thinking I had it figured out. The next, I felt like a toddler uncertain of its next wobbling step. I shared my fears with Kat; she'd smile, and wink, place a reassuring hand on my shoulder and tell me I could do it. It made me feel good, but I was dubious. I continued to plow ahead, however, because what else was there? The best thing was to not think about it, to not worry. So, I blared Stevie Ray Vaughan and stayed as stoned as possible while I worked.

Time was an anchor around my waist. What did the doctor say: six months, maybe a year, maybe less? I was used to duress, but I had a helper then. Now, it was just me. I bore the burden of life and death, or something much worse: perhaps a limbo state hanging in the balance between life and death. Lenny was right; hell is our own creation. I worried I was creating hell for me and Kat.

It was selfish, I know, but I couldn't help thinking about what would happen to me without her. I didn't want to live without her. I don't know if I could, anymore. Sure, I did it before—got lucky with a job—but I sold out. I quit my job, sold my trailer. I walked a tightrope and there was no net. If Kat died, I'd have to move. I had no claim to her estate. I'd have to find a job. I could go crawling back to Dick, but I'd rather not.

All these things: a job, the economics, friends, the minor details that make us human.... I never planned for them. I was too preoccupied with life to worry about the mundane motions of living. Sure, I cheated death, but living with life's requisite struggles had no cure. Man suffered. It was inevitable, as prescribed by the duality of the human experience. Without up, there is no down. Without bad, there's no good. It's suffering that gives meaning to joy, and solving one problem only gives rise to more problems.

I grew up believing in fairy tales, where problems could be resolved with a little cognitive power or a click of the ruby slippers. Eventually, I grew more enlightened, and yet, there was no going back; I was too far down the rabbit hole. The only solution was to plow forth, to extend life, and face the consequences later.

And so, I worked long hours, well into the night and with an intensity of a rabid bulldog. One moment, I glanced up at the basement window and admired the shafts of sunlight steaming in. The next time I looked, the window was pitch black. Missing time, it's called. It's when you're so deep into your work, you lose track of time. Sometimes, I'd wrap a cool, damp cloth around my neck to stem the fever. The next moment, I'd bundle up against a wave of chills. I wasn't comfortable, but comfort wasn't important. All that mattered was success. However, I was doubtful. I felt like Doctor Frankenstein, beholding the disembodied, beating heart for the first time. It was exhilarating and scary at the same time. Steely Dan helped. Pot helped more.

Kat visited me in the afternoons; she'd watch over my shoulder in silence and gawk at the images forming on my screen, then she'd tell me there was enough smoke in the room to set off the fire alarm. I'd remind her there was no alarm in the basement. I shared my joint with her and we'd both get lit. It helped calm my nerves and maintain focus. It helped Kat with her pain.

She'd try to get me to take breaks, and I reminded her there wasn't time for breaks. She'd extend her lower lip in an exaggerated pouty face until I relented. Then I let her trounce me at chess. I blamed it on the weed and lack of sleep, but she saw through my lies.

"Play your best," she said.

"I am."

"Bullshit. You're hanging pieces left and right."

"I need to get back to work."

I'd slink back down to the dungeon for the night shift, and Kat would check in before bedtime.

Kat rubbed my shoulders and said, "Hey, don't you think it's time for bed?"

"I don't have time for bed."

There was silence; the air felt heavy, and I felt Kat's eyes burning the back of my neck.

"Sorry," I said. "Maybe I do need a break. I'm making more mistakes. I've been working on the eyes for over an hour, and I keep hitting undo."

"Hey, be careful with that," she said in mock anger.

"It will be fine," I assured her.

"Come to bed," she said. "You've been working most of the day. I hardly see you anymore."

I remembered Tracy saying the same thing to me.

"The clock is ticking," I said.

"I know."

"So let me work, please."

"And then what?"

"What do you mean?" I demanded. "Then what? Then we live. We live, Kat."

Kat lowered her eyes and stared at the basement floor. "I suppose," she said.

"Do you want me to stop?" Kat shook her head.

Old feelings bubbled to the surface. Should I be doing this? I can do this, but should I? It was too late for me, but not Kat. *Let her go*, a small voice inside me said. *Don't cheat her out of normalcy.* The voice was wise and noble, but I ignored it.

I placed my hands on Kat's cheeks and pulled her in close. Then I planted a kiss on her forehead. "Go on up," I said. "I'll be there shortly."

Missing time swallowed me; soon, the morning sun poured through the window.

-Chapter 13-

I completed the design and placed my order. I waited impatiently for ten days, but when it finally arrived, I was that kid on Christmas all over again. Kat watched as I ripped open the boxes and pulled out packages.

"Is that me?" she asked.

It took a moment to comprehend. "Oh, no," I finally said. "But it will be. Help me inventory the pieces. I want to make sure I have everything."

Kat knelt down on the living room floor next to me and helped me unpack. "Jesus," she said. "How many are there?"

"Should be ninety-thousand," I said.

"Is that how much you are?"

"No, I'm only seventy-five thousand." Kat stared at me with a blank expression. "Bigger boobs and hips," I explained.

Kat threw the Lego-filled bag she was holding. It hit me square in the face, stunning me momentarily. "Okay," I said. "I deserved that."

With all the pieces accounted for, Kat and I carried the boxes downstairs. I thanked her and then asked her to close the door on the way out. When she protested, I told her I needed to do this part alone.

"Get some rest," I said. "In a few weeks, I'll need you for your part."

After she left, I locked the door behind her, put on some Steely Dan, and lit a joint. It was time to work.

For the next month, I was tireless, working eighteen hours straight, stopping only to replenish my weed supply from the upstairs bedroom.

On one of my upstairs forays, Kat startled me from behind. "It lives," she said.

I wheeled around and, for a moment, was at a loss for words. "Oh, Kat," I said. "Hi."

"Can we talk?"

The three words every man dreads hearing from his significant other. "Not now," I said, brushing her aside. "I've made a breakthrough."

"Look at you," she said.

"Well, that's hard to do without a mirror," I explained.

"Let me help. You look like shit. When's the last time you've been upstairs, other than to get some more weed?"

"Hey, we're almost out of Sativa. Can you run to the dispensary again?"

"When's the last time you've slept?"

"Well, I'm a Lego Man so..."

"You said you're embedded in your body, just as before. You get tired; you need sleep."

"I crave sleep. I technically don't need it."

"Look at your eyes."

I stepped in front of the dresser mirror and was irritated to see she was right. I looked like a disheveled addict tweaking for his next fix. My eyes were dark, thin slits. My body protested the long hours without rest.

"Yes, well, there's a lot of work to do," I said.

"I need you," Kat replied.

I turned towards Kat. She looked small and child-like and wore a grim expression. I pulled her in close and held her tight against my chest while resting my chin on her forehead. We embraced in silence, and I felt her heart beating against my chest.

"Be patient," I said. "Just a few more weeks."

Kat said nothing. When I asked her if she was okay, she nodded her head and sobbed.

It was late at night; I didn't look at my watch because I was afraid time was running out. The morning sun wasn't up, so this encouraged me. But something was off. I don't know if was the lack of sleep or I had lost my touch or what it was. I cocked my head to one side and then the other, and then I squinted to see if that made a difference; sometimes, I think it did. Other times, the proportions looked off.

The female body was different. I've sketched hundreds before, but I've never sculpted one, especially from Legos. The face was good. I spent hours on it, refining every detail and every nuance until I recognized the sweet, compassionate expression with a hint of mischief in her baby blue eyes. I smiled whenever I gazed into them. The legs were respectable; short, stout, but with a pleasing slope segueing into a plump, and very grabbable ass. But the torso was off. I couldn't quite place it. Maybe it was the proportion, the symmetry, the shape or some combination of the three. Whatever it was, I had no courage left tonight. Perhaps Kat was right.

The voice was booming and grated like a 5 am alarm. "I think her boobs are too big," the voice said.

I grabbed my chest and fell against the wall. "Jesus Christ," I whispered.

"Well, it looks like you need my help... again."

Tavarius's white mane looked like it had grown another foot since I last saw him. The amount of gel he must have used to get it to stand straight boggled my senses. Everything else about him was the same: thin, parched lips, beady eyes reminiscent of a mad scientist. At first, I feigned happiness, but then realized there was no need. I never liked him and so what if he knew how I felt? Besides, he was standing in my laboratory, a most uninvited guest.

"How the hell did you get in here?" I said.

Tavarius tilted his head back, opened his mouth wide, and laughed like it was the funniest thing he had ever heard. Then, as quickly as the outburst came, it went, and he just stared at me with unblinking eyes.

"Well?" I demanded. "How did you get in here? Answer me."

Tavarius solemnly looked at the door and pointed to it. "You left it open," he said.

I was in the habit of closing the door and locking it behind me. Perhaps I forgot this time, but that didn't answer the question.

"How did you get inside the house?" I said.

Tavarius shrugged and lifted his hands.

"Well?" I said.

"I don't know," he said. "I just walked in."

"What? You mean the front door was open too?"

Tavarius shrugged again. "Never mind that," he said. "I see you're in trouble. You need my help."

He looked at the mannequin, stretched out on the table like a lifeless body. He was right. I needed his help in the worst way, but I wasn't about to ask him.

"How did you find me?" I said.

Tavarius grinned, exposing a set of uneven, stained teeth.

"It wasn't hard," he said. "You didn't cover your tracks well—your social security number, your driver's license. I thought you were smarter than that."

I bit down on my lower lip; how easy it would be to strangle the wretch. I saw my fingers curl like tentacles around his throat. I wouldn't even need both hands; one would do. I could justify it in my mind and perhaps in the eyes of the law. He was, after all, in my basement, an intruder as it were. But then I thought about Kat sleeping upstairs. What a mess I'd leave behind. I certainly couldn't talk to the authorities, and it would leave her to explain things. Besides, I needed his help.

My eyes drifted toward the corpse on the table.

"What do you need?" Tavarius said.

"The assembly part is finished," I said. "Most of the code written, but I don't know how to transfer."

"Well, of course not. That was my genius."

Tavarius walked to the table and placed his hand on the white sheet. "May I?" he said.

I nodded my head, and Tavarius pulled back the sheet to reveal the head and torso. His cheek twitched as he stared, transfixed by what he saw.

"You always do such painstaking work," he said.

"Can you help me?" I said.

"You know I can."

"Will you?"

Tavarius inhaled deeply through his nostrils. "If you do something for me," he said.

I knew what he wanted, so I didn't bother asking. Instead, I looked at the mannequin's face, the perfect lips, the round cheeks.

"This is your girlfriend?" he said.

I shrugged. "You can call her that," I said.

"Don't worry. I'm here to help." Tavarius paused, took another deep breath, and nodded his head. "That is, if you're willing to help me," he said.

I felt like I was making a deal with the devil. Here is food and water and worldly riches if you just side with me. I looked into his malevolent eyes and then back at the mannequin and then back at Tavarius. He was smirking, confident that he had me.

"No thank you," I said in a quiet voice.

Tavarius's skin turned chalk white; lines spider-webbed across his face and then turned to chasms, wide enough to poke my fingers through. His eyes dropped from his head and dust poured from his black sockets. Fleshy white chunks dissolved and fell away, exposing the grey bone beneath. I stepped back. "What is this? What is this?" I said over and over.

The mannequin sat up and turned its head towards me. Its mouth fell open and a female voice came out.

"We didn't need him anyway," it said.

"We didn't?"

"No."

I waited for it to expound, but it never did.

"Oh, I see," I said. "You mean I know how?" The mannequin nodded its head. "It's inside of me?"

"That's right. Deep inside. You just need to access it."

"I understand."

But the only thing I understood was I needed sleep.

When I woke up, Kat was standing next to me.

"What are you doing here?" I said.

"Well, I live here. So—"

"Where's Tavarius?"

"Who?"

I looked around the lab and expected to see a pile of sand and rubble lying on the floor. The mannequin was tucked safely beneath its sheet, quiet and undisturbed.

"Doctor Tavarius," I said. "He was just here." Kat stared blankly. "Oh, never mind," I said.

Kat walked over to the mannequin and, before I could stop her, she pulled back the sheet. Then she stood, silent, pale, with her mouth open. I understood. I went through it myself. It was like hearing your recorded voice. You think to yourself, *that can't be right. That can't be me.* But it is.

"Me?" she said in a shaky voice.

"It is." I stepped in front of Kat and covered the mannequin's face. "What do you think?"

"I'm not sure what to think."

"Yes, well, that's a good sign. Maybe it's best not to think."

I placed my arms around Kat. She trembled beneath my touch and so I just held her. I held her tight.

-Chapter 14-

The results pleased me. She was magnificent, and she'd be the new show model, the Cadillac of mind transfer, robotic technology if I ever breathed life into her. But I wasn't God; I was a cheap imitation, a wannabe with an inflated ego who had overestimated his abilities. I was still bound by human limits.

I was sleep deprived, stressed, and scared. Tavarius visited me, sometimes in waking dreams and sometimes in my sleep. He taunted me like a demon, telling me I hadn't the ability to put the puzzle pieces together—mind, body, and code—into a cohesive image that would walk and talk and think for itself, autonomous in every way. I believed him. Well, I had no choice. I coded like LeBron James balled. I designed like Michelangelo painted, and I was one of the top robotics experts in the nation, perhaps the world. But when it came to neurology, neural pathways, brain waves, signaling, transference, and everything that made us human—our thoughts, our personality—that was Tavarius's discipline. He never let me forget it.

It didn't mean I would not try. When I looked at my beautiful Kat, I saw my rock and my reason for being. I was alive because she loved me. I loved her. Giving into my fear wasn't an option, even though the stakes were higher than life and death. If I failed completely, it meant the mind transfer never happened. Kat would succumb to her illness, and I'll be alone with a lifeless look-alike as a grim reminder. I'd be sad and forced to rely on Lenny's idealized version of an afterlife and the hope that she will reincarnate and have another chance.

My biggest fear, however, was partial failure in which I created my own Frankenstein, a creature so depraved that it wished death over the perverse life it was given. Kat appeared in my nightmares, always as the sympathetic creature, while I played the despicable scientist.

However, unlike Frankenstein, Kat gave her consent, and I took solace in this. She knew the risks, the rewards, what she'd be giving up, what she'd gain. Even so, I wondered if love blinded her. Did she want this for herself, or was she bending to my fervent desire to be together... forever? I don't think so. Kat was a strong woman with a beautiful mind and would never relent to another's will, not even mine. Still, I had my doubts.

One day she was sitting in a chair, quiet and reflective and I summoned the courage to ask: "Are you sure you want to live with me forever? I can be a real asshole."

"Well, you _are_ a real asshole," she told me. "But I'll take my chances."

However, as the days passed, I sensed her uneasiness. Her face held questions and trepidation. I understood, and I did my best to explain.

"Will it hurt?"

"No."

"Will I have to learn to walk and talk again?"

"No. I mean, I'm not sure. It will feel quite natural, I think."

"You think? Don't you know?"

"That part... well, it's hazy. That was part of my lost memory."

"Will all my memories be intact?"

"If I don't fuck it up." Kat glared, and I quickly walked it back. "All your memories will be there. I promise and your feelings, too."

"So, I'll remember you?"

"Of course."

"And chess? I'll still be able to play chess?"

"No doubt."

"What if something goes wrong?"

"Nothing will go wrong."

"But what if it does? Will I be in a state of limbo, a place neither here nor there?"

I hesitated and said, "No,"

"Does it feel weird?"

"It's just getting used to a new body, a new look."

"I see."

I felt obligated to ask if she wanted to continue, but I never did. I was a coward, afraid she'd say no.

I locked myself in the cellar lab and made it my sole purpose to study the human mind. What takes most individuals—under the tutelage of eminent scholars in great universities—years to learn, I had to teach myself in months. I didn't have to know all of it, just the parts that applied to the operation. Still, it was daunting. Mind uploading was akin to the first moon landing. Some people thought flying a man to the moon and returning him safely back to earth was impossible. And so too, the concept of storing a human brain on disk was a work of science fiction. Yet, the tools and theories existed, lying around like puzzle pieces waiting to be put together. It was a matter of applying our knowledge, some trial and error, and a little luck to make this hypothetical science fiction story into reality. And there I was, a walking, talking, thinking, scheming, loving, hating, laughing, crying, chess playing son of man and living proof of man's ingenuity, his genius and yes, his hubris. *Henry Ford said it best:* "whether a man thinks he can or whether he thinks he cannot, he is right." His words resonated with me and were my inspiration. *I think I can.*

Some people thought space was the new frontier and others thought it was the ocean; they're wrong. The human mind is as vast as any galaxy and as unexplored as any sea. Undiscovered breakthroughs, still locked away in the mind, are waiting to be released with the next firing synapse. Disease, hatred, bigotry, war, hunger—they're byproducts of our faulty thinking. Change our faulty brains, and we'll have utopia on earth. Imagine a world where every newborn is a genius—Mozarts, Einsteins and Oppenheimers proliferating the planet. I'd look developmentally slow by comparison. Imagine that new world. What couldn't we do then? Mind uploading is a step closer to that new world.

There are two methods. One produces a copy of the mind, a perfect replica of the thoughts, memories, and personality. That's how I was made. I am a copy stored inside a mechanical body; he the alpha and I the beta. The alpha lives on, unaffected and unperturbed by me and my life. Yet, I can't get past that I am him and he is me; it troubled me to think of my duplicate living with his thoughts and feelings, blessing and problems. Ruminating served no purpose. I had to live my life; suffer my tribulations and celebrate my blessings.

The other method is a destructive upload that copies as it deletes. The original neurons, from the original donor, degrade during the transfer, and the 5D drive takes over as the biological brain dies. It made me sad to think about a dying brain. This was always about extending life, never about destroying it. But it didn't matter if the donor was dying anyway, let's say of a terminal disease. They won't need their brain. They'll have a new one, a faster one, made of fused quartz, one that never ages and one that can be replaced easily in case of trauma.

Of the two methods, destructive upload was the easiest to execute, and it was the path I chose, or rather, it chose me. Keeping the original brain was not an option.

Kat picked up a rat, held it to her face, and showered it with kisses.

"Aw, what's up with the cute rats?" she said.

"I'll work on the rats first."

"What are you going to do with them?"

"I'm going to map their brains."

Kat scrunched her forehead and her voice rose in pitch. "What do you mean?" she said.

"It's what the name implies. I'm going to map their brain and create a model showing all the connections and pathways and create a database of the nervous system: the spinal cord, sensory receptors, and muscle cells.

From this, I'll reproduce their brain in a digital form that can later be stored on a disk."

Kat held the rat close to her bosom while stroking its back. "Does it hurt them?" she said.

"Uh, no."

"You know you're a shitty liar, right?"

"It's my eyes, right? They give me away?"

"Yes. They're shifty. But seriously, what does it do to the little guys?"

"I have to scan their brain tissue."

"Oh, so it's just a small sample, not the entire brain?"

"Okay, let's just leave it at that." Kat's eyes accused me of a horrible crime. "Okay," I relented. "It doesn't work that way. The human brain doesn't exist in just one state, it involves different hemispheres and many states that are connected, interacting, and changing. If I scanned just a small sample, it would be like taking a static picture of the subject, but it wouldn't contain the entire person or rat in this case; it would miss neurons, memories, you would lose the personality, and the very essence of the subject. In fact, it could not function at all with the missing data. I'll have to map the entire brain, Kat, and reassemble it in electronic form."

Kat's face was still, and she looked past me like I wasn't there.

"So, then, what happens to the original brain?" she said after a long pause.

"Well—"

"How many?"

"How many what?"

"How many of the rats are going to die?"

"I got six as a precautionary measure, but I only plan on using two or three."

Kat picked up a second rat and held both to her cheeks. "You're such a shitty liar," she said.

A full brain map takes about 20,000 terabytes or 20,000 trillion bytes or 2e+16. That's for a human brain, but a lab rat only takes about 10 gigabytes, which fits easily onto a USB drive. The entire rat brain, its memories of food, mazes and whatever else rats dream and think about, can be carried inside my shirt pocket.

The first subject was Ellinor. Kat named them all, but I wish she hadn't because it made my job more difficult. Ellinor's brain map took twelve hours, and it wasn't a complete success, nor did I expect it to be. It's one thing to research, to read about procedures and watch videos; it's quite another to perform the surgery. I wound up with a dysfunctional incomplete map. Think of an aerial view of the United States with a couple of states conspicuously absent. Okay, there were more than a couple of states missing, more like twenty.

Ellinor had huge chasms missing from her life—not just dreams of finding a large cache of cheese, but what a piece of cheese was, and what it was good for. She couldn't walk or squeak, let alone navigate a maze. Ellinor was a failure, but I felt some comfort in knowing I had succeeded in a small way. It was just a matter of learning from my mistakes, making corrections and filling in the gaps. Carey was next.

Carey was rat number two, and her brain map gave me a migraine. What I learned from Ellinor I applied to Carey, but my corrections only made things worse. Where Ellinor missed a few data points, Carey's scan looked like swiss cheese. I had two dead, miserable rats and nothing to show for it except an impending migraine and the onslaught of depression.

Kat was upstairs fixing dinner and was despondent over her newly minted rat friends. I could only wrap my hands around the back of my neck and repeatedly tap my forehead against the desk in hopes it would jog a memory, but it only made my migraine worse.

Scanning a mind for later storage was damn near impossible. I would think it completely impossible if it weren't for the fact it was done before, not only by Tavarius, but by other scientists as well. Their scientific papers were my textbooks, their knowledge was my hope.

"How's Carey?" Kat yelled down to me.

"Oh, she's fine," I yelled back up.

"You're such a liar."

"Well, yes. I am."

The process was daunting, especially for one not trained in medicine, let alone neuroscience. I had to stand on the shoulders of geniuses to make this work, but the mapping of electrical and chemical signal states, the synapses, the neurons, besides the intra-neural dynamic processes was, well, it was too much for me. I ran out of ideas and instead of killing more rats—Jennifer, Arnold, Rasputin, and Joy—I decided to do more research.

Damn. Why did she have to name her Joy?

Tavarius was a regular visitor. I tried extracting information from him, but he'd just snicker and wave a bony finger at me and told me I had to live up to my end of the bargain. I told him I would not.

"Then figure it out on your own," he said.

"I'm missing something. It's in the synaptic details. They're not coming through; I know that much. That's it, isn't it?" I said. "The neurons, they fire repeatedly. You told me it was like a light switch going on and off. Isn't that right?"

Tavarius had a habit of talking, even when he had nothing to say. His silence was confirmation I was on the right path.

"They fire on and off," I continued. "So, it's like... it's like a binary state. Current flows through a switch or it doesn't. It's a zero or a one. I understand that much. That's what I understand. That's it, isn't it?"

Tavarius turned his palms up and shrugged. I had the little prick. He was too arrogant to hold back.

"I don't know," he said. "Could be a thousand different things. Let me see your notes."

"My notes?"

"Oh, for fuck's sake," he said. "Your notes, your documentation. Don't tell me you haven't been documenting."

"Who has time to document? The clock is ticking, man."

"Well, how the hell... oh, never mind. What process are you using, preservation, or destructive?"

"You know I'm using destructive. I could never figure out how to preserve the donor brain in the time I have. Besides, she won't need it."

Tavarius puffed his chest out and a broad grin spread across his face. It was the look of an arrogant, proud, prick way too confident in his intellectual prowess. I'd hate him that much more if I hadn't recognized the look in my reflection.

"Well, that was smart," he said. "You're not using cryogenics, are you?"

"No. I'm using the room temperature method."

"Smart. Those chemicals really fuck with the brain structure. A warm scan is the way to go."

Tavarius's smile disappeared; his lip curled upward, and his expression turned to a menacing scowl. "You promised," he said.

"That was an old promise."

"You'll never get it on your own. You're a robotics engineer, a software engineer, not a medical doctor."

Tavarius's body pixilated and shattered into a million glass shards.

"Wait!" I said. "Just a hint."

The arrogant prick came back. He cocked his head and said, "A hint?"

"You're right, Doctor Tavarius. I'm not a medical doctor, and if I were, I'm still not as smart as you."

"You got that right."

"So, just a hint? It will be like a game."

"A game?"

"Yes, like a riddle."

Tavarius nodded his head and rubbed his chin. "Okay," he said. "Here's your riddle. Give me what I want or go fuck yourself and your girlfriend, too."

Her black king rocked side-to-side. He looked impotent lying on the woodgrain, checkered squares. He put up a good fight but succumbed to the relentless onslaught I placed on him.

"I don't get it," Kat said.

"What don't you get?"

"I'm Russian; my father was from Russia where chess was a subject they taught in school like math or literature. He was rated 2200 and taught me everything I know. My last rating was 2000."

"And?"

"And you continue to kick my ass like I'm a potzer. You're not even trying. Your mind is somewhere else, God knows where, but it's obvious you're not studying the board."

"So?"

"Well, how do you do it?"

"You're forgetting I have an electronic brain capable of executing five billion commands a second. Before you move, I've already calculated a thousand different combinations. Furthermore, I've read a hundred books on chess openings, defenses, and theory. Inside my head are all the documented chess games: Fischer, Kasparov, Karpov, Carlson, et al. It's all in there," I said, pointing to my head. "And I never forget. I never—"

I stopped mid-sentence and repetitively tapped my knuckle against the side of my head.

"What's wrong?" Kat said.

"I never forget."

"So?"

"Words, thoughts, ideas, conversations... they're stored on a small piece of glass, a 5D optical storage device capable of holding 500 terabytes. You'll have one too."

Kat stared and blinked repeatedly.

"I can go back in time," I said. "I see and hear everything, like I'm watching an old movie. It's a matter of rewinding, finding the right scene, the right frame."

"Okay?"

In the second it took Kat to utter those two syllables, I was back, sitting next to Tavarius and across from Doctor Ziegel, the right scene, the right frame. I heard Tavarius give me the answer, unwittingly, of course. He described the problem with the destructive process, the problem that made the scan incomplete and turned the rats into zombies.

"Lance?"

"Yes?"

"So, you're cheating?"

"I cheat?"

"Yeah, in chess. You're using your knowledge of chess, combined with the computing power of an electronic brain against me."

"Oh, oh, yes. Well, yeah, kind of."

"Will I be able to do that?"

"That and more. The technology has improved since they built me, faster processors, faster disk access times."

"So, I'll be able to beat you?" I closed my eyes and nodded my head. "That's something to look forward to," she said.

"Are you nervous?"

"Kind of."

"Don't be."

"But you haven't figured it out, have you? I can tell, the way you work, the long hours, drooped shoulders, resigned puppy dog look with your tail between your legs."

"I didn't think I looked that bad."

"Worse, even."

"I'm closer to figuring it out."

"Use that electronic brain of yours. Think. Think. Think," she said, rapping my temple with her knuckles.

I rubbed my head and told her I was thinking.

"I am," I said. "I swear I am. I've read everything I can get my hands on. I've studied. I've retained everything, the research, data, concepts, theories. I even watched YouTube videos."

"There are YouTube videos for this?" Kat said in a dubious tone.

"On neuroscience and mind uploading, yes. Much of its theoretical, but I was able to access material, let's say off the dark web, that allowed me to watch procedures on rats and monkeys. I'm a walking, talking, neuroscience encyclopedia. I know more about the human brain than most medical doctors. I could perform brain surgery if pressed into it."

Kat smiled. "You mean the patient would live?" she said.

"He'd live. He'd be a vegetable the rest of his life, but he'd live."

It was nice to hear Kat laugh. It had been a long time.

"Don't worry," I said, brushing the back of my hand against her full, pink cheek. "It will be fine."

"What happened to Doctor Lance?" Kat said. "Mind uploading kills the donor, right? That's why the rats die?"

"Yes, there is a degenerative process that destroys the donor brain. That's the approach I'm taking with you. But they uploaded me using another process that keeps the original brain intact, healthy, and able as ever. I am simply a copy of the donor. Doctor Lance lives; he's healthy and walking around; out there, somewhere."

Kat scrunched her nose and cocked her head to the side.

"I know. It boggles the mind," I said.

"Yes, but why are you choosing the destructive method over the other?"

"It's not a choice. I had a partner, and he was a real prick, but he was also a genius. He did the bulk of the transfer work, and he's the one that discovered the non-destructive process. The problem is, I don't know how he did it."

"It makes me sad."

"It won't hurt. I promise."

"I'm not sad for me. My brain is going away one way or another. I'm sad for Ellinor, Carey, Jennifer, Arnold, Rasputin, and Joy."

"Yeah, Joy is a real heartbreaker; the cute one. I'll spare her if I can."

I held Kat by her shoulders and pulled her in close, then I kissed her forehead.

"I have to go back downstairs, now," I said.

"So soon? Stay with me. You should rest."

"I'm good. This was a delightful break, but I'm on the verge of a breakthrough."

-Chapter 15-

The flea-bitten white rat made its way up my arm, crawled onto my shoulder, past my ear, before settling on my head. I had no idea what it was looking for. Probably a morsel he could scavenge from the cracks in my skull. Its soft pads tickled, but its sharp teeth felt like pinpricks. I was tempted to grab the pesky rodent and hurl it into the living room wall, but Kat was sitting across from me with a delighted look on her face. She would not approve.

I was indignant, but Kat's laughter was disarming.

"Would you get this pesky rodent off me before I launch it into orbit?" I said.

Kat removed the rat from my head. "Aw," she said. "She's not a pesky rodent. Her name is Joy, and you'll not harm a hair on her chinny chin chin."

Kat kissed Joy on the head, then thrusted her at my face. "Say hi to your mean Grandpa Lance," Kat said.

Joy's two beady eyes and a pink nose bobbed up and down. She was cute for a rat, but that didn't stop me from opening my mouth and trying to bite her head off. Joy's eyes doubled in size as she retreated to the safety of Kat's palms.

"What's wrong with you?" Kat said. "You scared her."

Kat showered the rat with kisses, and Joy returned the favor in kind. I watched in amazement and disgust.

"Sometimes I think you love that rat more than you love me," I said.

"Well, yes."

Kat placed Joy in the middle of the chessboard where she crawled and sniffed the pieces, starting with my pawn, and then my bishop, before addressing my very exposed King. Joy talked to him, a rather one-sided conversation in rat-speak, explaining why it was time for him to give up. After a few seconds, they seemed to agree. Joy rose onto her hind legs and swatted my king down with her front paws; thus slaying the once proud monarch. I stared in disbelief, and then I looked up at Kat. She bit her thumb while trying to stifle a laugh.

"Oh, you think it's funny?" I said.

"No," she said, chuckling.

Kat was about to pick up my slain king, but I told her to leave him.

"Joy made the right move," I said.

A big smile waxed over Kat's face. "That's the first time I beat you," she said.

"More like crushed me."

"You let me win?"

"No. Honest. You did it on your own."

Kat picked up Joy and stroked her back. "Well, I'm not so sure I believe you," she said.

"What do you want to do now? Netflix?"

"Oh, I need flowers. Would you be kind enough to run to the nursery?"

"I told you. I'm not a gardener. I nearly killed Lenny's pot plants."

"And I saved them, remember?"

"Yes. And for this, I'm eternally grateful."

Kat smiled and bounced Joy up and down in a playful, happy dance.

"Okay," I said. "I'll head out. Do you want to come?"

"I'm tired. I'll just stay and rest, play with Joy."

"How are you feeling?"

"Never better."

I held out my hand. "Are you sure?" I said.

"Of course. Why do you keep asking?"

Kat placed her hand in mine, and I squeezed it gently. She smiled and nodded her head. "I'm fine," she said. "I'm just tired."

"What's her favorite color?" the kindly, elderly lady behind the counter said.

I scratched the back of my head.

"Well, does she like roses, tulips, marigolds, petunias, sunflowers?" she continued.

"Yeah, okay."

"Okay, what?"

"Those sound good."

The kindly lady let out a deep breath. She smiled and appeared to take pity on me.

"Okay," she said. "Why don't you try marigolds, daylilies' and petunias? They're beautiful and easy to grow, and I'm sure she'll love them."

"I guess I should have asked, but she's not picky. I think those will look fine in our garden."

After paying for the plants, pots, potting soil, fertilizer and a bunch of other stuff I never thought I'd need, I loaded Kat's car and headed back. I thought about stopping at Walmart and picking up some items for the house, but decided against it. I still didn't feel comfortable out in public. People were scary and could ruin everything I've worked so hard for. Besides, I didn't think it was a good idea for Kat to be alone for too long, at least not so soon.

I saw the white pickup truck as I pulled into Kat's driveway. It sent a chill down my spine. I ran through the different narratives. Was it a utility man? No. There'd be signage on the side of the truck. What about a salesman? I didn't think a salesman would drive a white pickup. I could be wrong. It wasn't the cops. That was good. Was it one of her children? Kat told them what was happening, so I wouldn't mind if it was one of her kids. It was just awkward meeting this way. I wanted to be there to soften the blow.

If it was a stranger, I wondered if Kat had her mask on, her hat, and her glasses. It was easy to forget.

I got out of my car and left everything inside and then hurried through the side door and into the kitchen. I stopped suddenly and felt the hairs stand on the back of my neck. Then I prayed this was another daydream, the same specter I had conjured before. But it had been a long time since he visited and by the look on Kat's face, I wasn't the only one seeing him.

"Well, well. Here you are," Tavarius said. "Finally."

"How did you find me?"

"Well, for a smart man, you didn't cover your tracks very well. Social security number, the post office. Somehow, I can't picture you as a mailman. How's that working for you?"

Kat looked up and questioned me with her eyes.

"Why did you let him in?" I said.

"I didn't," she said, motioning towards Tavarius.

Tavarius wore that ever present eat-shit smile like a wet rag across his face; but in his hand was something more menacing.

"He let himself in," Kat said.

"Yes, I see that."

My pulse quickened. Options played through my mind like rolling credits at the end of a movie. I could talk to him. I was a good talker; maybe I could use some psychology and perhaps diffuse the situation. But with my abrasive personality and disdain for Tavarius, it would only escalate things.

I could charge him. I'd take a bullet for sure, but I'd survive. Probably. And if I got my hands on him, I'd wrap my Lego fingers around his pencil neck and squeeze. Game over. Knowing Kat, she'd be there too, in case I needed help. But there was always the other possibility. A bullet could rip through my vitals and render me helpless. Doctor Tavarius knew where to aim, and he'd probably get several shots off before I could disarm him. It would leave Kat on her own, and my stomach turned just thinking about that.

Kat looked at me. I told her silently, with my eyes, not to worry. Then I flashed her a smile, hoping she would reciprocate, but she sat there, her face frozen and disconsolate. I turned to Tavarius and tried to bluff the smug look off his face. I wiggled my fingers at Tavarius and reminded him of the 960 psi.

"About the same force needed to crush a bowling ball," I said. "What's stopping me from popping your skull like a grape? No one would press charges seeing how you entered my home uninvited and held me at gunpoint."

Tavarius's confident expression withered and cracked. His jowls twitched, and his grey eyes shifted from side-to-side. Instead of rebutting my claim, he took dead aim at my nose.

"You wouldn't make it a step," he said. "Now, sit down next to your—well, next to your lovely bride."

The Doctor's scathing grin returned, and it made the back of my ears burn.

"I'll stand," I said.

He motioned to the chair with his gun. "No," he said. "I insist."

Kat nodded her head. I sat next to her, and she grabbed my hand. Her fingers were cold and clammy, and I held them to my lips and kissed them repeatedly.

"That's better," Tavarius said. "Now, there's no need for this. You know what I want. Let's agree to terms and a delivery date, and I'll be on my way."

"Yeah, that's not going to happen," I said.

"What does he want?" Kat said. "For fuck's sake, just give it to him."

Tavarius looked at Kat and smiled. "Wow," he said. "She's magnificent, a real work of art. The bride of Ziegel. But how? How did you manage without my help? I know you're a genius, but I never thought you could pull this off, not without my help."

"What the fuck is he talking about?" she said.

"Nothing," I told her. "He's a crazy old man."

"Oh, she doesn't know, does she?" Tavarius said. "Neurons were lost; just like with you. Was there extensive memory loss? Did you do a destructive or preservation scan? Where's the body?"

A Glock was pointed at my skull, but Kat's icy stare was more worrisome.

"What's he saying?" Kat said.

"He wants me to make another Lego man for him. He wants immortality."

"Exactly," Tavarius said. "And after all, that was the agreement. I'd help you and when the time came, you'd help me. Don't tell me you want to renege on your word."

"What do you need me for?" I said. "You have Doctor Ziegel, the original. Just go to him. He knows everything I do. He can build your pathetic likeness if you like."

Tavarius's face turned solemn.

"What," I said. "Did he wise up and run out of there too?"

"He's dead," Tavarius said in a matter-of-fact tone.

A picture of Lance appeared in my mind's eye. I saw him bandaged and bleeding from the gunshot wound I inflicted.

"Oh, don't look so sad," Tavarius said. "You didn't kill him. He was dying anyway. Cancer. Don't you remember?"

"No."

"Well, that must have been part of those lost neurons. It was a nice funeral. I didn't attend, but I heard about it. You would have been proud."

I looked at Kat and saw a thousand questions written on her face.

"So, shall we decide on a delivery date?" Tavarius said. I didn't answer. "C'mon now. Don't be so stubborn. I helped you not only with my skill, but financially as well. You couldn't do this by yourself. It's time to live up to your end of the bargain."

"That was an old bargain. One I made before I realized..."

"Realized what?"

"People like you should never go on living. It's good you have an end."

Doctor Tavarius squirmed in his seat; His gun wavered as if rocked by a breeze.

"Now, listen here, you little prick," he said. "Save your self-righteous bullshit for someone else. I helped you when you needed it and now you're going to help me. You promised."

"Oh, for God's sake," Kat said. "Give him what he wants."

"You don't understand," I told her. "He wants me to build another Lego man so he can inhabit the body."

"Then just do it."

"No. It stops here."

Tavarius gestured toward Kat with his gun. "What about her?" he said.

"She's the last."

"What the fuck are you two talking about?" Kat said. "Just do what he wants and get him out of here."

Tavarius pointed the gun at Kat's head. His hand was steady.

"You should listen to her," Tavarius said.

I didn't care about myself. I'd gladly take a bullet if it would make this go away. What I couldn't reconcile was living without Kat.

"How much time?" I said.

"Three months."

"I can't do three months. If you want quality, you'll need to give me more time. There's the design phase, assembly—"

"I don't have more time," Tavarius said.

His voice was soft, and his eyes locked onto mine.

"Okay," I said. "And the money?"

"You'll be fully banked. Spare no expense."

"So, I'll deliver a fully equipped mannequin, ready to accept a neurological transfer, and you can handle the rest?"

"Exactly."

"Put down the gun, Tavarius. You have what you came for. Now leave me to my work."

Tavarius smiled, shook his head, and said, "No."

"Well, you can't stay here. Leave us be, so I can work in peace."

Tavarius waved his gun at Kat. "I'll need collateral," he said

"She's not going anywhere."

"It's a fair trade. I'll return your Lego bot when you give me mine."

"You're an asshole."

"I'm desperate. There's a difference."

I was on my feet; six feet, four inches of me, coiled and ready to explode at the slightest provocation. Tavarius stood up and aimed the gun at me. I was ready to step forward when I felt a warm hand around my wrist.

"Stop," Kat told me. "I'll go."

"You don't understand," I said. "This man is mad. You can't trust him."

"I have no incentive to harm her," Tavarius said. "I have as much to lose as you. She'll be safe as long as you hold up your end of the bargain."

Kat's eyes were cold, calculating, and calm; they spoke to me. "*Go along*", they said. "*I've got this*".

It was an odd feeling: trust. I believed in myself. I was always the smartest one in the room, the only one who could make everything right. Kat was asking me to step aside: "I've got this."

I nodded my head, and Kat gave me a reassuring smile. She's got this.

Kat turned to Tavarius. "If I'm going on a trip, I'll need my makeup," she said.

Tavarius laughed, and Kat wanted to know what was so funny.

"My dear, lady," Tavarius said. "You kill me. You don't need a damn thing. That's the beauty of being you."

Kat looked at me, and I shrugged.

"Well, I'm not leaving without Joy," Kat said. "Fetch my purse, will you, Lance?"

Tavarius raised the gun and aimed it at my head. "Wait there," he told me. "Who's Joy?"

"Joy is my pet rat," Kat said. "She was a present from Lance."

"And what's he doing in your purse?"

"He's a she and she is napping."

"Your pet rat is napping in your purse?"

"Oh, yes," I said. "Joy loves Kat's purse. She crawls in there and finds a cozy, warm spot, and sleeps for hours. Besides, I think you'll want to meet Joy."

"Oh, I see. This Joy is one of your lab rats?"

"Yes. May I fetch her?" Tavarius said nothing. I raised my hands in the air and said, "Her purse is just there in the living room."

Tavarius waved me along with his gun. I sidestepped past him and into the living room. Inside Kat's purse, Joy's eyes were shut tight, and her tiny nose bobbed up and down with each breath. I thought I heard her snoring, but I must have been hearing things.

I carefully picked up the purse, then walked back into the kitchen and handed it to Kat. Joy didn't stir.

"Ah," Kat said. "There's my little Joy."

Kat picked Joy out of her purse and rained kisses on the rat's face. Joy squirmed and opened her eyes as she slowly came to life. Tavarius looked amazed by what he saw.

"Oh, my," he said. "Would you look at that? Look at him?"

"It's a she," Kat said.

"Whatever it is, it's a fine piece of work."

"It wasn't easy," I said.

"Well, nothing worthwhile is, Doctor Ziegel. That's what separates us from the rest of humanity. We're willing to take the risks, to obtain the knowledge and apply it for the betterment of man. You and I aren't that much different. We were born to be giants, and giants we've become. There's nothing wrong with that."

The old Lance would have concurred with Tavarius. The new Lance knew better.

"Indeed," I said.

"Yes, indeed. And Lance, I hope when this mess is over, we can return to civility. Believe me, I don't like this any more than you."

"Really? You seem to take great pleasure in this."

Tavarius made sweeping, circular gestures with his gun as he spoke. "You backed me into a corner," he said. "Time's running out for me. You-you have all the time in the world. You have what gods have. Immortality."

Tavarius was a man addicted to his delusions. I pitied myself because I recognized my own delusional thoughts in his words.

"It's not what you think," I said. "This eternal life. It's not an easy one."

"Perhaps, but it's better than death, better than worms eating your flesh."

"There were times..." I stopped, bit my lower lip, and exhaled deeply before continuing. "... there were times I wish I opted for death."

Tavarius looked at Kat. "Yes," he said. "I bet you don't feel that way now."

Kat held Joy to her bosom and stroked her back. They looked serene, so calm and undisturbed.

"Would you like to hold her?" Kat said to Tavarius.

Tavarius recoiled. "No, no," he said. "You stay right there."

"How about if I place her on the table and you can call her to you."

"She can do that?" Tavarius said. "I mean, she can walk?"

"Of course she can. Why wouldn't she?"

Kat placed Joy on the kitchen table and the rat began scurrying around, sniffing the air and looking for food, just like any other rat would.

"Oh, would you look at that," Tavarius said. His voice was high and excited, and his face lit up. "Oh my, look how it moves, how it stops, and starts. Look there, it's wiggling its nose. It's fully autonomous, aware."

"Call her," Kat said. "Tap your finger on the table and she'll come to you."

Tavarius tapped the table with the index finger of his left hand. Joy stopped, pinned her ears back and looked towards the sound. Tavarius tapped again, and Joy ran across the table and into Tavarius's outstretched hand.

"See?" Kat said. "She likes you."

Tavarius giggled like a boy as Joy scrambled up his arm and onto his shoulder. The rat nibbled on the old man's ear, but this didn't make him angry like I thought it would. Instead, Tavarius laughed. I guessed it was the most attention he's received from a female in a long time, maybe forever.

"Oh, oh, oh, oh," Tavarius said. "That hurts, you little booger." He smiled as he said this.

"I think she likes you," Kat said.

"Oh, I think he does too."

"She's a she," Kat reminded him. "I think you should remember that from now on."

I heard a click. I looked over at Kat. She had the slightest, but most evil, fuck you grin on her face and a glimmer in her eye. *Ah, clever girl,* I thought.

I braced myself for the pop. When I opened my eyes, I saw Joy scrambling for safety. She chattered like an excited monkey.

-Chapter 16-

Joy sat on top of Kat's head and vacuumed the smoke coming out of Kat's mouth into her tiny nostrils. The rat had a dopey look on its face (more dopey than usual), and she looked high. Whenever Kat passed me the joint, Joy would crawl down, sprint across the table and climb on my head. My first instinct was to grab the squirmy little varmint.

I fantasized about launching her over the hedges, but Kat's loud voice stopped me in mid-thought.

"Don't you dare," she said.

"What? I was just going to scratch the little critter."

"Of course you were."

The spring sun felt warm on my cheek. Kat and I talked, but not always with words. A touch on my shoulder, holding hands, or sometimes a knowing glance was enough to convey what a thousand words never said. Sometimes Joy would barge in with the nonsensical chatter of a stoned rat, and we just laughed.

I thought to myself: *how easy this is?* I never felt more normal than I did at that moment on the porch looking out over the garden. I don't know; maybe I was getting sentimental in my old age. I had nearly lost her twice. The first time, I saved her. The second time, she saved the both of us. Oh, and Joy too.

"I am grateful for..." I said, stretching the last word for a beat. Then I turned my head and smiled at Kat before completing my sentence: "...Kat."

Kat smiled. "I'm grateful for you," she said.

"I'm grateful for the beautiful flowers. I bet you never guessed I was such a talented gardener."

"Well, that special fertilizer helped."

I took a deep breath as I watched the petunias swaying in the wind. "Yes," I finally said. "That fertilizer worked well."

"Did Dick take care of the truck?" she said.

"Yes. He has some friends in rather low places. They took care of it—no traces."

"Did he ask questions?"

"I think he wanted to, but he didn't. He asked me if I was in trouble. I told him I was good. He sends his love, by the way."

Kat's droopy eyes and perma-smile told me the pot was working. She nodded off, and Joy fell asleep on her chest. I was content to let her sleep while I enjoyed the scenery and the mild temperatures. After a few minutes, however, the silence made me uneasy and so I nudged Kat awake.

"Kat," I said.

Kat slowly opened her eyes and turned her head to me. "What the fuck?" she said.

"What happens to us when we die? What do you think happens to us?"

"Jesus Christ. I was having such a delightful dream. It's amazing. You never told me I could still dream."

"Yes. You can still dream."

"Gee, thanks."

"But what about my question?"

Kat thought for a moment and then told me we never die.

"We don't?" I said.

"No. When our bodies cease working, we go through a life review, and we see everything we did. We see how our actions affected other people, and we experience what they felt and how they treated others based on what we did. It's a ripple effect, like throwing a pebble into a pool and watching the ripples spread out from there; these ripples are our feelings, and emotions, our words, and actions and they're magnified by a power of ten and we experience them as others experienced them in life."

I looked over at Kat as she spoke. Her eyes were closed again; Joy was still sleeping.

"It's like a magnificent, colorful tapestry hanging over our head," Kat continued. "And each of us contributes our thread to be woven into the overall pattern."

Kat told me about our team of light—deceased relatives, angels, and spirit guides—and how they help us decide what we should come back as in our next life and what lessons we should learn.

"How do you know all this, Kat?"

Kat opened her eyes, then she picked up the half-finished joint and lit it. She took a drag and let out a puff of smoke that slowly drifted over the flower bed.

"I read a lot of Deepak Chopra," she said. "And I smoked a lot of weed." I shook my head and laughed. It sounded strange—this from a person living inside a Lego body; who was I to talk about strange?

But I suppose reincarnation was no less palatable than the Christian view of death: fall into the arms of Jesus, but only if you lived a worthy life, obeyed the rules, prayed the right prayers, attended the right churches, and adopted the right doctrine. Heaven was your reward, hell your punishment.

It all sounded like hell to me. What's heaven, and why should I want to live there, anyway? It sounded terribly boring with its harps and wings and floating on clouds for an eternity. Living meant pain and suffering, but I wanted to live every miserable, wonderful second of it. I wanted a body, arms to hold, legs to walk. I liked my brain, and I enjoyed thinking even if I thought too much. My heart thought too, and I learned to listen to it. Yes, it was a mechanical heart, but I still felt things. And my feelings for Kat went beyond what my intellect could ever dream of.

Still, I wondered about past lives. If we reincarnate, it made my pursuit of immortality a moot one. I wasted a lot of time and energy to solve a problem that was never really a problem.

"Where do you think Lance is right now?" I said. "The original Lance."

"Probably hanging out with the original Kat," she said, laughing. "Why do you ask?"

"I want to know about life and death. What's more important than that? In knowing death, you know what life is, just as up teaches us down; left teaches us right and so on. It's the duality of life. Isn't it?"

"I suppose, but maybe we're not meant to know everything. Maybe it's better we don't. Ignorance is bliss, right?"

"Ignorance is ignorance," I countered.

Kat held her up hand to the sunlight and spread her fingers wide.

"You like?" I said.

"It takes some getting used to."

"It took several weeks before I realized what I was. With each passing day, your reflection will make more sense to you. You're lucky. You have me to guide you."

"You did a wonderful job. I look kind of steam punky."

"That's the look I was going for."

Joy opened her eyes suddenly, then she raced across Kat's arm and hopped onto the table. She ran to the ashtray, sniffed the joint and started eating it.

"Hey!" I yelled.

Joy looked at me with a *what's your problem* look in her eyes and Kat backed her up.

"What?" Kat said. "It's finished."

"There were some good pulls left on that joint," I said.

"We have plenty more."

"Yes, but she shouldn't swallow it. It will gum up her electronics if she forces it down."

Joy nibbled the pot in contempt of my complaint. Kat sat back in her chair; her sleepy eyes studied Joy while I studied them. My two greatest creations, my David, my Venus. Okay, David was a rat, but my Venus, well, she was my love, my life, my muse.

After all these years, the emptiness, the searching, the fear, the restlessness—I finally discovered what's important.

The End

About the Author

Stephen Kanicki is a father, a teacher, and an award-winning writer and photographer. His novel, *There are no Saints*, explores religious, spiritual and metaphysical themes woven into an imaginative narrative. *There are no Saints* won first place in both the 2021 Maxy and Pencraft Awards and has been a category best seller on Amazon.

When he's not writing books, Kanicki enjoys songwriting and playing guitar. He recently got a ukelele and is having way too much fun playing it.

Note from the Author

Word-of-mouth is crucial for any author to succeed. If you enjoyed *Lego Me*, please leave a review online—anywhere you are able. Even if it's just a sentence or two. It would make all the difference and would be very much appreciated.

Thanks!
Stephen Kanicki

We hope you enjoyed reading this title from:

www.blackrosewriting.com

Subscribe to our mailing list – *The Rosevine* – and receive **FREE** books, daily deals, and stay current with news about upcoming releases and our hottest authors.

Scan the QR code below to sign up.

Already a subscriber? Please accept a sincere thank you for being a fan of Black Rose Writing authors.

View other Black Rose Writing titles at www.blackrosewriting.com/books and use promo code **PRINT** to receive a **20% discount** when purchasing.